FEED A FEVER

From where she sat in the grass, Sarah looked at Jesse, her upturned mouth poised to ask her next question. She must have read the answer in his eyes, for the unspoken words melted from her lips, vanishing into an expression of childlike wonder.

Beneath her fleeting look of confusion, he saw a beauty her recent illness couldn't hide, a depth of emotion as appealing as the first dawn. He leaned toward her, the sun's warmth on his face no match for the fever burning inside of him.

Starve a fever, the folk remedy went. Or was it feed a fever? He was starving all right.

He put his arm around her waist and pulled her closer, feeling her curves beneath his fingers as he drew her near. This wasn't the innocent schoolgirl he'd had a crush on his whole life. This was a woman through whose eyes he was beginning to see his whole world anew.

She gazed up at him, her fingers clutching his arm, her ragged breathing mirroring his hunger. Every ounce of common sense he possessed warned him to run like hell.

He traced the soft angles around her mouth with his thumb and felt her quiver beneath his touch. *Feed* a fever, he heard echoing in his brain. He wasn't sure he was thinking straight, but it sounded right to him. She'd soon be well...and so would he.

She tilted her mouth up to welcome his, and then it was too late to change his mind. He pressed his mouth to hers and heard a soft moan escape her lips as she returned the kiss.

Other *Love Spell* books by Victoria Bruce:
PROMISES FROM THE PAST

Windmills In Time

Victoria Bruce

LOVE SPELL BOOKS NEW YORK CITY

LOVE SPELL®

October 1998

Published by

Dorchester Publishing Co., Inc.
276 Fifth Avenue
New York, NY 10001

ISBN 0-505-52280-2

To Georgia Nelms, who first introduced me to the romantic timelessness of the Nebraska Sand Hills.

Many Thanks to:
Barbara Benedict, Angie Ray, Sandra (Paul) Chvostal, and Colleen Adams, who keep me writing.

Windmills In Time

Prologue

Nebraska Sand Hills, 1887

Jesse Colburn flipped his frayed collar up against the falling temperature and, looking up at ominous black clouds, nudged his horse into a canter on a road nearly washed out by the last rain. The weather wouldn't hold. And he didn't care to be soaked to the skin after an already miserable day of cooling his heels at the bank.

Hat in hand, he'd met with the bank president, Lindsey Seymour, about a loan. Seymour had hemmed and hawed, spouting stock phrases about bank procedures and final loan approvals as if they were a creed. Then he'd finally swallowed with an Adam's apple so large it barely fit inside his high starched collar, and said he'd prefer to postpone the transaction—especially seeing as Mr. Morgan, Chairman of the Board, was away for ten days selling cattle in Ogallala.

Jesse had left empty-handed, but he wasn't finished with Lindsey yet. He needed the money or he'd have no crops come spring.

Slowing Sage to a trot, he surveyed the devastation along the side of the road and swore under his breath. Last month, John Morgan's cattle had broken through a weak section of his fence and destroyed his corn and wheat. As greedy as the old man himself, the animals hadn't been satisfied with ravaging his ripening crops. Like scavengers come to pick his bones clean, they had trampled his garden too, systematically devouring the table crops he'd planned to live on through the winter. Now he'd have to repair the damage to the fence and hope it was enough to keep them out when he planted again.

As he came up over the rise, his thoughts were interrupted by a wagon blocking the road, one of its wheels lodged in a rut. Old man Morgan and his ranch hands were the only others who regularly traveled this stretch of the Sand Hills. Except for Sarah Morgan. Not that Morgan's daughter would choose a lumbering hay wagon when she had her pick of sleek black buggies.

Jesse rode up to the stranded cart and noticed a still form huddled next to the wheel, a cloak covering the body. A bloodless hand clutched the hub. He swore again, dreading having come upon someone who'd fallen ill on such a lonely stretch of road.

He hunkered down next to the wagon and lifted the edge of the cloak, exposing a richly embroidered skirt stained with bright red blood. The woman gripped her crimson-streaked belly as desperately as she clung to the wagon. Peeling back the hood of the cape, he uncovered the ashen face of Sarah Morgan, her drawn features sending a shaft of fear through him that made his own troubles wax pale.

"Sarah," he said hoarsely. "It's Jesse Colburn. What's wrong? Did you have an accident?"

She shook her head, the motion nearly imperceptible. "The baby," she murmured.

She opened her eyelids and looked at him, her big brown eyes reminding him of the frightened little girl he'd befriended in first grade.

"What baby?" She was the only woman of childbearing age on the nearby ranch. Seeing her weakened condition and the blood, he hoped there was another explanation. Twenty-five and unmarried, Sarah was John Morgan's only daughter, the one thing Morgan worshiped more than his land.

"My baby. . . ." She struggled to sit up, only to collapse back into his arms, her eyelids fluttering and then closing in a way that chilled him to the bone.

The magnitude of the situation pressed down on him like the impending storm, and he wished he were still sweating under the critical eye of Lindsey Seymour. Long before Morgan had begun try-

ing to grab up all the land he could buy—
including the Colburn property—Jesse had felt
protective of the man's daughter. But if she'd gotten herself pregnant, there'd be no helping her.
Morgan's rage would know no bounds. From the
looks of her slim waist, she couldn't be far along.
Perhaps she had a fever and was hallucinating.

The nearest doctor was at least ten miles away.
He couldn't leave her here alone, and it would take
too long to dig out the wagon and drive her there.
The comfort of her father's house, and her own
bed, was still three miles ahead.

"What am I going to do with you, Sarah?" he
whispered, knowing she couldn't hear him. "If I
make the wrong choice, it could cost you your
life."

He'd been making his own decisions since he
was fourteen, and he'd learned that once you
made them, you couldn't look back. Covering her
again with her cloak, Jesse lifted Sarah in his arms
and carried her to his horse. Straining every muscle, he managed to mount with her in his grasp,
the reins tied over Sage's neck.

Her sod house was the closest shelter. He
wished he had a better place to leave her while he
went to get the doctor. Everyone knew that the
hovel Morgan had built for his daughter was just
so she could homestead the place in name only,
leaving him to claim the land as his own.

Still, there wasn't time to be particular. It would
have to do. He'd take her there and then bring
back Doc Mabe. If the doctor were sober, the

choice would prove a wise one. But if he'd been on a week-long bender . . .

Well then, Jesse would have the blood of another woman on his hands, and old man Morgan would have one more reason to try and make his life a living hell.

Chapter One

Surrounded by the written legacies of ten thousand men and women, Dierdre Brown expectantly curled up in an antique leather chair with one of the rare-book store's latest arrivals, an 1887 diary from the Sand Hills of Nebraska. Three years ago she'd been hired to authenticate and catalogue the late Samuel Vanderbrief's massive collection of rare books. Mr. Vanderbrief had been an eccentric collector, buying entire estate libraries—sight unseen—and hoarding the more than 80,000 volumes in a climate-controlled vault beneath his nineteenth-century mansion on Long Island Sound. Dierdre had always thought it sad that until his death, the only other person permitted to see the books had been his son, Sam, Jr.

Sam had apparently thought so, too, for almost

immediately after hiring her, he'd opened a museum over the bookstore where anyone, whether of means or not, could view the priceless first editions and century-old manuscripts—all under glass, of course. As soon as she catalogued each new lot of books unearthed from the vault, Sam sent his favorites home to the austere library on the Vanderbrief estate, culled a few of the rarest finds for the museum, and advertised the rest to the bookstore's most discriminating collectors.

Dierdre pulled on a pair of acid-free cotton gloves and opened the diary. Manuscripts from pioneers who'd settled the prairies would never find their way into Sam's museum, or even into his private library, but to her the stoic personal accounts of untamed life on the Great Plains were just as precious as the valuable first editions.

She'd authenticated hundreds of such journals, and found them all unique in some way. Yet, from the moment Dierdre had spied the halting, almost childlike signature on the flyleaf of the delicately bound journal, she'd felt an unusual connection to its author, a pioneer named Sarah Morgan.

As strange as it may seem, the woman wrote, *I believe that life must surely hold something more than hostessing and needlework for an unmarried woman of twenty-five. Having no one else in which to confide, I can only reveal my unconventional feelings within the uncensored forum of my journal.*

The fan squeaked overhead, its blades throwing shadows across the mahogany paneling, the sound of its protesting gears echoing through the two-story-high reading room. Heat strong enough to peel the smell of summer right off of the concrete rose from the Manhattan sidewalks outside, but Dierdre only had eyes for the story unfolding on the weathered sheafs of paper before her. As a historian, she considered the fact that someone would actually pay her to read a work of art like this a lucky bonus. Had she not needed the income, she would have done it for free.

Sarah's halting script was ornamented with tiny loops and swirls, hinting at fanciful dreams which she had probably never achieved. She had been young for her twenty-five years—at least it seemed that way to Dierdre. She'd spent the bulk of her years isolated on a large cattle ranch in Nebraska. And as was not unusual for a woman during those times, she'd been dominated by the man in her life, her father.

She'd also been pregnant out of wedlock, her reputation facing certain ruin. Dierdre pushed her horn-rimmed glasses higher on her nose, immersed in the woman's touching account of her predicament. Even as her first maternal instincts awakened within her, Sarah had lived in fear of what her father would do when he found out.

Twenty-seven-year-old Dierdre closed her eyes, trying to imagine how she would feel in the girl's place. It wasn't difficult. Although Sarah had been beside herself with worry at the prospect, Dierdre had always longed to have a baby of her own. Diagnosed with a unique seizure disorder, she'd been cautioned that having a child would be a risky endeavor.

Like Sarah, she had no husband. Nor did she have any prospects for one. Maybe that explained why, despite the century that separated them, she felt a special bond with the pioneer woman.

For years, Dierdre had hoped to meet the perfect husband and father for her child, but she'd finally come to grips with reality. If men were intimidated by independent females, they were even more alarmed by a headstrong woman with an unexplainable brain disorder that showed up on EEG's and responded only to drugs with frightening names.

Growing up, she'd wanted to be part of the rough-and-tumble sports that had always occurred on the rolling acre of front lawn on Thanksgiving morning. She hadn't understood why she hadn't been allowed to play like all the other children of the family, but her mother had taken a hard line against physical exertion by her only daughter, the runt of a litter including four others, all strapping boys. "Don't overstress Dierdre," her mother would say. "She's too delicate." Coddled and sheltered until she'd felt that a piece of herself had been stunted at the embryo stage, she'd eventually formed a wall of defenses that isolated her from the world more than her malady did.

She needed her own family, she'd decided, one where she wasn't handled with kid gloves—even if it meant learning how to be both father and mother to a child. So, after a lifetime of being overprotected by those closest to her, she'd embarked on a series of artificial insemination procedures.

Her medical condition demanded that her progress be carefully monitored—unnecessarily, as it turned out. A year of fertility treatments had passed without success. At first, the excitement of conceiving a child had buoyed her spirits from month to month. But lately, a hollowness had set in that she'd had trouble shaking in between visits to the doctor. The aftermath of failure seemed to linger a little longer each time.

While waiting for the outcome of her latest *in vitro* procedure, she'd finally decided if she wasn't pregnant, she'd have to accept that it wasn't meant to be. The emotional ups and downs were growing too painful to bear.

Dierdre sighed and turned the page of Sarah's journal. She'd soon know the direction her future would take. The lab report was due in at four.

Time passed unbidden, the sunlight gradually deepening to a shade of gray distinctive to New York City. The stairway door creaked open, but Dierdre only heard it in the background, her mind envisioning Sarah's waist growing thick as she nurtured the child within. After all the years of imagining what it would be like to carry a child of her own, she felt as if she were living and breathing Sarah's words.

"Dierdre, you'll hurt your eyes reading in the dark. Didn't your mother ever tell you?"

Startled, she glanced up from the page and noticed her boss standing in the shadows. "Yes, she told me that all the time, but it hasn't come true yet." She tapped the frames of her glasses. "Still the same prescription since eighth grade."

Sam flipped on a wall switch, throwing a cone of light over her shoulders. "I know that faraway look in your eyes. Which cause are you ready to take up now? Women's right to vote? Or the protection of the residents in a prairie dog town?" Sam's tone was light, a break from his usually reserved demeanor. His passion for history was the common ground they shared, and usually the context in which they related.

"I've been reading the most intriguing diary by a pioneer named Sarah Morgan," Dierdre said. "I don't know why I'm so enthralled with her. Maybe because she was with child at the time she wrote the account."

"How delightful." Sam smiled broadly.

"So you like children?" she asked. With all the doctors' appointments, she'd had to tell him about her efforts to have a baby, but she'd never realized he had an interest in kids.

Sam looked surprised. "Oh, no. Children have sticky fingers and faces. Hardly compatible with my father's collection of rare books. What I meant was that the woman's condition makes her journal a more interesting collector's item."

"Of course." Dierdre smiled wanly, wondering if she'd ever get the chance to feel a child's sticky hands hugging her neck. She turned the page to find the outcome of Sarah's plight.

"That reminds me, aren't you supposed to be calling the doctor for your results?" Too young and handsome to be as old-fashioned as he was, her boss had turned out to be as overprotective as her mother.

"Mmm," she said absently. Through Sarah's eyes, she could see the vast Morgan ranch; through her ears, hear the rustle of wind through the cottonwood trees.

"So, have you called?" he asked again.

"Not yet," she murmured, anxious to finish the diary. "They won't have the results until four . . ."

She glanced at her watch. Yikes, it was already ten after. "You're right. I almost forgot."

Tucking the journal under her arm, Dierdre jumped up. The room began to spin. As if she'd stepped onto a merry-go-round, she watched the rich dark walls dance around her. Grabbing the chair arm for support, she slumped into the brass-studded chair. She shut her eyes, trying to stop the reeling room. It was the second dizzy spell she'd had that afternoon. Maybe she was catching the cold that was going around. She didn't want to even consider that her seizures might be returning. She'd managed fine for over a year without medication.

When the unsteadiness finally passed, she stole a glance at Sam. Thankfully, he was busy stocking new inventory. If he suspected she was having problems, he'd bundle her off to the clinic, and she certainly didn't have time to sit in a doctor's office simply for a pesky flu bug.

Moving cautiously this time, she rose and walked behind the Victorian counter. Lifting the phone receiver, she punched the speed dial to her doctor's office and waited while the office voice mail listed options. She pressed "0" for operator.

The recording told her thank you, that she was being connected. Tapping a toe, she watched Sam climb a rolling ladder to shelve the handful of first editions she'd authenticated and catalogued that morning.

"May I help you?" a voice on the other end of the line asked.

Dierdre told the receptionist her business, and waited on hold while the nurse checked the lab results. Growing bored with the easy-listening music playing over the phone, Dierdre opened the diary and began reading where she'd left off.

It seemed Sarah's panic was increasing. According to her calculations, she was three months gone and couldn't keep her secret much longer. Beside herself with worry and guilt, she'd never said how she'd come to be with child. Dierdre had the feeling Sarah could barely face the truth herself. Not knowing who else to turn to, Sarah had decided to travel into town to visit her best friend, Becky Simmons, until her father returned from Ogallala.

Underlined in a shaky hand she had written: *Now marriage to Simon is inevitable*.

Dierdre's heart went out to the poor girl. Raised by overprotective parents herself, she recognized

21

how ill-equipped Sarah was for handling the situation. She suspected Sarah's naiveté might be partly responsible for the circumstances in which she'd found herself, yet Deirdre would have gladly changed places with her in a minute. With the benefit of over a hundred years of progress on her side, she was far better prepared for the uphill struggle Sarah faced.

The other line rang. "I'll get it," Sam said, climbing down the ladder. His shoulders cast a shadow across the page as he walked past.

Sebastian, the long-hair Maine coon and resident bookstore cat, hefted his massive body down from a velvet-cushioned chair and brushed up against her leg, reminding her it was time for his afternoon feeding.

As Dierdre reached under the counter for the cat's dish and food, clenching the receiver between her neck and shoulder, another wave of dizziness washed over her, a fluttering of the eyes warned her she should sit down. Drops of sweat beading on her forehead, she collapsed into the nearest chair. Maybe she should call the doctor.

She laughed to herself. She *was* calling the doctor.

Sebastian meowed, reminding her she was still holding his food dish. She put it down, then turned slightly, thinking she heard the wind whistling through an unseen crack in the wall. Her lightheadedness intensified to an almost pleasant sensation of floating, of being lighter than her body. She felt as if the sun beat down on her.

Looking for the source of the bright light, she tilted her head back. The light overhead pulsated with each revolution of the fan, making it seem as if it were flashing in time with the blowing wind. No. There wasn't any wind in Manhattan. Not today anyway.

"Dierdre, are you all right?" She could hear Sam's worried voice through the fog clouding her senses, but she was mesmerized by the flashing lights, the rhythmic glint of silver off the blades. Never had she seen anything so beautiful.

You shouldn't be upset, she wanted to tell him. Sam was a nice man, but he'd never understood her passion about having a child. And he probably never would. She had everything she wanted. What was it she had? Oh, yes. Joy built up inside her. She had a baby growing right there inside her.

No, she thought distractedly. That had been Sarah Morgan.

The blades sent out a ripple of light in an electrical river of sparks. She felt drawn to the pulsing lights, pulled there by a strangely familiar sensation. She floated up until she felt her knees buckle. Her hand flew to her abdomen. The baby! She had to protect the baby.

She heard Sam moving toward her, but not in time. She was falling. . . .

Protectively clutching her belly, she dropped the phone and felt the floor come up to meet her, driving a shaft of pain through her abdomen. From the dangling receiver, she heard the words, "Good news, Miss Brown. You're pregnant."

23

You're pregnant. The words she'd waited so long to hear. Finally, she was going to have the family she'd always wanted. Or was she?

Her concentration fading, she tried to cling to consciousness, but the effort was too difficult. The scene beneath her clicked onward, frame by frozen frame. Huddling beside her still form, Sam shouted instructions into the phone, while outside the constant blare of horns and traffic droned on.

She couldn't leave. She needed to stay here with her baby. She wanted to bounce her child on her knee and feel tiny sticky hands around her neck. She couldn't lose it all now, not when she was this close.

As she fought to stay alert, her fingers closed around the diary on the floor next to her. The binding, worn smooth by time, felt cool and comforting beneath her grip. And then her mind floated away, leaving her body behind.

Chapter Two

Jesse found the tiny baby's body behind the soddie.

While Doc Mabe examined Sarah, Jesse stood over the blood-smeared earth, holding the remains of the unborn child. A drop of rain struck the baby's cheek and he carefully wrapped it up again.

Sarah had been telling the truth about the baby.

The rain came down harder, and he slipped the bundle under his jacket. The knowledge of the cold, still body next to his sent a sense of desolation through him so strong that he felt fourteen again and all alone. A dozen years had passed since once before he'd had to dig a tiny grave, and it still struck him as the hardest thing he'd ever had to do.

Did Sarah share his feelings? Or had she come here to hide her mistake? And who was the father of the child, the bastard who'd left Sarah to deal with the baby alone?

Carrying the pitiful bundle protectively under his jacket, Jesse located a shovel among the rusty tools in the barn and trudged back out into the deepening mud. In the fading light, he paused to survey the vast, virgin prairie, wondering where Sarah would have chosen to bury her child. Attired in the soggy browns and yellows of a summer that had tenaciously outstayed its welcome, the endless, rolling line of the horizon stretched unbroken, save for a grove of cottonwoods along the far creek. A shaft of sunlight suddenly broke through the rainclouds, illuminating the stoic assembly of trees, casting a beacon of light over the shimmering leaves that danced in the rain.

Then the heavens inexorably closed again, extinguishing the light, leaving him with only the sodden chill of the stillborn child cradled next to his heart. Jesse began slowly walking toward the darkened clump of trees. Sarah's only utterances had been about the baby, but he suspected that this was one grave that would go into eternity unmarked.

Rain streaming off the brim of his hat, he finished his thankless task and pondered whether he should say a few words over the babe. He hadn't spent much time in church, but he didn't think it right to send the child back to God without a prayer.

He tried to remember what they'd said over his mother's grave, but his mind went blank. Shoving his hands into his pockets, he finally settled on something simple—the truth.

"There's not many that survive the fires and blizzards and fevers here, but those that do must bury those that don't. Amen."

Looking up from the newly turned soil, he stared at the windmill in the distance, its blades spinning like a silver top. This was one more baby who would never laugh, who would never know what it was like to play. He'd learned to harden himself against the sufferings of most everything, but the deaths of animals and children still got to him. Drenched to the skin, he didn't think he'd ever change.

The soddie door opened and Doc Mabe emerged. Stretching his stooped shoulders, he signaled for Jesse before hastily disappearing back into the soddie. Jesse returned the shovel to the barn and approached the house. Reluctant to get any more involved than he already was, Jesse paused at the threshold. With its low ceiling and small windows, the sod house was as crude and meager as Sarah was refined and beautiful.

Inside, Doc took a swig from a flask and offered it to Jesse. Thankfully, Doc Mabe hadn't drunk himself into a stupor that morning, but then his hands weren't all that steady anyway. When Jesse didn't immediately reach for the bottle, Mabe wiped the lip with his soiled sleeve and offered it again, destroying whatever temptation Jesse might have had to ease his apprehension with a drink.

"How is she?" Jesse asked, taking off his hat and stepping inside. He'd stay just long enough to find out her chances for recovery.

Mabe shrugged and took another swallow. "The bleeding's stopped. If I don't miss my guess, I'd swear she had a miscarriage, but I couldn't find any sign of the fetus. Probably just as well. Her father would disown her if she got herself in the family way, being unmarried and all. She's of strong stock, though. I reckon if she makes it through the night, she'll live. I've got another house to visit, so I'll be on my way."

Jesse froze just inside the doorway. "Doc, you can't leave now. Who will take care of her?"

"I'm a doctor, not a nursemaid." He slipped his flask into the pocket. "Did you want to pay me or shall I send the bill to her father?" he asked.

Jesse thought of Sarah facing her father's anger alone. If she lasted until morning, she still might wish she were dead. His instinct to wash his hands of the whole business warred with an innate desire to protect her. He was already strapped for cash, while his fields lay fallow. Helping Sarah was one more strain he could ill afford.

Then he remembered how vulnerable she'd looked lying in the road. He could still hear her soulful voice as she mentioned the baby. "No. I'll take care of it. In fact, I wish you wouldn't mention it to anyone." He dug out his tattered wallet and removed a dollar bill.

The doctor gave him a knowing look. "As far as not telling her father," Mabe continued, pulling out a matchstick and poking it at a fleck of tobacco caught between his stained teeth, "he and most of his hands are in Ogallala, but I can't keep something like this a secret. I'm beholden to the Morgans. John brings me a side of dressed beef nearly every year."

Jesse slipped another dollar into Mabe's hand and waited for him to leave. He didn't know the first thing about caring for a sickly woman. Yet, if he fetched one of her father's men, they'd want to know what was wrong with her and Morgan would then find out for sure.

Doc frowned. "The weather really is frightful. I hope I don't catch my death." He shrugged on his cloak and stood in the kitchen, unmoving.

"How much?"

"What?"

"How beholden are you?" Jesse bit back an oath and counted out five dollars. Without a miracle, there went his last hope of making it through the month without a loan. "Is that enough to swear you to secrecy?"

Mabe leafed through the bills with a dirty thumb and grinned broadly. "Well, yes. That's very charitable of you. After all, I really have no proof that the girl has been free with her favors."

The doctor must have seen the disgust in Jesse's expression, for he picked up his black bag as he left the house, quickly mounted and rode off, his full-length black slicker slapping against his horse.

I've really done it now, Jesse thought as he watched him disappear into the night. He'd taken up for Morgan's only daughter, a girl who would never stand against her father on her own. He might as well have just signed away the deed to his soul.

Chapter Three

The next morning, the rain retreated, leaving behind a cloudless sky. Sunlight streaming through her window, Dierdre squinted into the glare, amazed by the sun's blinding radiance. She'd never been a morning person, but she was sure that she'd been up early enough—at least once or twice—to notice whether the rain had ever had such a profound effect on the air before. Last night's downpour had barely registered in her subconscious, but apparently it had been sufficient to leave the sky fresher and blue than she'd ever seen it.

As her eyes adjusted, Dierdre noticed something shiny outside reflecting the sun's dazzling rays. It looked strangely similar to the spinning rotor of a helicopter. Head pounding, she reached over to her nightstand for her glasses, but they weren't where she always left them.

In fact, the stand wasn't where she'd left it either. She'd often fallen asleep while reading—on the couch, at the kitchen table, or even in the bathtub—but disorientation upon awakening had never taken this long to pass. And she was tired. Very tired. As if she'd had the blood forcibly wrung out of her.

Confused, she pulled the covers up under her chin, suddenly aware of how rough the sheets felt. It was odd, because for as long as she could remember, she'd bought expensive sheets of Egyptian cotton; they were the only thing she could stand against her skin at night. These weren't her luxurious sheets. These were more like hospital-grade linen.

Wider awake now, Dierdre tried to sit up, but a catch in her side thwarted her efforts. What was going on? The last thing she knew, she'd grown lightheaded—just like when she'd had seizures as a child—a signal that she was losing control of her body. Then she remembered falling. . . .

The baby!

Alarmed, she bolted upright and inadvertently moaned. My God, how she hurt. Abdominal muscles cramping, she crumpled back against the pillows, but the sensation of pain clawing at her gut was nothing compared to the shaft of dread piercing her.

What if something had happened to the baby?

Protectively, she cradled her belly where she

hoped the seed of her child still grew. The doctors had warned her that going off her anticonvulsant was risky—that even though she'd been seizure-free for twenty years, there were never any guarantees. But it was a chance she felt she had to take. The medication could harm the fetus.

But so could a seizure.

What if in her determination to become pregnant, she'd somehow damaged the new little life? While reading about the pioneer Sarah Morgan, she'd become mesmerized by the strobe-like effect of the lights playing off the blades of the ceiling fan. She knew that flashing lights sometimes triggered convulsions. The doctors who'd tried to diagnose her had even used special strobe lights to alter her brain waves for testing. As much as she wanted to deny it, she must have had a seizure.

"Sarah?"

She glanced up, expecting to see her boss. Instead, a man with a gun on his hip stood in the doorway, his sky blue eyes filled with concern.

"Sarah," he repeated more softly. "Are you in pain? I heard you from the other room."

She wanted to tell him that her name was Dierdre, but the words stuck in her throat. Like a settler captured in a black and white photograph from the late 1800s, he was dressed in dark pants, a white shirt and a vest. The only thing missing was a wide-brimmed hat.

Yes, she must have had a seizure all right. She'd had moments as confusing as these when she was little, but it had been so long ago that she'd almost forgotten how frightening they could be. She'd learned to play a game then. It seemed to help calm her so she could surface to consciousness more quickly.

"I'm dreaming," she said aloud. "I can wake up now."

Closing her eyes, she concentrated on making the dream go away. It was easy to dispel the strange night terrors and fleeting memories from her seizures when she recognized them for what they were: a release for her subconscious mind—a mental circuit-breaker for an overloaded system. She could wake up now.

Opening her eyes, she looked around. A crudely crafted nightstand leaned precariously against the opposite side of the bed. On it, a speckled blue metal pitcher held a single white daisy. And still staring at her from the doorway was one of the most ruggedly handsome men she'd ever seen—dressed in vintage clothing.

Okay, she could play along. Her mind might still be scrambled, but she'd get answers. Little by little, she'd put the pieces back together.

"You don't look like a doctor."

"I'm Jesse Colburn. Doc Mabe left last night."

She nodded. Okay, that was progress. She was in a hospital. "Did he say anything about my being pregnant?"

"He mentioned it."

"And . . . should I begin crocheting baby booties?" She held her breath. She needed reassurance. She'd longed for a baby so long, endured the insemination procedures, only to have her hopes dashed each month when her period started.

Jesse frowned. "Don't you remember? You lost the baby."

Dierdre felt the smile dissolve from her face. As his words sank in, she felt as if she'd been kicked in the stomach. Doubling over, she moaned, the searing ache in her heart far more terrible than the pain in her womb. "How did it happen?" she asked weakly.

"I don't know. When I found you, you were nearly unconscious. You were collapsed on the ground."

Oh no. Drawing up her knees, Dierdre hugged herself, a tangle of hair hanging in her eyes. She'd fallen and lost the child she'd so desperately yearned for. For years, she'd imagined how the first few months of pregnancy would feel, how joyous sharing life with another human being would be. After coming so close, the loss seemed even more painful.

"You almost died," he said, as if that could soften the blow.

"Everyone warned me about the risks," she said, shaking her head, "but I wouldn't listen."

"Your father's not back yet," the man said.

"He didn't know," she mumbled. "No sense in upsetting him."

"I didn't think so," Jesse bit out.

His sudden sharpness caught her by surprise. It was strangely out of keeping with the caring look he'd worn when she'd asked him the fate of her child. Like rubbing salt in a wound, his caustic retort made her recoil, longing for the comfort of a friend.

"What about Sam? Does he know?"

"Who's Sam? The baby's father?" If anything, the wariness with which he regarded her grew.

"Oh, no," she said. "Nothing like that."

Sam would be worried. She'd phone the bookstore and let him know what had happened. She carefully rolled over, searching for a phone. That was odd. The only thing within reach was the rustic side table and antique metal pitcher. Hardly the kind of furniture one found in a hospital.

Unlike the sterile white of a hospital, the walls were as dark as the earth, and smelled more like rich sod after a rain than an antiseptic sick ward.

She glanced out the window. She wasn't wearing glasses, but she could clearly see something far less high-tech than a helicopter. Spinning silver blades of a windmill reflected the rays of the sun, reminding her of the flashing glint of light on the fan she'd seen in the bookstore the day before.

She choked down her rising panic. It was apparent she'd suffered a seizure, but instead of fading, the delusions were becoming more realistic.

Until she had been nearly seven, she'd awakened from each convulsion with stories of rural fields that stretched forever. Her tales had so distressed her parents that she'd finally learned to keep them to herself.

Then, with the medication, the seizures and the dreams that went with them had finally stopped.

Until now. The difference was that this was not one of the vague, fleeting visions of her childhood, hovering just out of her mind's reach. Now, with startling clarity, she could see the patchwork quilt on the bed, a rag rug on the dirt floor.

The man in the doorway had called her *Sarah*.

While she'd waited for her test results, she'd wished she could change places with Sarah Morgan. Metaphorically, of course. Sarah had been an unmarried girl in a woman's body, alone and frightened. But she'd had the one thing Dierdre wanted most in all the world. She'd been pregnant.

Dierdre felt her lower lip tremble. Had she somehow wished herself into Sarah's life—just when she was getting everything she'd ever wanted in her own? The aroma of damp earth filled her senses, but its rich promise of life mocked her. Struggling to gain control of her emotions, she pursed her lips tight. She couldn't fall apart now.

She pressed her hand to her forehead, trying to drive out the confusion. If her mind was playing tricks on her, maybe losing the baby was part of the illusion. Maybe she was having a bad dream, an incredibly realistic nightmare from which she still hadn't awakened.

Desperately, she clung to the hope, trying to rationalize away the seeming evidence to the contrary. She couldn't be anywhere but in her own time. It wasn't possible.

She clasped her hands together to stop their

shaking, only to discover that she didn't recognize the length of her fingers or the shape of her nails. These were more the sturdy hands of a pioneer woman than Dierdre's own fine, tapered hands of which her mother had always been so proud.

Dierdre didn't know where she was, or how she'd come to be here; but if there was any chance her own child was still alive, she knew she couldn't stay. She had to go home. Home to her baby.

Chapter Four

Journal of Sarah Morgan

*I met a man today. He has gray eyes, a glorious
moustache and an expression serious enough for a
family portrait. I realize that given the unusual circumstances of our meeting, I should not make any
judgements, but I cannot help but believe him to be
a man of the highest character.*

*The events leading up to our introduction were
some of the most distressing moments of my life.
Because of their private nature, I will begin when I
collapsed while trying to free my wagon from a rut.
I'd planned to go into town to stay with Becky, but
I foolishly got stuck in the mud.*

After what seemed like hours, Jesse Colburn

stopped to help. I could see the fear in his eyes when he assessed my condition. I couldn't blame him. I was frightened too.

I must have passed out, but when I awoke, I was looking into the kind face of a stranger. On first impression he might well have appeared dispassionate and aloof, had not his eyes revealed a deeper sensitivity. He explained that he was my employer, Samuel Vanderbrief, and that I was in the hospital. The next day, he hired a nurse and insisted on taking me to his home. It is a grand place with immense turrets and impressive stonework, surely equal (if not in size, then in craftsmanship) to the finest castles of Europe. However, despite its exquisitely crafted medieval tapestries and massive fireplaces, it feels cold and empty—as if something integral to its core is sadly missing.

The trip from the hospital to Mr. Vanderbrief's ancestral home was quite a departure from anything I've studied in my lesson books. Along city streets, I saw buildings so tall I grew dizzy looking for their tops, and strange vehicles that honked and traveled at amazing speeds without using horses. He called our conveyance a "limo" and I believe it to be far longer than any wagon my father owns.

The doctors tell me that without my medication to help prevent it, the strain of my pregnancy produced a seizure. They worry that if I don't start taking the medicine again, I may have more severe seizures, which could hurt the baby. They caution me that if I do take the drugs, it could be a signifi-

cant risk for the child as well. For now, I have de-cided not to take their pills.

I try not to worry that I have made the wrong decision, for they tell me too that too much worry-ing—they call it stress—is bad. So I patiently lie in bed swaddled by the softest sheets I have ever felt.

I should perhaps be completely disconcerted by my inexplicable situation, but I feel strangely at home in this exciting new world.

Mr. Vanderbrief frequently visits, and reads to me from Greek and Roman classics. Judging from his occasionally dour nature, I feel that taking time away from work is not his habit, but I welcome his thoughtfulness as I had no one before with whom I could discuss such ambitious works.

Perhaps the event of my recent illness has awak-ened a sentimentality in him that had previously gone unexplored.

Whatever the cause of his demeanor toward me, he is infinitely polite. When he visits, he modestly insists the nurse remain in attendance at all times. He calls me Dierdre, and I answer to the name.

I do not know how I came to be here, but I am sure that the child I carry was conceived out of love. Because of his apparent concern for me and the child, I wonder if Mr. Vanderbrief could be the fa-ther, though I cannot bring myself to discuss some-thing this intimate with him.

I cannot fathom what has happened to the real Dierdre Brown, but I fervently pray that she is as happy as I. If I am dreaming, my only hope is that I never wake up.

Chapter Five

There had been no easy way to tell her.

From the shadows of the low doorway, Jesse watched Sarah's bowed head, her folded hands. When she looked up at him, the confusion in her brown eyes had given way to an unbearable yearning. He'd seen that look of deep longing before and it scared him to death.

He searched her hollow cheeks and dry, cracked lips for pretense, but found none. Sarah's beautiful smile, long coveted by the county's most eligible bachelors, could never have affected him as did her obvious pain at the loss of her child.

Maybe he had underestimated her.

"I can't stay here," she protested, weakly waving a hand at her surroundings. "I've got to go home."

Home to a yellow and white mansion with tall

corner towers, arched windows and fancy carvings beneath the eaves. Jesse felt his sympathies waver. Sarah Morgan was used to the best her father could provide. The rumors in town were that she ate breakfast on plates imported from Italy and supper on dishes from France.

With its mean furnishings, the soddie was little more than a hovel. Old Man Morgan had left just enough furniture and supplies to fool a government agent—if he didn't look too closely. She wouldn't want to stay here any longer than she had to.

"You're in no condition to walk yet," he told her.

"I doubt where I'm going will be on foot," she said with a quiet laugh.

"Of course not," Jesse said, fighting down his anger. John Morgan's spoiled daughter was accustomed to traveling in style. Even the wagon he'd pulled from the mire in the road was better than any transportation he had to offer.

"I have to get back," she said fervidly. "Especially now when things seem to finally be working out with the pregnancy. At least I hope they are," she added, her voice dropping low.

Jesse stiffened at her callousness. So she was pleased to have shed the bundle that now lay in the ground. Her grief had certainly been short-lived. Now she was free to go back to her fancy house, unconcerned about her father or her reputation. He glanced out the window toward the tiny fresh mound of soil among the cottonwoods. He'd even helped by burying the evidence.

"My spells have never lasted this long," she continued, as if she considered her miscarriage no more distressing than a spring cold.

"How convenient for you," he forced out, "but the doctor says you need strict bed rest."

"And I'll get it," she said, struggling to sit up. "Just as soon as I'm myself again."

Jesse frowned and stepped farther inside the room. He'd thought Sarah to be a spineless young woman with no will of her own, vacillating in the breeze like the delicate blooms of the beautiful windflower, her opinions directed by the winds of her father's wishes. But her eyes were now bright with growing determination, an emotion he'd expected John Morgan to have long since broken in her.

Unless she has a fever.

An old fear curled up Jesse's spine, and he moved into the light streaming through her window, staying well away from her bed. He wanted to touch her forehead and check her temperature as he'd seen the doctor do, but he dared not behave so boldly.

"I can ride to your ranch and bring help," he said, "but the doctor said you shouldn't be moved yet."

"There's no time," she said, dragging the quilt aside and exposing the nightgown the doctor had exchanged for her soiled clothing. She pushed herself to her feet, swaying there only for a moment before she began to lose her balance.

With an oath, Jesse rushed to her side, catching

44

her as she collapsed. Cradling her feminine curves
as disinterestedly as possible, he lifted her up in
his arms. Apparently jostled by his swift actions,
she moaned softly, her fingers reflexively curling
around his neck as delicately as a child's.

Sweating now, Jesse settled her gently back
onto the pillows. The decorative tatting across the
front of her gown rose and fell with her rapid
breathing, signaling how much energy she'd exhausted trying to get up. Grasping her hand, he
unwrapped her fingers from his neck, and would
have left the room, but she held on, her grip surprising him with its strength.

Wondering what he'd gotten himself into, he
studied the hand clutching his. Sarah had the
bones of a strong pioneer woman, but the pampered skin of a lady who'd never had to work a day
in her life. She'd be useless for anything but box
socials and fancy parties at her father's ranch. He
firmly loosened her grip. At least her skin was cool
to the touch. No fever.

"Baby . . ." she murmured.

Jesse glanced up sharply. Why was she mum-
bling about her baby? If anyone heard her, she'd
be ruined. No respectable man would marry her—
no matter how large her dowry.

"Help me," she murmured, her eyes fluttering
closed.

He shook his head, not wanting any part of her
dilemma. He didn't owe Sarah anything. Her father had given him nothing but trouble. When
he'd told Morgan about his cattle breaking

through his fence and destroying his crops, the man had laughed and offered him a pittance for his farm. When Jesse had refused, Morgan had threatened he'd get the property one way or another. If John Morgan was anything, he was a man of his word.

Jesse knew he should be working on getting the loan from Morgan's bank before the man got back from Ogallala—not inviting his ire by keeping company with his daughter.

As he wrestled with his predicament, the clouds outside suddenly shifted, plunging the soddie into near-darkness. One defiant beam of light reflected off the windmill outside her window, haloing Sarah's golden-brown hair like in a picture of the holy Madonna. Her rapid breathing slowed. She drifted into a peaceful sleep, her face glowing with the beauty of innocence.

Sarah certainly wasn't pure, he thought wryly, studying the play of sunlight around her face. And hers surely hadn't been a virgin birth.

She'd made her bed . . . now she'd have to lie in it.

Jesse grimaced, realizing where he'd last heard that old adage. The years hadn't softened the pain. Reminded of another brown-eyed, honey-haired woman who'd needed help and gotten none, he covered Sarah with the quilt, tucking it over her shoulders.

Shutting out the too-fresh memories, he contemplated the woman whose future rested upon his decision. He might despise her disregard for the child she'd so casually discarded, but what would happen to her if he abandoned her now? He could take her home as she'd asked, but that would raise questions about her condition.

If her secret got out and ruined her life, he didn't know if he could live with himself—no matter what he thought of her father. His mother hadn't raised him that way.

The only alternative was to care for her himself. It meant extra hardships, and he knew nothing of nursing—save how fragile and fleeting life could be—but he could think of no one else he could trust. No one else he'd ask to risk John Morgan's wrath.

Damned if he did, damned if he didn't. It wasn't much of a choice, but gazing at Sarah's lovely, vulnerable face, he knew he hadn't much choice anyway. His conscience had always been louder than John Morgan's squawking.

Muttering an oath, he stomped from the room, knowing he'd better get to his chores or there would be no farm for John Morgan to take away from him.

He'd take care of his responsibilities, and then he'd get back here to watch over the fallen angel sleeping in that bed.

Chapter Six

The following morning, Jesse dismounted and tied Sage's reins to the rail outside the General Store. The smell of coffee wafting over the rain-scented air reminded him he hadn't had breakfast, but that was a temptation that would have to wait. He had more important things to think about.

"What? Back so soon?" Becky Simmons asked as he walked through the door. "You were just here yesterday."

She patted her tightly braided hair and batted her eyelids. Jesse felt his appetite subside. Becky was not unattractive, but she always paid him more attention than was comfortable. "I need a jug of molasses," he told her.

"Splurging on molasses. What's the occasion?"

"No occasion." Not unless Morgan came home

48

too soon and decided to have a lynching party. "Uh—got a calf that won't nurse."

"Isn't it kinda late for calving?"

"Its mother died last week," he lied.

"What a string of bad luck you've had."

You have no idea, he thought, remembering Sarah back at the soddie.

"I just wish there was something I could do to help." She leaned over the counter, her gaping neckline revealing a flash of bone-white chest. Jesse looked away.

"You can give me a five-pound bag of beans." He nodded at an open barrel of pinto beans.

She laughed. "You're such a kidder. I meant, did you need anything more from me?"

"Five pounds of cornmeal," he answered.

"Cornmeal? Don't you usually grind your own?" Another customer entered the store, but she didn't seem to notice.

Not this year. Thanks to John Morgan's cattle. "Mealworms got into it," he mumbled, reaching into his pocket.

She placed his order on the counter. "Want me to put that on account?"

Jesse grimaced. Until recently, he'd always paid in cash.

"You don't need to be ashamed if you're a little short," Becky said too loudly, making him want to throttle her. "I know you're trying to get a loan. We carry lots of farmers until they sell their crops. Only problem is, today's bill puts you over the limit."

"You could trust me for it," he said, hoping Lindsey Seymour from the bank hadn't spread the details of his finances all over town. There weren't many things that bothered him, but having others think he'd let his mother's homestead go to ruin was one of them.

"You'll have to leave something for security." Her gaze drifted south and paused suggestively at the level of his hips. "Your gun maybe?"

Under her unwelcome scrutiny, Jesse's blood burned cold. The gun had been his father's. Once he'd strapped it on at age fourteen, he'd never been without it. It felt as much a part of him as his arms and legs. On the prairie, you never knew what danger might threaten you or your livestock.

"Becky, you've known me all my life. Surely you can trust me this once." He hated having to beg, and he hated that trying to help a Morgan had reduced him to it.

"I have known you long, Jesse Colburn," she said, smoothing her hands slowly down over her hips, "but I haven't necessarily known you well. Maybe we could change that. You could give me a ride out to see why my friend Sarah Morgan didn't arrive yesterday."

"No," he said. The last person he wanted to find out about Sarah's condition was the town's biggest gossip.

Becky's smile shriveled, age lines around her mouth showing in spite of how tightly she'd wrapped her braids. "I mean the roads are too bad to get a wagon through," he said. "I'm sure Sarah will come in to see you in a week or so when they dry out."

"You could take me on your horse. We could ride together."

"I don't think Sage would like us riding double that far," Jesse said. *And neither would I.*

Becky frowned. "What a shame. Well, that's all right. I've got the evening off. We can find something else to do for entertainment."

"I don't know . . ." He needed to get back to check on Sarah, but he didn't want Becky deciding to travel out to see her before she was well.

Becky glanced impatiently at the other customer. When he wandered out the door, she whisked off her apron and came around the counter. She stood so close, Jesse could feel the heat from her body spelling out a message that a blind man could read.

Hell. What was he thinking? He couldn't spend an evening pretending he was interested in Becky Simmons—no matter what the stakes. "Sorry, I've got chores to get done."

He slammed down his gun on the counter, grabbed the supplies and walked out, feeling Becky's stare boring into his back as he left. He had his self-respect. That might be all he had left, but his mother had taught him that when a man loses his self-respect, he might as well be dead.

Of course, without his gun, he thought mirthlessly, it could come to that.

An hour later, Jesse rode up to the soddie. The front door banged against its canted frame, swinging wide, then banging shut again, at the whim of the wind. He'd made sure it was firmly closed when he left. Had one of Morgan's hands come for Sarah? He hadn't noticed any fresh tracks from that direction.

A prickle of fear darted up his spine. What if someone passing through had stopped at the cabin and discovered the defenseless woman inside? Wishing like hell he still had his gun, Jesse dismounted and cautiously approached the house, his mind filled with harrowing pictures of what might have happened in his absence.

He glanced through the window. When he was fairly certain that no one lay in wait for him in the shadows of the kitchen, he slipped through the gaping door. The bedroom door hung ajar, a crack of light spilling from within. He'd closed this door too. He peered through the opening. The bed was empty. He crossed the threshold and threw back the pile of rumpled bedsheets, even checking under the bed. Sarah was gone.

Forgetting to be careful, he charged outside, searching for clues to what had happened to her. Among the crisscrossed pattern of his boot prints leading to and from the cabin, he found the indentation of a small bare foot in the damp earth. It was the right size for Sarah's. Heart in his throat, he followed the prints around back.

Twenty yards behind the house, he found her. She lay facedown, claw marks trailing through the mud where she'd tried to drag herself after she'd fallen. Her nails were dirty and broken, and her lustrous brown hair was a tangled mat of dried mud and sandburs.

"Sarah . . . Sarah . . . Sarah," he murmured as he turned her over, fearing the worst.

Her face was terribly pale. He put his ear to her chest, listening for signs of life. He thought he felt some warmth from her body, but he couldn't detect a heartbeat. Filled with dread, he pressed his ear firmly to her breastbone and the soft breast shielding her heart. Nestled against her chest, he finally picked up a faint beat. The rhythm was irregular. But she was alive.

"What the hell are you doing out of bed?" he muttered, more to himself than to her. He never would have suspected that she would try to get up on her own.

Her eyelids fluttered open. Looking up at him, her big brown eyes still reminded him of the girl he'd known so long ago. Yet, as she struggled to focus, he recognized the determination in her gaze that had been missing when she was a child. The newfound resolve in her eyes was accentuated by the gauntness of her pale, drawn face.

"If trying to find the bathroom by myself is considered poor patient etiquette," she said in a raspy voice, "then pardon me."

Bathroom? He looked up and saw that she'd made it halfway to the outhouse a dozen yards away. Was she too proud to use the bucket he'd left for her under the bed?

Victoria Bruce

His fear dissolved into anger. "If you're trying to kill yourself, you'll have to do it without me," he said. If he hadn't come back when he did, he might have found her dead from exposure.

She wasn't out of the woods yet. If anyone rode by, they'd see him alone with Sarah Morgan, her nightgown twisted up around her knees. Swearing under his breath, he took off his shirt and covered her with it. Then he lifted her and carried her into the soddie, trying to ignore how pleasantly her body molded into his.

"Do you want me to take you to your father's?" he asked, laying her on the bed. He was ready to relinquish the responsibility. Lord knew he was better at caring for cows and pigs than for a human being.

"No," she said adamantly.

"Then what is it you want?"

He thought he saw a look of desperation in her face that she'd hidden from him so far. Her lip quivered and she rolled over against him, hugging him around the neck.

"What I really want is to be near my baby." A hot tear splashed on his bare chest.

Her words echoing in his ears, Jesse glanced at the copse of cottonwoods where he'd dug the grave. Was she so despondent that she wanted to die? He'd thought she didn't care about the baby, that all she wanted was to go home to her pampered life. Realizing how little he understood the woman Sarah had become, he pulled her to him. Humming to her as he would a startled mare, he

54

gently rocked her, letting her cry in his arms.

Even after her shoulders finally relaxed and her breathing slowed, she clung to him like her heart was breaking.

Dierdre didn't know how many hours had passed, but before she opened her eyes and saw him bending over her, she sensed Jesse Colburn's presence. Strong hands holding the torch steady, he turned up the wick of the kerosene lantern next to the bed. As the light caught, the flames threw a shadow larger than life across the earthen wall.

She hated the helpless feeling of being waited on by someone else. It was a holdover from her childhood, she knew, but that didn't make it any easier. Even a handsome man doing the waiting made it no more palatable.

After lecturing her like one would an irascible child, Jesse had carried her inside and put her to bed. She supposed she should be grateful for his help, but, given the bizarre circumstances in which she found herself, she felt as if she were just another piece on a strange chessboard, being moved at will. She kept waiting to wake from the nightmare, but the dream only seemed to become more real.

"So, you're awake," he said gruffly. The gentleness with which he'd hummed to her earlier was gone. "I was hoping you could sleep a little longer."

"I tell myself the same thing every morning," she mumbled. As the haze of exhaustion wore off,

Dierdre could increasingly feel the stinging of scrapes, scratches and sunburn, and the cramping in her abdomen from the exertion of going outside. She'd hoped the exercise might help jog her mind out of the strange groove in which it was stuck. But instead of speeding up her return home, apparently all she'd done was annoy Jesse and cause herself a setback.

She was vaguely aware that Jesse had pulled a chair up to the end of the bed and lifted the sheet, exposing her feet. "Hold still now," he said, firmly grabbing her ankle.

"What are you doing?" she cried, trying to yank her foot away.

"Got to pull out these stickers. You must have found every sticker patch from here to the outhouse."

"I never made it to the . . . outhouse," she said, remembering her ill-fated trip outside. Her nightgown was still damp and muddy, she realized with chagrin.

He tugged her foot toward his chest and wedged it in the crook of his arm. She watched him unsheathe a nasty-looking knife. When she realized what he meant to do with it, she jerked again. "Aren't you going to sterilize that?"

"What do you mean?" He looked at her as if she spoke a foreign language.

"You know, use some alcohol to disinfect it?"

He stared at her with a curious expression, then got up and came back with an open bottle. She could smell the strong scent of liquor in the air. "I never heard of wasting good brandy on the outside of the body," he said, nevertheless saturating a rag from the bottle. He wiped the knife and then her foot.

The alcohol stung, but she'd been prodded and poked by doctors her whole life, and knew ways to distract herself from discomfort. "I've got a problem," she said, trying to take her mind off the hot poker in her heel. "Ouch, that hurts."

"Sorry," he said, backing off for a moment.

"That's better. As I was saying, I've got a little problem."

"Only a *little* one?" he said.

"I need to know where I am."

He looked up in surprise. "You don't remember?"

"I can't remember . . . anything." That wasn't exactly true. She knew all about her life before she met Jesse and she knew lots of things about the past—things she'd learned about from books. It was the dated feel of her surroundings—the sudden absence of taxicabs and skyscrapers—that she was having trouble explaining away.

"You mean when you . . . got sick . . . you lost your memory too? Like amnesia?" He looked doubtful.

She nodded, hoping she could convince him. As much as she hated needing anyone's help, if she was going to make sense of her predicament and get back to her baby, she needed answers.

He studied her as if suspecting a practical joke. Finally he cleared his throat. "You're Sarah Morgan," he said. You and I went to school together through the sixth grade." His voice softened. "You've changed some since I last saw you."

No kidding. She hadn't seen herself in a mirror recently, but she knew she didn't recognize the golden tones in her skin, the larger flare of her hips . . . or her fuller breasts.

"Ouch. That's a deep one," she said, pulling her foot away.

Jesse stopped, sweat glistening on his forehead. He took a swig of brandy and offered her some. She wasn't supposed to have alcohol. The doctors said it scrambled her brain waves. But how much worse could that be, she thought, allowing herself a sip. The brandy warmed a trail to her empty stomach.

"I remember the first time I ever saw you," he continued. "You were wearing the prettiest white ruffly pinafore in the first grade. Your hair was blond then," he said, his voice slipping into a soothing, easy rhythm.

"Your braids went down your back and were plaited together with a ribbon the color of a robin's egg. You sat up front without being told to, and I sat next to you because Mrs. McFadden put me there."

"What year was that?"

"Well, let's see. You were six and I was a year older. That would make it 1868."

1868. A chill shot up Dierdre's spine, and she reached for the liquor bottle.

"You were terribly shy that year. Whenever the

teacher would call on you, you blushed and hid your face."

"Surely not," Dierdre said indignantly. "I loved school."

"So you do remember," he said, giving her another taste of brandy.

"Well, not exactly," she said. She'd loved the school she remembered from the future. She wasn't so clear about what, if anything, she knew firsthand about the past. She had hazy bits of memories that she'd never considered to be anything but the circuits in her brain misfiring. Now she just didn't know what to believe. "It was a long time ago."

"You're not that old," Jesse teased.

Two years older than Sarah's twenty-five, she thought, allowing herself a small smile. "Go on," she said.

"You had a miniature cloth doll filled with corn kernels. You played with it in the corner of the schoolroom instead of going outside with the others. You'd sit on the floor, legs bent out to the sides, completely alone. And during the lessons, you carried the doll in a bag that hung from your belt. Whenever you wanted to cry, you'd rub your fingers over the sack like a good luck charm."

"How did you know I wanted to cry?" Dierdre asked quietly.

Jesse smiled, remembering the time she'd wanted desperately to go outside and been too shy to raise her hand. He'd known from her fidgeting what was the matter, but he didn't know how to help. Then he'd thought of a diversion. He slipped the horny toad he had in his pocket under the teacher's desk. Mrs. McFadden disliked most animals, but especially anything small and slimy. When the toad jumped onto her foot, the startled teacher had screamed to high heaven and cleared the schoolhouse like a shot.

"I just knew," was all he said, head bent over his work.

He'd sat next to her until he'd grown so tall that Mrs. McFadden had moved him toward the back, but he'd never forgotten the girl in the front row with the braids.

He hadn't seen much of her after the sixth grade. His mother had taken over his schooling when he'd dropped out to help on the farm, and John Morgan had brought in tutors from the East and as far away as Europe to teach his daughter.

"Is this your house?" Dierdre asked, wincing as he painstakingly worked at another sticker.

"No. This is your homestead. I've got a farm just west of here. You actually live in the big house on the hill three miles due east. Don't you remember anything about your ranch or your father?"

She shook her head, not appearing as frightened as he would have expected of someone who'd just lost her memory. But maybe that wasn't so strange. After all, he too had memories he would happily erase.

"Are we good friends?" she asked. The innocent question hung suggestively between them.

Abruptly, he put down her foot. He hoped she

didn't think he was the baby's father. He knew it looked bad the way he was caring for her here, unchaperoned, but surely she couldn't mistake him for more than a bystander who'd reluctantly gotten in over his head.

"You have your own set of friends. We don't travel in the same circles," he said brusquely.

"But why aren't you and Sarah . . . I mean, why aren't we still friends? You live so close."

He'd once thought they would be friends forever. Jesse picked up her other bare foot and knew he'd never again get this close to Sarah. Though she'd apparently forgotten, she was from another world. When her father returned, John Morgan would make sure she remembered.

"If it's something I've done . . ." she began.

He shook his head, skimming his thumb over her foot to see if he'd gotten all of the stickers out. "You've done nothing but be yourself."

"Something happened you're not telling me. Did it involve the Morgans?"

Jesse put down her ravaged foot. "John Morgan would rather see me run out of town than tip his hat."

"Maybe I can speak to him on your behalf," she began.

He cut her off. "What's done is done," he said, resentment welling up like a raging prairie fire fanned by the Nebraska wind. Considering she'd gotten with child out of wedlock, she of all people should understand that.

Jesse moved his chair to the head of the bed and

tried to work a burr out of a clump of her matted hair. "Our families don't get along. In fact, if your father knew I was helping you, he'd probably disown you."

She nodded, but still looked puzzled. "If I'm homesteading this place, then why don't I live here?"

She'd just asked the question that everyone in the county knew the answer to, but no one had the backbone to mention. "You live at your father's. He takes care of this place. He's put ten acres under cultivation and manages the cattle."

"But the cattle are mine?"

"According to what I've heard . . ." Jesse winced. He hoped she didn't think he was so interested in the Morgans that he dallied in town listening to gossip. "The cattle are part of your dowry. As to when you'll be married, that's apparently up for conjecture."

"So, this is my house," she said thoughtfully.

"I suppose you could say that," he said, doubting John Morgan felt that way. "To prove your claim, you're supposed to live on it for five years and demonstrate that it's a thriving concern."

Sharp burrs pierced the skin of his fingers as he labored to free the sandburrs from her mud-encrusted hair. He bit back an oath, trying not to pull the entangled locks, but the burrs refused to release their prisoners. "I'm going to have to cut your hair."

"Oh, that's too bad," she said. "I've always dreamed of having it this long."

She'd always worn it this length, Jesse thought. She must have forgotten that, too. He took out his knife again. Did she expect him to "sterilize" it again? Well, why not? After cleaning the blade, he took a drink of brandy and passed her the bottle.

"Why don't I live here?" she asked, taking a not-so-dainty swig.

"I don't really know . . ." He dropped his voice, wishing she'd fall asleep before she trapped him with any more tricky questions. But like a dozing child who's just noticed that her bedtime story isn't finished, she grew alert, her eyes widening.

"But you must have some idea," she pressed.

Reluctantly, he cut out a matted tangle. "I would imagine that your father wouldn't like you living alone . . . you being a single woman and all."

"Of course not," she said. "That would be too modern. Even though a third of all homesteaders in South Dakota are women, it just wouldn't do."

Jesse hadn't known that fact. And he sure hadn't expected Sarah to know something like that either. He hoped she wasn't getting any dangerous ideas. The prairie was no place for a woman on her own.

He painstakingly sheared the rest of her hair until it was the same length as his. Her haircut finished, he rinsed out a rag and began to wash the dirt from her face.

"Hmm, that cool cloth feels good," she said as he scrubbed a stubborn patch of dirt on her neck. She arched her head back so he could better reach her neck, exposing the hollow of the throat.

Noticing how the warm golden glow of the lantern had chased the pallor from her face and neck, Jesse felt a quickening inside. Even with her face smudged with dirt and her hair shorn short as a cap, she was a beautiful woman.

"That's enough," he said, quickly standing up. "I brought you something to eat."

"Food just doesn't sound good to me right now."

"But you need to build up your strength."

"I'm really not hungry," she protested, "but could I put on some dry clothes?"

"Oh, of course." He fumbled through the meager selection of women's clothing in the armoire until he found a tattered nightgown. It looked more like a rag than something to wear. "Do you need help changing?" he asked, praying she'd say no.

"I'll manage."

Relieved, he turned his back to give her privacy. He wanted to make sure she was asleep before he left her this time. When she signaled she'd finished, he noticed her soiled gown on the floor and picked it up. He'd rinse it out in the horse trough.

"How many cattle do I have?" she asked drowsily.

"About a dozen head, I suppose. If what I've heard is true." He rolled up her shift and awkwardly stuffed it under his arm. God help him if anyone saw him leaving with her nightgown.

"And how many acres?"

"Three hundred and twenty, including the one hundred and sixty for your tree claim." John Morgan had planted just enough saplings to qualify for the extra acreage.

"I like that . . ." she said, her voice trailing off as she finally succumbed to exhaustion. "There must be a lot a woman can do for herself with a house and a herd of cattle and a windmill."

He figured she was right, but she obviously didn't remember the strength of John Morgan's will. A half-section of land was nothing compared to her father's vast holdings, yet he'd probably go to his grave and beyond to take them from her. What John Morgan wanted, John Morgan got. Not even his daughter could stand in his way.

Jesse glanced down at the sleeping woman. Her hand rested over her heart, her fingers delicately fanned out. He pulled the quilt up higher around her, and watched the pampered hand reflexively curl into a fist. She was fighting his help even in her sleep.

He supposed she'd change when she got her memory back. Yet, seeing the strength of her resolve in that fist, he grudgingly admitted there was something about the new Sarah he liked. If only he didn't sense that this new side could also lead them both into trouble.

Chapter Seven

"Open your mouth," Jesse ordered, guiding a spoon toward her mouth.

From her sickbed, Dierdre skeptically watched the tar-like black mixture approaching. Its strong odor was unpleasant and unrecognizable. So this was what he'd been so anxious to feed her last night. Wrinkling her nose, she turned her head away.

"If I'd known you were going to be so stubborn," he said, shifting closer, "I'd have put it in a bottle with a nipple, like I use to feed my orphan calves."

His face was unrelenting, but underneath the gruffness in his voice, she detected a note of tenderness when he mentioned his animals. "You feed this to cows?"

"Sometimes."

Despite her reservations about eating cow food, she let him feed her the spoonful. Closing her eyes, she swallowed the bittersweet goo. "What the dickens is that?" she exclaimed, looking for something to wash the awful taste out of her mouth.

"Sorghum molasses," he said. "To build up your blood."

"Oh, good, some milk." She gratefully accepted the tin cup he offered her and took a long drink. She nearly gagged on the gamey liquid.

"Are you trying to kill me or cure me?" she spat out.

"I had thought I'd keep you around awhile," he said, "but I still may change my mind."

"If the rest of the menu is like this, I wish you would—change your mind, that is."

"I'm saving the cornmeal mush for the main course," he said, nodding toward a plate on the nightstand.

"Oh, goody," she said unenthusiastically. It was one thing to read accounts of pioneers eating mush, it was quite another thing to be fed it oneself.

Apparently undeterred by her lack of appreciation, he refilled the cup with more of the odoriferous milk. She submitted to drinking another mouthful. "I don't know about feeding calves sorghum. But from the taste of this milk, I can definitely tell you you're feeding your *cows* the wrong thing."

A slow smile pulled at his mouth. "That's because it's goat's milk," he said. "Even a newborn baby could digest it."

She made a face. "It tastes like one already has."

He shook his head with a mixture of irritation and amusement, which he made no attempt to hide. "When you were little, you didn't used to put up such a fuss."

She thought of the unborn baby she'd left behind. "I didn't used to have so much at stake," she said quietly.

He looked up at her in surprise. "Living where you do, what kind of responsibilities do you have to worry you?"

"It's kind of complicated," she hedged.

"I wasn't prying." He cut off a slab of fried mush and wielded a forkful of it toward her mouth, patiently waiting until she worked up courage enough to try it. It was bland, but edible. He fed her bite after bite until the plate was clean.

"Do you have children?" she asked.

"No. I'm not married."

He would probably make a good father for a child one day. Too bad she hadn't found someone like Jesse in her own time. Making a baby with him would surely have been more enjoyable than artificial insemination. Realizing the direction her thoughts were taking her, Dierdre grew suddenly uncomfortable.

"Are you all right?" he asked, leaning closer, his nearness making her flush.

Virile and strong, Jesse was certainly pleasant to look at. As she gazed at him, the wind outside howled a lonely cry and rattled the windowpanes. Inside, in the haven of the room, the heat climbed.

"I'm just a little warm all of a sudden," she said, fanning her face.

"A fever?"

"No, I'm fine," she insisted.

"You were in pretty bad shape last night. I'm going to check your feet." When she nodded, he turned back the bedclothes just enough to inspect the soles of her feet.

"Is this sore?" he asked.

Dierdre watched him examine the results of last night's handiwork. He ran his thumb along the arch of her foot and lightly stroked the sole, avoiding the sore spots. Rather than hurting, it felt good. "Nothing special," she lied.

"I could have left some stickers."

"Not the way you were mining for gold."

He replaced the covers, studying her intently. "I don't know . . . you seem flushed." He hesitated, then felt her forehead with the back of his hand, his warmth threatening to raise her temperature even higher.

Her impulse was to pull away. She'd told the truth about her situation. It *was* complicated. Waking up in another time, not to mention in another body, wasn't something that was easy to accept. She didn't need any more complications. Still, despite her best intentions, the emptiness inside her responded to the comforting touch of his hand.

Apparently unaware of how he affected her, he

69

Victoria Bruce

brushed his hand across the hollow of her cheek, the tiny hairs on the back of his fingers further awakening her senses. "You're a little hot to the touch, but I don't think it's a fever."

A frown further honed the chiseled features of his weathered face. Stubble shaded his strong jaw. He drew his hand from her cheek, the sudden loss of contact making her long for more.

"I've got to leave now, but I'll be back later." He grinned. "There's a chamber pot under the bed. Think you can stay out of trouble while I'm gone?"

Automatically, she started to agree, but affected by his warm smile, she allowed the reply to die in her throat. If he'd asked her that a week ago when her ordered life was still under control, she would have unequivocally answered *yes*. Raised with four overprotective brothers watching over her when her parents couldn't, she'd never been allowed the chance to get into trouble.

"Well?" Jesse got to his feet.

Towering over her, his long legs encased in worn, snug denim, he was a man from a different era, ruggedly handsome and unaware of his earthy sensuality. Under different circumstances, she might have been tempted by Jesse.

Hell, she *was* tempted. But attractive or not, he was no match for the baby who needed her in the future. After years of feeling like a misfit with a strange affliction, she knew that her only chance of happiness lay with her baby, in the future.

"I'll behave," she promised. Her place was with

70

the child she'd created. She had too much to lose to ask for trouble now.

The following day, Jesse raised the hammer over his head and smashed it down with all his might, splitting the gate post with his unnecessary force. He swore at the soft wood, at his own impatience, and at the beautiful woman who lay a stone's throw away. She'd never need this corral after the next few days, and he was only helping Old Man Morgan by repairing it, but he couldn't stay inside the house another minute.

He drove in another nail, more deliberately this time, using every ounce of restraint he possessed. He'd thought he'd come to terms with the fact that they traveled in two different circles, that he'd never be more to her than the gangly schoolboy who'd once watched over her.

Why now, when he least needed any more problems, would he feel any differently? He angrily pounded in another nail, narrowly missing his thumb.

Somehow he managed to finish mending the busted gate without injury. He led Sarah's mare into the corral. Happy to be out of its tiny stall in the barn, it rounded the perimeter of the fence, nickering into the air, ears alert.

Maybe being penned up with Sarah for so many hours was what had made him edgy, Jesse thought, watching the horse frolic like a colt. He'd come back late last night and tried to sleep in the chair by her bed, but instead kept watch over her as she slept, her lovely face a puzzle he couldn't decipher. Had she changed, or had he?

He went back into the barn and saddled Sage. It just wasn't natural for a bachelor to be in such close confines with an unmarried woman. Now that she was on the mend, he should limit the time he spent with her.

Soon she'd be back home where her every desire was met. She wouldn't need him. And he sure didn't need the kind of problems that falling for Sarah Morgan would inevitably bring.

Chapter Eight

Jesse yawned, rolled over and nearly fell off Sarah's kitchen table. *Damn.* Thinking he was snug in his own bed, he'd dreamt he'd gotten the loan and that his wheat crop was safely in the ground.

Nice dream, but wrong on both counts.

He'd planned on leaving Sarah alone last night, but he'd heard her whimper in her sleep and his conscience had gotten the best of him. He knew he wouldn't be able to live with himself if he let anything happen to her.

Still fully clothed, he slowly got to his feet. He'd left the bedroom door ajar and stretched out on the hard slab of rough-hewn ash in the kitchen, then drifted in and out of a restless sleep, listening in case she called out for him. The dirt floor would have been softer, but he'd forgotten his bedroll. All in all, he hadn't had a good night's rest since he had found her.

Trying to work a kink out of his neck, he heard her stirring in the bedroom. He glanced inside her room, ready to avert his eyes if she needed privacy.

"Good morning," she said winsomely, eyelids heavy from sleep. Wisps of the hair he'd hacked short curled enticingly around her face. *The woman would look good even during a hailstorm.* .

"Mornin'." He hastily retreated from the door. He wanted to give her another tablespoon of sorghum molasses for her color, but she had put up such a fuss yesterday, he'd rather force-feed a bull while waving a red flag.

He'd fry up some cornmeal mush instead, and sweeten it with sorghum so she couldn't taste it.

"Did you sleep well?" she asked from the other room.

"Oh, yeah," he grumbled, stoking the fire.

"So did I. It's surprising how comfortable a bed without springs can be."

"Is that a fact?" he said, melting a dollop of lard in the cast-iron skillet. Rich folks sure weren't the same as common folks. Even the worn-out mattress Morgan had put in his homestead looked to be better than anything Jesse had ever slept on— especially the past few nights.

Jesse added the doctored mush to the fat. It popped and crackled, filling the sod house with the sweet smell of corn. When it was browned on both sides, he scooped half of it onto a plate and took it in to Sarah.

"Can you feed yourself this morning?" He placed the food next to her bed.

"I think I can manage." She sat up in bed, exposing the lacy tatting on the top of her nightgown.

He raised his gaze from the gently sloping mounds beneath her gown to her face, determined not to think about the curves so poorly concealed by her clothing. Even in the low light, he could see how pale her cheeks still were. Maybe she needed some fresh air and exercise. Nothing that might wear her out.

He opened the armoire and examined the two dresses he'd brought back last night. One was stiff and brown, but very functional. The other was softer, but more worn. They weren't what she was used to, but they were better than the clothes John Morgan had left in the cabin.

"Put this on and I'll take you out for some air," he said, tossing the blue flowered garment onto the bed. "You can dress yourself, can't you?"

"Since I was four," she said, grinning at his expense.

He stifled a smile. The new Sarah was unpredictable, like a half-broken filly.

"This cloth is lovely," she said, picking up the dress. She fingered the faded fabric as if it were loomed with the finest thread. "Modern reproductions just don't capture the same feel."

Unsure whether she was still making fun of him,

he watched her rub the garment across her cheek. The hue of the cornflowers and daisies deepened the shade of her dark eyes.

"Do you like blue?" she asked. "I noticed you debated over which dress I should wear."

"Blue's your favorite color," he said softly. "At least it used to be."

"How do you know?"

"I gave you a robin's egg when you were six, and you told me it reminded you of your mother's eyes. You said whenever you missed her, you just looked up at the blue sky so you wouldn't forget."

And then she'd shyly kissed him on the lips, Jesse thought, uncomfortably shifting his weight to the other foot.

Even without her memory loss, he doubted she'd remember; but it had been his first kiss and he hadn't washed his face for a week.

He looked at the lips which no longer belonged to a girl, but to a grown woman. The quiet between them grew to a roar. He was close enough to kiss her. "I best get to the chores," he said suddenly. "Whistle when you're ready to go outside."

He turned and left the room. He'd worked up a powerful appetite. Even sleeping all night laid out like a stiff at Newly Carson's Undertaking Parlor had done nothing to pacify it. He kicked the door open and strode out of the house, ignoring the other piece of mush in the skillet.

It could be manna from heaven for all he cared. His appetite wasn't for food.

* * *

Dierdre watched Jesse pumping water into the horse trough with a vengeance. After chopping wood like a fiend, he'd tossed his shirt across a tree limb and primed the pump by pouring water in it from a bucket. He splashed fresh water onto his face and chest and under his arms, the pioneer man's version of a cold shower. If anything could convince her that she'd traveled to a different time and place, it was the very real way this handsome man of the land affected her.

Gazing out the window, she bit into the cornmeal mush cake he'd made her, smiling as she detected the faint taste of molasses. He had such definite ideas about what she needed to regain her strength.

She knew she was a nuisance to him. She also knew she had more important things to think about than how Jesse Colburn looked without a shirt. She should be concentrating on getting well. She needed to figure out how to get out of this time-warp. But watching the sun glance off his rippling back muscles as he worked was mesmerizing nonetheless, and she could not look away.

The simple sod house, the seamless virgin prairie, the animal attraction of a man who survived on the land, and earned his living by the honest sweat of his brow. . . .

Dierdre blushed, realizing how far her observations had wandered from strictly a historian's point of view. She pushed the plate of food aside and picked up the dress Jesse had laid out for her. She'd seen such humble clothing displayed in museums, but had never hoped to try on such a piece herself.

She took off her nightgown and slipped on the dress. Instead of buttons, it had ties on each side to let out the waist to accommodate weight fluctuations . . . including pregnancy. Untying the straps, Dierdre adjusted them to her size. Then, in a moment of fancy, she released them again, blousing out the substantial folds of material that would allow for the growth of a baby.

If her ill-timed wish to change places with the pregnant Sarah hadn't come true, she might be buying maternity clothes in stores where she'd only window-shopped before. Smoothing her hand over her flat stomach, she felt a pang of sadness. She didn't even know whether her own unborn baby had survived the fall.

A shadow passed in front of the door, startling her from her thoughts. From the doorway, Jesse watched her, his shirt back on and buttoned, an intensity behind his stare that she hadn't felt from him before.

Embarrassed, she tightened the laces, wondering how long he'd been standing there. "It's lovely," she said. "So different from what I'm used to."

He shuffled his feet, remembering the last time he'd seen a woman in that dress. His heart lurched with the memory. At the time, he'd thought he was grown, that he'd seen it all. He'd been fourteen, and although older than his years, far from being a man. He just hadn't known it yet.

"Ready to go outside?" he asked hoarsely.

Sarah nodded and stood up. What little color had been put back in her cheeks drained out. Swaying, she grabbed the wall for support and dislodged a chink of sod, raining dirt onto the floor.

Jesse grit his teeth. "Do you need me to carry you?"

He hoped she'd refuse. He'd undertaken this job and now had to see it through, but he wasn't at all sure he wanted to get too close to her again.

"No. I just got up too fast." Coughing, she dusted off her hands, wobbling on unsteady legs.

"Maybe, but you look like a newborn filly trying out her legs for the first time." Surely he could handle helping her just this once. After all, he didn't want her to fall.

"I'm fine."

"Lean on me," he insisted. "It's just until you get the blood circulating again."

"That's really not necessary," she said, taking an uncertain step. "I'm quite capable . . ."

A knee buckled and she nearly went down. He caught her, tucking her arm firmly in his. "Proud as a peacock," he muttered, helping her through the narrow doorway. She had a hidden stubborn streak a mile long. From what he knew of her as a child, he would have never guessed.

He guided her through the kitchen and out the front door, his arm resting against her rib cage. With each step, he could feel her womanly softness, appealingly unbound by any corset or foundations. He hadn't thought to bring her any

79

undergarments. To his chagrin, he realized he wasn't completely sorry.

As they crossed the uneven ground outside, her breathing grew labored. He felt her lean more heavily on him—in spite of her pride. "We can rest now if you need to," he said.

"No. I can make it. There's so much I need to see."

A little further on, she stopped. "Is that soap weed?" she asked excitedly.

"Of course." He glanced at the look of wonder softening her face. Sarah had to have seen a thousand of the thistly bushes in her life.

"Isn't it beautiful? Too bad we'll have to dig it up."

"Why would you want to do that?" he asked.

"So a calf won't accidentally poke its eye out on the spikes," she said innocently.

He stared at her in amazement. "Where did you get that idea in your head?"

"My mother told me that when I was little." She shifted her weight off him until she was standing straighter.

"You'll have your hands full if you're planning on digging up every thistle you find. They're everywhere."

"Oh. I suppose you're right," she said with a sigh. "But one can dream."

Not if he's smart, Jesse thought, dragging his gaze from the rich depths of her brown eyes. Slowly he led her to the nearest shade, a cottonwood tree under which he'd scattered hay from the barn.

She tilted back her head and inhaled deeply. "The smell."

"The straw's fresh," Jesse said, his jaw tensing. "If there's an odor, it could be from that stagnant pond down by the creek. It'll dry up in a few months."

"What I mean is, the air smells wild and fertile, like a place where things can put down roots and grow for a thousand years." She sat down on the ground and lifted a piece of straw to her nose. "The city never smelled like this. In some ways it's going to be hard to go back home."

Standing under the sweeping arms of the cottonwood, Jesse studied Sarah, wondering for the second time whether she was teasing him. Surely she was anxious to return to the comforts of her fancy house. He knew for a fact that the governor's wife had given Sarah a rocking chair crafted during the American Revolution. He'd heard it sat next to a marble hearth that came all the way from Italy. Since outgrowing braids and pinafores, Sarah had probably never had to sit directly on the ground with just a cushion of straw.

Yet when she talked this way—as if everything were new and fresh to her, as if she felt the same things for the land that he did—he could almost forget that she came from a different world . . . that her father was his enemy.

He leaned back against the trunk and gazed at the distant hills. Nestled in the cradle of a nearby valley, a dozen pronghorn antelope grazed with their young.

"What are you looking at?" she asked.

"Just antelope." Glancing down at Sarah, he noticed that she'd folded her legs under her much as a doe might—stately, maternal.

"Where?" she asked enthusiastically.

He patiently pointed out the pronghorns camouflaged among an outcropping of rocks. She searched the horizon, following his direction, for a sight that should have been as natural to her as the dawn or the setting sun. When she shook her head, he sat down beside her.

"In the valley beyond the nearest hill," he said, sighting down his arm for her like the barrel of a shotgun. She moved closer, tilting her head toward him until her chin nearly touched his shoulder.

"There. Look for their white markings. The fawns have spots for protection." His breath growing shallow, he was a boy again, sitting next to little Sarah Morgan. He could almost imagine that the years between them had melted away and he was still the unjaded youth who had watched out for her when she needed help.

"Oh, I see them now," she said suddenly. "They're beautiful. There's three, no, four . . .Oh, there's a whole herd." Sarah's eyes lit up, twinkling in the sunlight that dappled the leaves above.

And then he wished she would kiss him again.

"I don't ever remember seeing such a spectacular sight," she said, her hands fisted under her chin as if she could barely contain her pleasure.

A puff of wind kicked up her short, curly hair, tousling it as effectively as a restless night's sleep. He fought down the urge to comb his fingers through the wayward strands.

He shouldn't be wasting time with her, letting his mind drift in impossible directions, he told himself. Then she licked her lips against the dry wind, leaving an inviting sheen of moisture, and all he could think about was how sweet the taste of her mouth would be on his.

He fixed his gaze on the antelope, denying himself another look at her, but she shifted positions and the wind filled his nose with her scent. He turned his head, trying to escape her unsettling assault on his senses.

"I don't suppose you ever get lonely out here, do you?" she asked, her voice floating over the natural harmony of the prairie sounds.

Jesse wanted to snort. It could get so empty and cold on the Nebraska plains, he sometimes wondered why he didn't give it up and move away.

"Although I suppose people can feel alone anywhere," she continued. "Even in a place as big as New York City."

He looked at her against his will. What did she know about feeling alone? Given her father's circle of friends and the allure of her dowry, she must have a social life that rivaled anyone in the Sand Hills.

"There's enough work to keep me busy year-round," he said. He wasn't about to admit how often he longed to see another human being during the long Nebraska winters.

"I'm sure there is. Though I think one of the dangers of progress is becoming too busy. This is the first opportunity I've had to stop and take stock—and it was a forced vacation at that." She laughed.

He knew she'd lose interest in the simple life once she returned to her privileged home, but the lightness of her carefree laugh made that time seem a long way off.

"What do you do for fun?" she asked. "Surely you can't work all the time. What do you do when the fields are planted or the crops harvested?"

Jesse tried to remember when he'd last had any real fun. He went into town whenever he needed supplies, but that had ceased being an adventure and had become just another chore when his mother died.

If he had to pick one thing he really wanted to do, it might be to sit right here with Sarah, watching her eyes light up as she discovered the world all over again.

She looked at him, her upturned mouth poised to ask her next question. She must have read the answer in his eyes, for the unspoken words melted from her lips, vanishing into an expression of childlike wonder.

Beneath her fleeting look of confusion, he saw a beauty her recent illness couldn't hide, a depth of emotion as appealing as the first dawn. He leaned toward her, the sun's warmth on his face no match for the fever burning inside of him.

Starve a fever, the folk remedy went. Or was it feed a fever? He was starving all right.

He put his arm around her waist and pulled her closer, feeling her curves beneath his fingers as he drew her near. This wasn't the innocent schoolgirl he'd had a crush on his whole life. This was a woman through whose eyes he was beginning to see his own world anew.

She gazed up at him, her fingers clutching his arm, her ragged breathing mirroring his hunger. Every ounce of common sense he possessed warned him to run like hell. After all, hadn't she just miscarried another man's baby? But if he could just get Sarah out of his system, he told himself, then when all this was over and she had gone home, he'd be able to walk away without regrets.

He traced the soft angles around her mouth with his thumb and felt her quiver beneath his touch. *Feed* a fever, he heard echoing in his brain. He wasn't sure he was thinking straight, but it sounded right to him. She'd soon be well . . . and so would he.

She tilted her mouth up to welcome his, and then it was too late to change his mind. He pressed his mouth to hers and heard a soft moan escape her lips as she returned the kiss.

Warm and willing, her ardent reaction dispelled any doubts about her interest in him. As she melted against him, the vast prairie seemed to shrink. The deliciousness of her warm mouth shut out everything else around them.

Beneath his lips, she whimpered her pleasure.

Reluctantly, he reminded himself that it was John Morgan's daughter he was kissing like there was no tomorrow. He was attempting to save her reputation, not contribute to its ruination.

"I better get you out of the sun," he said, pulling away.

She brushed the grass off her skirt, her cheeks coloring. "Yes, it's certainly heating up."

He stood up, extending his arm to her, but even the warmth of Sarah's hand in his told him he'd made a big mistake. He'd tasted heaven, but it hadn't satisfied his appetite. Her sweet kisses had only stoked his hunger for more.

Tonight, he was *definitely* going home to his own place.

Chapter Nine

I woke up today to the bustling sound of the city, wondering with anticipation what the new day might bring. In Nebraska, my only reprieve from the endless boredom of the ordinary was the moments I dreamt about a different kind of life.

Once while my father was out riding the range, a traveling peddler with a trained goat for a companion stopped at our ranch. He showed me postcards from around the world with pictures on the front colored in pastel. Hidden deep in a trunk, he had colorful can-cans, dresses which he said came all the way from the theatrical stages in Paris, France. I blushed and fingered the stiff crinoline as if it were magical, before remembering my strict upbringing.

Eschewing the eye-catching frills and colorful garters, I debated whether to buy a collection of sweet-

Victoria Bruce

smelling tea leaves imported from exotic countries, or something more practical. I finally settled upon a serving spoon, a tin of biscuits, and a pair of warm gloves like I'd seen advertised in the newest Sears catalogue.

The peddler let the goat bring over my purchases from the wagon in his mouth. After I wrested the dented tin from the animal, I rewarded him and myself with a few of the biscuits. Savoring the tasty crackers, I listened in rapture as the salesman regaled me with fascinating stories of his travels. Unfortunately, not content with just the crackers, the goat nearly chewed clean through the newel on the gatepost before my father returned and chased off both the man and his pet.

I was heartily lectured about talking with strangers and restricted to my room for several days, yet every time I saw that gnawed-up post, I'd think about what adventure might lie just around the corner.

To my grave disappointment, when I finally traveled "around the corner"—from Prairie Bend east to Omaha and north to South Dakota—I only found more of the same: prairie, cattle and tumbleweeds.

New York. Now that is as far around the corner as I am likely to ever get. I have yet to see a tumbleweed. I never want to leave.

Selfish as it may seem, I just hope Dierdre doesn't decide she wants her body back. I've never felt so petite. My skin feels smooth and silky, and Mr. Vanderbrief has brought numerous jars of creams and lotions to help me keep it that way. I've learned words like collagen, emollient, and sunscreen.

My fingers are long and narrow and lily-white—
what my mother would have referred to as refined.
With these hands I can actually learn to play the
piano if I want, instead of merely driving my music
teachers mad with my clumsy efforts. My nails are
long with perfect half-moons at the base. Among the
presents Mr. Vanderbrief has brought to cheer me, I
found the most startling array of nail lacquer. I
haven't the courage to paint my fingernails, but
I applied a different color of polish to every toenail.

As I discover this whole new world, I do wonder
what has become of my life. Has Dierdre Brown
taken my place in society? Is she more comfortable
than I representing the Morgan family at prominent
social functions? More adept than I at handling the
suitors who line up, wanting to court my father's
land?

And what of the father of my dead baby? Did he
want anything more of me than a quick, rough mat-
ing? He could have gotten that in town at far less
dear a price than I paid.

I fear he was no different from the others. Perhaps
only less restrained. I hope his clever ways don't fool
the new Sarah Morgan as they did me. For I would
not like to exchange that kind of life with her for
anything.

Even though my conscience dictates that I
shouldn't enjoy taking someone else's life as much
as I am, I cannot bring myself to trade places
again—even if it were under my control.

Mr. Vanderbrief is the perfect gentleman. In a

*time when men are apparently much more forward
with a woman, he is teaching me that a true gentleman controls his desires, considering the wants of
the lady even above his own wishes.*

*Surely this chivalrous approach would have put
him in good stead had he lived in 1887, but I find
it even more attractive in its stark contrast to relationships of the present.*

*When it is deemed safe for me to be up and
around, he will take me to something he calls Central Park, an outing he hopes will bring the color
back to my cheeks. I can't wait.*

Chapter Ten

Even though she'd read Sarah's personal account, along with the writings of a hundred others, Dierdre had had no idea what life on the plains for a pioneer woman was really like. She hadn't realized how affected she'd be by the untainted beauty of her simple surroundings. She hadn't known how tempting it would be to lean on someone as solid and virile as Jesse. And she didn't know what she might have done if he hadn't gone home last night.

With the sun just peeping over the horizon—its early-morning rays gradually coloring in the black, shadowy scene outside her bedroom window—she chided herself. She'd indulged her curiosity enough. It was time to get serious about finding a way home. She replayed her last memories of the future, looking for answers.

That final day in the bookstore, she'd sat beneath an umbrella of light, doing what she loved best: reading about history. Accompanied by the soothing hum of the antique ceiling fan, she'd felt an instant kinship with Sarah as she'd read her account of a woman's life on the prairie.

She'd been reading the journal right before she blacked out. The last thing she remembered after falling was closing her fingers around the worn binding of the diary. Was Sarah's diary the key to her time-traveling? And if so, with the journal in the future, what good could it do her now?

Except it wasn't just in the future, Dierdre realized. It was also in the past. Sarah had written in it just a few days ago. Her last entry had described how she'd decided to visit Becky until her father returned.

She had to find it, Dierdre decided. Jesse hadn't wanted her even stirring when he wasn't here, but this was something that couldn't wait. Maybe Sarah had hidden her diary here, away from her father's watchful eyes. She'd thoroughly search the soddie. Jesse wouldn't even know.

As she rolled over to get out of bed, a spasm knifed through her back. Unable to get up, she realized how ill-advised her overexertion had been the previous afternoon. After their kiss Jesse had charged off, claiming he had chores, and she'd decided to take on a task of her own. By the time he had returned to make her dinner, she'd been back in bed, with no apparent after-effects. Fortunately, he wasn't here to see her now.

Trying to get more comfortable, she rolled onto her back again and gasped in pain, frozen in position by the newest wave of spasms. She felt as if her spine had been twisted into one of the pretzels street vendors sold in Manhattan.

Involuntarily, she moaned and clutched her back—just as the front door opened. "What's wrong?" Jesse hurried into the room.

Like a kid caught with her hand in the candy jar, Dierdre jerked her head around and sent another dagger down her back. When the hell had he ridden up? "It's nothing," she lied. "Just a little twinge in my back."

"I can see it's a lot more than that," he said. "You're gritting your teeth from the pain. I'll get the doctor. He probably won't want to come, but—"

"No. It's all right. I'll live. I may not want to," she said dryly, "but I will."

"That's nothing to joke about," Jesse said fiercely. "You could have died."

That would have been horrible for Sarah, Dierdre thought, *but then maybe I'd be in the future where I belong*. "It wouldn't have been your fault. You did everything you could."

"But how would I have known that?" he asked, the pain in his gaze so intense it was nearly palpable.

"I just tried to do too much," she said, wondering what could be the source of so much suffering.

Certainly his distress went far deeper than the casual concern of a neighbor.

"What did you do?"

"I'm always taking on more than I'm capable of," she said, stalling.

"Tell me," he growled.

"I dug up the soap weed."

"You what?" He swore under his breath. "Yesterday, you couldn't even stand without help."

"Once I got up and around, I started feeling much better."

"But to dig up a soap weed? No one in their right—"

"You can say it." She'd concede him the point. Her sanity was definitely in question, and he didn't know the half of it. Her only hope was that Sarah was in the future, taking better care of her life than Dierdre was of Sarah's.

Jesse watched the tight ball huddled on the bed. Her carelessness infuriated him. He clenched his fists.

"I wanted to help. I was wrong to overdo it, but maybe there's a lot that could be done to protect the animals," she argued.

"Like digging up every soap weed plant within fifty square miles?"

"I didn't want a lost calf who hadn't learned about things like sharp soap weed plants to get hurt." She changed position and softly moaned. "It was a lot harder to get out of the ground than I expected," she admitted.

The Morgans had two thousand head of cattle.

While Jesse was trying everything he knew to keep Sarah safe, she was more worried about a stray calf than herself. He didn't know which he wanted to do more—yell at her or pull her into his arms. He was dangerously close to the latter.

Abruptly, he turned on his heel and walked out of the soddie before he could do something crazy.

Without looking back, he mounted Sage and rode like the wind: unfeeling, relentless. He wished he could just keep on riding until she was out of his life. She'd go back to her father at the first pressure Morgan put on her, and where would that leave *him?* While she was snug in her fancy home, he'd still be facing bankruptcy; he'd just be further behind in his work.

He made up his mind. He wouldn't go back. He'd take care of his stock, then ride five miles to see his neighbor, Mrs. Dickens. He'd report Sarah's illness like he should have in the beginning. He'd be free from her by nightfall.

The door creaked open. Dierdre hadn't heard anyone come up and she felt herself automatically tense. The twinges in her back flared up and she gritted her teeth.

It had been dark for hours. She'd slipped in and out of a restless sleep, trying first one position then the other.

"Sarah." Jesse's voice carried through the cabin. "I brought something for your back."

"A hot bath, I hope," she murmured.

She heard him sit down in the chair next to the

bed. "Something better. Can you roll over so your back is toward me?" he asked, lighting a candle.

Jesse watched her painfully work her way onto her side. "I'll need you to lift up your nightdress."

He felt a flush rise up his neck. He shouldn't be here. If anyone knew what he was doing, they'd hang his hide on the barn door to dry. Why hadn't he gone to the Dickens's farm like he'd planned? He'd be home in bed right now instead of losing sleep over someone who didn't seem to understand the seriousness of her plight.

"Uh, okay," she said after a moment's hesitation. She inched her nightclothes up to the level of her chest, but kept herself covered with the bedsheet.

"Now this may feel hot," he cautioned. He removed the lid of the tin. Holding his breath, he dipped his fingers into the ointment and replaced the lid. With a tentative motion, he slid his hand under the sheet and applied the balm to her back, in big circles just like he'd done to his Lucy when she'd strained a tendon.

"Ow, that burns. What the hell are you using on my back?"

Astonished, Jesse stopped rubbing her muscles. He'd never heard a lady swear before. "Horse liniment," he answered, holding his hand as far from his nose and eyes as possible.

"Do I look like a horse?" she hissed in the darkness.

"Of course not."

"Then why did you think you'd treat me like one?"

Without letting her secret out to the whole town, he hadn't known what else to do. The way she was hollering, the town might hear anyway.

He shook his head. "Thank God Lucy didn't put up such a fuss when I rubbed her down. I'd have had to shoot her."

"Who's Lucy?"

"An old mare of mine."

"Oh. Will it help?"

"Shooting you? I doubt it."

"Very funny." Her tone changed, went shrewd. "By the way, what happened to your pistol? I haven't seen it since that first day."

"Fortunately for you, I turned it in," he said, applying the liniment. He massaged the corded muscles between her shoulder blades down the length of her spine, his fingers on fire.

"That really stings," she complained. "Are you sure this is okay for human use?"

He snorted. "No idea. But my daddy used to say, what doesn't kill you makes you stronger."

"I'm going to be a regular Goliath then," she muttered. "Do you have to rub so hard? I'd like to save some skin . . ."

She broke off, her complaint dying in her throat, replaced by a sudden purr of pleasure. "Oh, right there. That's the spot."

"I believe Goliath was bested by the young David," he pointed out.

"All the more reason to be gentle with me."

She quit pulling away and her muscles began to relax beneath his touch. He felt the gentle curve

97

of her waist and the small of her back. The fire in his fingers faded, leaving them acutely attuned to the softness of her hot, silky skin.

Massaging the swell of her muscles at the hips, he realized that except for her nightgown, she was completely naked. He felt a tightening in his groin and concentrated on working out the knots, trying to ignore the pliant feel of her skin beneath his hands. Doctors had to think this way all the time, he reminded himself, struggling to keep his hands from trembling. Knowing he must remain impartial, he massaged the tightest area. She groaned and arched gently against his hand. "That feels great."

He blew out a long breath and put the lid back on the jar. He found it easier when she was complaining. "That's enough," he said.

"Are you sure?" she asked.

He was far from a doctor and had the wandering thoughts to prove it. "Quite sure."

"Oh." She sounded disappointed.

He forced himself to his feet. "I may not be able to come by tomorrow. I'll leave the liniment on the nightstand in case you want to use it again. Think you can manage?"

"Of course," she said, the vulnerability going out of her voice.

Jesse wiped his stinging hand on his pants and left without another word. He didn't trust himself with her. Not anymore. Not tonight. Maybe not tomorrow. He should have told the neighbors about her like he'd planned. But since he hadn't, he'd stay away as much as possible.

He walked Sage past the place where Sarah had seen the soap weed. In the moonlight he could see that she'd carefully dug up the plant and replaced the hole with dirt, probably worried that the hapless calf who'd narrowly avoided poking an eye out might now stumble and break a leg.

With a snap of the reins against his thigh, he urged his horse into a canter, hoping the night air would clear his mind. He'd thought Sarah defenseless without his help, just like the "poor cows" she hoped to protect.

Even as he left her far behind, he could feel each stroke of his hands on her smooth skin. He'd been a damn fool. While he'd been worrying over her, he'd been the one who needed protection.

True to his word, Jesse didn't show up at all the next day. Dierdre had no intention of using the liniment he'd left for her. Fortunately, her back felt much better.

In spite of what her erstwhile masseuse would probably say, she searched the soddie for the diary. It didn't take long to realize that it wasn't inside the sparsely furnished place. Unless Sarah had buried it outdoors, which didn't seem likely given the condition of the journal's pages and binding, she probably kept it somewhere in her bedroom. Dierdre spent the rest of the day planning how to get inside the Morgan house.

Yet as hard as she tried to keep her thoughts on

getting home, she kept remembering how Jesse's sure hands had expertly strummed the taut muscles of her back like a priceless guitar, nearly driving her wild before he was through. For that reason alone, straining her back again was tempting.

It wasn't until the morning of the following day that she heard the sound of his horse slowly trotting toward the soddie. Unable to control her excitement over seeing him again, she ran outside to greet him.

"How's the back?" he asked.

"Very well. I'm thinking I should find something else to dig up." If not to get another back rub, at least just to annoy him. With satisfaction, she watched a look of dismay cross his face before it melted into a testy grin.

"You didn't get enough liniment?" he asked.

"Oh, yes." She'd gotten more than enough of the smelly stuff, if not of the hands that had applied it.

"I do believe you're right." He lifted his nose into the air and sniffed. "I must be downwind."

She laughed and took a deep breath, but she'd become accustomed to the scent of the liniment. She was sure, though, that she still smelled like a locker room on game day. "I think what I need is a bath."

"Can't argue with that."

"How would I go about getting one?"

"Unless you favor washing in the horse trough,

there's always the creek down by the cotton-woods."

"That sounds fine." In her position, she couldn't expect Crowne Plaza.

"I can take you there," he offered.

"That isn't necessary. I can manage on my own."

"I'm not letting you go off half-cocked again."

She grinned. "Afraid I might find some more soap weed?"

"No. But if you're going to bathe in the creek, you'll need someone watching out for you."

Jesse had "watched out" for her the night before last, and had her muscles, bones and body singing three-part harmony before he was done. Just the thought gave her goose bumps. She rubbed her arms, trying to erase her reaction. "I haven't seen another soul besides you for a week. What are the chances of someone stumbling across me the minute I take off my clothes?"

"You never know," he said stubbornly. "You can't be too careful."

She stared at the deep creases around his mouth, worry etched in his furrowed brow. To look at him, one would think she'd just told him she was going to walk through Central Park alone after dark.

"All right," she finally relented. "You win."

"I'm glad you're willing to listen to reason."

"It wouldn't hurt if it went both ways," she pointed out.

"I'm a very reasonable man."

She lifted an eyebrow. "If you say so."

"Climb on," he said, slipping his boot out of the stirrup.

"Excuse me?" She automatically stepped back from his horse.

"It's a good ways to the creek. I doubt it's smart to walk that far yet."

She inspected the horse's back, and Sage swished a fly off his back with his tail as if inviting her to get on. She didn't want to admit that she didn't know how to ride. Jesse already thought her helpless.

"Ready?" Jesse held down his hand to her. "If it's supplies you're worried about, I've got soap and a clean towel in my saddlebags."

"Uh, no. It isn't that."

"Is it too soon after losing the baby?"

She saw a shadow of worry cross his face and quickly rushed to dispel it. "I'm feeling surprisingly fit," she said. She wished she had such a resilient body in the future. It was getting on this damn animal that she was having trouble with. She took Jesse's extended hand with her right one and tried to figure out how to get her right foot into the stirrup.

"That's fine, Sarah," he said wryly, "if you're planning on riding facing me. I'll have to warn you, though. Sage isn't used to that kind of thing."

She snatched her hand away, her cheeks flushing. "I guess I'm just a little rusty at riding double."

"Put your left foot in the stirrup and give me your other hand."

Now, why hadn't he said so in the first place?

She lifted her bent leg and her foot missed the stirrup by a mile. Even with Sarah's long legs, she was too short!

Jesse slid back his hat and grinned. "I've seen old tin cans less rusty. For someone who was raised on a horse you seem to be mighty out of practice."

Lifting her skirts, she glared at him. With a grunt, she lifted her leg a little higher and pushed off the ground, hanging on to his arm with all her might.

"You can let go of my arm now."

Releasing her grip, she noticed how far she was above the ground. She'd done it! She was riding a horse. Well, they were still in neutral, but at least she'd gotten on.

"Are you ready?"

"Uh-huh." She looked for the closest handles. The only thing she could find were tiny leather braids on each side of the saddle. They looked more decorative than functional, but she grabbed one with each hand, just as the animal broke into a brisk walk.

"Whoa," she cried, losing her balance.

"Sage doesn't answer to verbal commands," Jesse said, reaching back and steadying her before she fell.

"It was you I was talking to." She searched for something more substantial than the two tiny braids to hold on to. Jesse's waist was the obvious choice, but she chose the back of the saddle rim instead. It might not be as secure for her physically, but it certainly would be safer emotionally.

"I'm not sure I mind much better," he said, nonetheless slowing the horse to a walk.

"I don't doubt it." She peered at the moving ground. "But I'll get the hang of it soon."

"You've got plenty of time," he drawled. "At this rate, we'll get to the creek sometime next week."

"At least I'll arrive in one piece," she muttered under her breath.

"Did you say something?"

She tossed her head, letting the wind blow through her short hair. Let him make fun of her. She might not know how to do anything more athletic than catch a bus, but she'd be damned if she'd let him get the best of her.

Just as she was congratulating herself on keeping one leg on each side of the horse, Sage started climbing a short steep rise. Dierdre lost her grip on the rim of the saddle. Feeling herself slipping backwards, she threw her arms around Jesse, holding on so tightly that her body pressed against his.

She told herself it was better than having to listen to his griping if she fell off. Unfortunately, the expanse of his broad back against her chest was even more warm and inviting than she'd imagined. Maybe it was the adrenaline rush of fear from her first trip on a horse, but her breath quickened and her pulse began to race.

As she clung to him, she absently speculated what his work-hardened back would feel like without his shirt. A thrill coursed through her, sending her blood pressure higher. Jesse's earthy masculinity was proving far more appealing to her than any Wall Street hotshot.

Thankfully, they reached the copse of tall, shimmery trees. "Need a hand?" Jesse agilely threw a leg over the saddle horn and got down.

A gentle rustling stirred through the cottonwood leaves, whispering over the trickle of the creek. She started to refuse the offer of help, as she'd done most of her adult life. Suddenly tired of fighting the specter of dependency, she submitted to his outstretched arms, letting him swing her from the horse. With the ease of a man accustomed to hard manual labor, he set her gently on solid ground, his capable hands encircling her waist.

That hadn't been so bad, she decided, when he had released her. Relying upon someone besides herself might occasionally have its advantages.

While Jesse tied Sage to a tree, she sat down on a grassy outcropping. She plunged her feet into the shallow water and let the stream flow over her legs.

It was cool and invigorating.

Jesse watched her kick her feet in the creek. "Maybe I should have taken you back home for your bath. You seem well enough to go when you're ready."

"I do want to go back where I came from," she said quietly, "but it's not going to be quite that easy."

Sensing that Sarah's thoughts were a long way

off, Jesse felt a jealous twinge. "Sure it is," he said, frowning. "I can hitch up the wagon and see you get there today." He wanted her to agree, he told himself. Then he could forget about her, get his mind back on his crops.

She nodded. "If you're talking about me going to the Morgan ranch, I would like you to take me there, but I don't want to stay."

His heart leapt in his chest, betraying his common sense. He knew things couldn't go on as they were, but while not seeing her yesterday, he'd had trouble staying away. The sooner he made the break with her, the better. "Your father will expect it."

"I don't care. I'm not the same person I was when you knew me before."

Hearing the conviction in her voice, he was tempted to believe her, but what about when she got her memory back wholly? "You have nothing to lose now," he explained. "No one else ever need know about what happened. I fixed it with the doctor so he won't tell."

"How did you do that?"

He shrugged. "I paid him off."

"Oh," she said, smiling. "That was very kind of you. Still, there's only one place I belong, and it's definitely not with John Morgan." Although she was gazing right at him, her eyes seemed to be looking far into the future.

"You'll see things differently when he gets home. No one goes against your father and gets away with it."

"No." She shook her head, chasing away the distant look in her eyes. "This has nothing to do with him. I have more important things at stake. I won't knuckle under to his pressure. I have enough obstacles in my way as it is."

He watched a leaf float past, get caught in an eddy and swirl round and round until it finally broke loose and disappeared downstream. That sparkle in her eyes when she'd run out of the soddie might have been for him, but it didn't matter, he told himself.

Sarah didn't remember him. She'd barely given him more than a few words of polite conversation in years. Even if she hadn't lost her memory, how much notice had she paid him as he toiled on his farm? She wouldn't have given him a moment of her time if she hadn't gotten into trouble. Jesse suddenly went cold inside.

"You don't know what it's like to struggle," he told her, his tone likewise chilled. "To worry about where the next meal's coming from. You've known only luxury. Now that you've decided to stoop to the level of a homesteader, you think you can spend a week or two here, and show your father how strong you are. But there's more to living off the land than play-acting."

"You're right," she said pensively. "I don't know what living off the land is like. Not firsthand anyway. And I have been spoiled. But it's not what I wanted. Don't hold it against me."

"You're well enough to go home now," he said

sharply, "but what you do from here on out is none of my business."

She scooped up a fistful of water and let it drain through her fingers. "Whatever's eating at you, you can't go on keeping it bottled inside."

That was easy for her to say. All the times he'd worked for Morgan as a boy, the man had made no secret how he felt about poor farmers. Even while Jesse was still mourning the loss of his father, Old Man Morgan hadn't let him forget his place.

After the death of his stepfather, his mother had worked herself to the bone. Morgan's neighborly response had been to turn up the pressure for her to sell him the farm. Once, on the outside looking in, he'd seen Sarah dancing at her thirteenth birthday party. That was during a moment stolen from his never-ending list of chores.

The memories were imprinted on his heart and his mind, but he forced the thoughts back into the recesses of his brain, unwilling to dwell on the seething anger that had fueled him for so long.

He couldn't change history. It was time he quit imagining he had anything Sarah might want. He'd take her home if that was what she wished, but he'd leave her there. Then he'd go see about his loan before Morgan got back from Ogallala and made things any harder.

Suddenly, Sage lifted his head and sniffed the wind from the south, his grazing forgotten. Jesse searched the horizon. A dozen riders crested the hill riding three abreast, led by a great black horse garbed in silver tack that sparkled in the sunlight.

Jesse's throat tightened, dry as the cloud of dust following the hard-riding posse. The devil had returned. John Morgan was home.

Chapter Eleven

The thunder of hooves crashed through the stillness of the prairie, growing louder, and Deirdre noticed a nearby herd of antelope bound away, white tails erect, bodies stiff with fright. The rhythmic blowing and wheezing of the galloping horses, in contrast to the absolute silence of the riders, blended into an unnerving symphony with the tympanic rumble of hoofbeats.

If Dierdre had needed further proof that the dream world in which she'd awakened was real—or that the harshness of 1887 Nebraska spared no one—the alarming sound echoing across the quiet prairie sufficed. Forsaking her bath, she pulled on her shoes and socks. She reached out to Jesse for reassurance, but he was gone. He'd disappeared as stealthily as a highwayman in the night, leaving her to face the unknown alone, abandoned.

Dread and uncertainty escalating, she prayed the horsemen would continue over the hill, but the lead man motioned with his gloved fist and the band veered directly toward her.

Heart beating an irregular tattoo, she gladly would have fled, too. Confronted by a motley band of men with pistols on their hips and rifles strapped to their saddles, she longed to return to the relative safety of a Manhattan apartment guarded by a safety chain, two dead bolts, and a motion-activated burglar alarm. Never had the hazy skyline of New York City and the constant din of street noise held such appeal.

The riders remained mounted, chaps tanned by a coat of dust. Only the leader, an imposing presence in black, appeared unsullied by the trail. He halted his equally intimidating steed ten paces from where she sat. Above his ruddy cheeks and full jowls, his eyes had a dark intensity that made it difficult to look away. "What the devil have you done to your hair, girl?" he bellowed.

Instinctively, she ran her fingers through the tattered remains of her hair before realizing how easily the man had put her on the defensive. She jerked her hand away from her shorn locks. From the entries in Sarah's diary, she knew this powerful stranger with the broad shoulders and silver hair had to be John Morgan.

"Hello, Father," Dierdre said, as calmly as her nervousness would allow.

"You look like a trollop instead of the daughter

of one of the richest men in Nebraska. Did you think you would defy me this way?"

"Actually, it was an accident. I tangled with a rather formidable patch of stickers out back, and it had to be cut." She watched him digest this information as if she'd force-fed him spoiled meat.

"What were you doing here in the first place? You belong at the ranch." His shiny black horse pawed the ground, apparently no less impatient with the inconvenience she'd caused than the man who thought she was his daughter.

Trapped, she held her ground. "I'm not sure how I got here," she began. That much was true. One moment she'd been in the bookstore, the next she was gazing upon Jesse Colburn, the most incredibly handsome man she'd ever seen.

Morgan stared at her as if she were the spawn of some imbecile, and no way could she have descended from his own venerable family. "You'll have to do better than that." His hardened expression warned her that he'd long since stopped dealing with his daughter from the heart.

Yearning for an escape, Dierdre searched the endless vista for Jesse, hoping she'd been wrong about him deserting her. The only movement she could detect was the undulating expanse of grass stretching out before her. He'd undeniably left her alone.

She took a steadying breath and raised her chin. "I was on my way to town to see Becky. . . ." She tried to remember the fateful last entry in Sarah's diary. "It started to rain. My wagon got stuck in the mud and I couldn't free it."

Morgan shook his head like a massive buffalo shaking off a troublesome fly. "You know how to read the sky for weather. You should never have let the rain catch you by surprise."

Dierdre hid her clenched fists in her pockets—for Sarah's sake trying to pose as the dutiful daughter. "I realize that. When I couldn't get the wagon dislodged—"

"Forget the damn wagon," he shouted. "You can ride a horse. Mason Diggs here taught you himself when you were four years old. Now tell the truth, girl."

"Of course I can ride," she lied. "But I became ill, and I came here to recover until I was well enough to travel."

"I hope you're not taking after your mother. She was the weakest willed woman who ever walked the face of the earth."

"Now, wait just a minute." Dierdre jumped to her feet. This was Sarah's fight, not hers, but gaining her own independence had come hard and not without a struggle. "That's my mother you're speaking about."

Morgan shifted in his saddle and the leather creaked ominously. "Watch your tongue. I won't have you talking back to me—not as long as you live under my roof."

"I'm not living under your roof."

"You're on my land, drinking my water and standing under my tree."

"I thought I was homesteading this land."

"You?" He laughed. "You couldn't actually homestead any land."

"The land commissioner must think I can."

The men behind him glanced at each other uncomfortably. "Leave us," Morgan barked. "All except Mason."

Dierdre waited until the men rode off. "To keep to the terms of the Homestead Act, the person homesteading the property must live on it for five years. How would your high-placed friends feel if they knew you were defrauding the government?"

"You haven't had to lift a finger a day in your life. Manage on your own?" He gave another disbelieving laugh. "You couldn't last here a fortnight."

"We'll see, won't we?" she said, folding her arms at her chest.

John Morgan's ruddy complexion darkened. "I order you to give up this foolishness and come home now."

Jesse might not be coming back, but Dierdre didn't want to go anywhere with this tyrant. "I'll stay where I am, thank you," she said defiantly.

Morgan's dark brown eyes glittered dangerously. "You'll do as I say, girl. I'm your father. Mason will bring you home. I have company coming for supper tonight and I expect you there to act as my hostess."

Dierdre gritted her teeth to keep from telling Morgan what she thought of him, but she wanted to search the house for Sarah's diary.

"I'll come," she said, "but just for supper." She wouldn't spend the night under the same roof with Morgan.

"Where's the wagon then?" he barked, as if he'd never doubted her compliance.

She frowned, wishing *he'd* forget about the damn wagon. "In the barn."

He signaled Mason with a wave worthy of a cavalry commander. "Go get it and bring it back."

Dierdre held her breath. Jesse might be hiding in the barn until Morgan and his men left. But Mason returned alone driving the wagon, its horse tied to the rear. "There's mud up to the hub on one wheel," he said, corroborating her story.

"Let's go." Morgan reined his horse around, obviously dismissing them both.

Reluctantly, Dierdre lifted her skirts, only the hope of seeing Sarah's diary getting her into the wagon. As they rode away, she glanced back at the tiny soddie. It stood alone and desolate, just like her.

Chapter Twelve

Standing amid the cottonwoods, Jesse watched the procession head toward the Morgan place. Sarah rode in the wagon beside Mason, her father galloping ahead, his pace quickly outdistancing them. The gate Jesse had repaired stood open— there were no animals left to guard.

He'd waited, just in case she'd really needed him, but Sarah had made her allegiance clear. Jesse couldn't compete with mighty John Morgan. But then neither could she.

He hadn't wanted Morgan to find him with Sarah—that would be the surest way to ruin her reputation. Then all his efforts to conceal her secret would have been for naught. Still, he'd hoped that for once she'd stand up to her father.

As Sarah's wagon climbed the rise, he saw her

glance back at the soddie. He held his breath, wondering if she'd change her mind and come back. She'd nearly driven him crazy with her foolish stunts—dragging herself out of bed to go to the outhouse, wrenching her back digging up the soap weed plant. But she'd surprised him, too. He smiled, remembering how tenderly she'd talked about protecting a young calf who hadn't yet learned about all the dangers of the world.

Watching the wagon disappear over the horizon, the dust settling on the road to the abandoned homestead as if nothing had ever happened, Jesse felt a swift gut-kick of understanding knock the wind out of him. Judging from the way he'd mooned after her, he was no wiser than the poor calf Sarah pitied.

He'd risked a great deal for Sarah, but nothing had changed. She'd gone home just as he'd always known she would. Most likely, she'd already forgotten about him.

He lay the reins across Sage's neck and urged him toward town. Now that Sarah Morgan was back where she belonged, he could see about saving his farm.

Seymour looked down his crooked nose at the loan application and then at Jesse Colburn, who sat as restless as a contrite sinner on Sunday morning. He'd made up his mind to grant the loan, but Seymour's philosophy was that it didn't hurt to put the fear of the Lord in folks while they sweated it out.

"How will you pay back the money?" Seymour steepled his long fingers. He'd already run Colburn through his standard list of questions the week before, but he never grew tired of asking them. It made him feel important. Although he'd never admit it, his apparent attention to detail was more self-serving than in the interest of efficiency.

Jesse sat straighter, eyeing him as if he watched him from the opposite side of a magnifying glass. Had Colburn seen through his little charade? He resisted the urge to loosen what seemed to have become his noose of a collar.

"I'll repay the loan with the profits from next year's harvest."

"And what if there's a drought, or a herd of cattle break through your fence again?" Reassured, Seymour settled into his routine, his voice echoing comfortingly off the walls of his office and perhaps even to the tellers' cages beyond. With the chairman of the board out of town, the loan committee hadn't met in two weeks, but as president of the bank Seymour had the authority to approve certain small loans. He made sure he exercised his power whenever he had the chance.

"This is the first year I've had a crop fail. I've always paid my bills."

"I understand." Seymour nodded and ceremoniously penciled a note on an officious-looking piece of paper. *Write your mother*, it said. He covered it with his sleeve and continued. "If you mortgaged your property as security, I'd have less problem approving your request."

Colburn frowned and glanced out the window as if waging a battle with his conscience. "I can't do that. I promised my father I'd never sell or mortgage the land."

"You'd receive the note back as soon as you paid off the loan," Seymour pointed out. "You can't expect the bank to take all the risks."

Colburn didn't answer. Seymour tapped his pencil against his chin, then solemnly bowed his head, adding another notation to his monogrammed stationery. *Send shirts to laundry*.

"Have you access to an alternative source of funds?" he asked when he was done.

Colburn had to admit he hadn't.

Without the bank, this man would be finished, Seymour thought, permitting a small measure of pride to wash through him. So charitable was Lindsey, so tolerant of his fellow men, he could look past the fact that Jesse would never rise above the stigma of his unfortunate upbringing and limited formal education.

Seymour had to admit that to Jesse's credit, he was a hard worker and had always been self-sufficient. More important, he had a steady temperament and had never been in any legal trouble. Seymour took out his handkerchief and wiped the lenses of his spectacles. He had always detested violence. He didn't mind stooping down to help a man with dirt under his fingernails, but he abhorred the lack of self-control in those who couldn't govern their temper, and those men always ended badly, usually with the law involved.

Setting his spectacles back on his nose, Lindsey played his final card. "No other source of funds? What about next year's crops as security?"

He anxiously waited for the applicant's initial refusal, which often erupted into full-blown anger, then usually deteriorated quickly into self-blame and finally acceptance.

"All right," Jesse said unwaveringly, surprising the bank president. "Draw up the papers."

Seymour felt his jaw drop. Never had he witnessed such decisiveness in a potential borrower. He'd expected a lively argument at best.

"Excellent," he said tonelessly, somewhat disgruntled at the bloodless victory. "I'll be back in just one moment." He retreated to the bank's outer sanctum. Jesse had passed his test without giving him any of the satisfaction. He'd make him wait another week before releasing the money.

Jesse stared out the gilded bank window, his patience growing thin. If the wheels of banking all moved as slowly as the decision on his loan, how did any business get done? The waste of valuable time made his having to depend on others for his livelihood even more irksome, but he would wait all day if he had to. Without the loan, nothing else mattered—not preparing the soil for planting, not even putting up the winter hay for his animals. If he didn't get the money, there would be no farm.

Ten minutes passed. To Jesse, staring out the window, it felt like ten hours. On the dusty street outside, a stranger rode up and dismounted, his horse lathered into a foamy sweat and favoring its back left leg. The man wrapped the reins around the hitching post and entered the bank, the jangle of spurs marking his every step. He glanced into the president's office, saw that it was empty except for Jesse, and dismissively turned his back.

Instead of taking his place in line, the man announced to the teller that he was Simon Brolyn. When he had everyone's attention, he smoothed down a sleeve of his perfectly tailored jacket and in an accent hailing from much farther south, most likely Texas, demanded to see the bank president.

Lindsey Seymour rapidly appeared from a back room, conspicuously missing his loan papers, Jesse noted with disappointment. "Mr. Brolyn, it's a pleasure to meet you again. How may I help you?"

The lights glared off the stranger's wavy black hair as he looked down at Seymour and smiled. "I have a rather sizeable bank draft written against John Morgan's account. I want to cash it immediately."

Through the open door, Jesse unwillingly listened, along with the entire bank, as the president tried to reassure the stranger that the funds for his bank draft could be approved as soon as John Morgan returned to town.

"He's back," the man drawled, "and he expects his order for farm machinery to go out today." Still smiling, he said, "I'd hate to inform him the hold-up came from his own bank."

Seymour dug a finger under his shirt collar. "Well, I'm dealing with Mr. Jesse Colburn, but maybe he won't mind waiting a moment." The bank president poked his crooked nose into his office and made his excuses to Jesse, then ushered the stranger through a door marked "Private."

Jesse had hoped to complete the loan before anyone knew Morgan had returned. He worked the crease of his old hat, wondering how the news might affect his getting the money.

When the door opened again, Brolyn exited and shook the bank president's hand, his tight smile and cold glance belying his easygoing manner. "Tomorrow then."

Lindsey Seymour reentered his office and resumed his position behind the desk, his brow twisted into a sweaty knot. "Excuse the interruption. Mr. Brolyn is a valued customer. . . . Just as you are, of course," he added hastily. "Now, where were we?"

Over the bank president's shoulder, Jesse watched Brolyn mount his horse, jerking sharply on the reins. Still favoring its leg, the bay shook its head. Jesse tensed. "It's been a real pleasure doing business with you, Mr. Colburn," Seymour was saying. "The modest amount of the loan, and your history as an upstanding citizen weighed heavily in my decision to overlook your lack of credit." Lindsey Seymour offered him a fountain pen.

Jesse reached for the pen, his gaze pinned on Simon, outside. The Texan spurred the lame horse

122

and it gave a half-hearted buck. Angrily, the man snapped the ends of the reins across the animal's face. The horse shied away, fear showing in the whites of its eyes.

"Now, if you'll just sign these papers, we can have the loan for you within a few days." Seymour slid a stack of officious-looking sheets toward him.

Jesse closed his fingers around the pen. He knew his most pressing matter of business sat across from him, but somehow he couldn't pull his attention from the scene unfolding outside the bank window.

When the horse shied, Brolyn nearly was unseated. Pulling roughly on the horse's bit, he repeatedly struck the animal across the face with the butt of his whip until a gash appeared dangerously close to its eyes.

Jesse leapt from his chair, remembering another beating he'd watched on this very street. He and his mother had come in for supplies just after his father had died. A man had staggered out of the saloon with empty pockets and a powerful anger. With no one to take his rage out on, he'd picked up a board lying across a mud hole and used it to beat his horse over the head. It happened so fast, there had been no time for anyone to stop him. Her heart going out to the helpless animal, his mother had bought that blinded horse with the money she'd been saving for supplies and nursed it back to health. They'd eaten beans flavored with sorghum for a month, and he'd grown to like the taste. The pony had outlived his mother.

"Mr. Colburn, are you all right?" Jesse could hear doubt in the bank president's voice. His confident ministerial tones had been reduced to the shaky vibrato of a junior deacon.

Jesse dropped the pen and shot out the door, just as the horse threw Brolyn unceremoniously to the ground. Brolyn picked himself up. On the backside of his fancy suit was the imprint where he'd landed in the dirt.

"You no-good son of a . . ." Simon raised his whip to strike the horse again, but before he could club the poor animal, Jesse coiled back and connected with an efficient punch to the jaw.

Simon Brolyn reached out for balance, grabbing Jesse's sleeve, but when he stood firm, it tore, and Simon dropped like a sack of potatoes. With a measure of satisfaction, Jesse noted that the man's jacket now matched the rear end of his dusty pants.

Jesse grabbed up the whip, tempted to use it on Simon. Instead, he broke it over his knee. Keeping Brolyn in his sights, he eased up to the frightened horse. Speaking in soothing tones, he slid his hand down the animal's rump and lifted its left rear leg, balancing the shank against his thigh. Just as he'd thought. A rock was wedged in the hoof.

"Don't think you can interfere in my business and get away with it," Simon growled from the ground.

"If I see or hear of you harming a hair on this horse again, I'll do more than interfere," Jesse answered, digging out the stone with his knife. He let go of the leg and felt the tendons for damage. No swelling. Both the leg and hoof were sound.

"Your threats don't scare me," Brolyn yelled, but he didn't get to his feet.

Leaving Brolyn sprawled in the dirt, Jesse retrieved his hat from the ground and turned back to the bank. Lindsey Seymour was peeking out from behind the safety of the plate glass window in his office. When he saw Jesse start toward the bank, he quickly hung a sign in the window and pulled the shades. *Closed for Bank Holiday*, the sign read.

Jesse tried the door and found it bolted fast. His gut tensed like the snap of a lariat around the hoof of a headstrong calf. There would be no charity today at the Prairie Bend Community Bank. And it was his own damned fault. Again he'd stuck his nose where it didn't belong, and look where it had gotten him.

He slapped his dusty hat against his leg in disgust. It had been a bad week all the way around. Starting with his neighbor Sarah. She'd wasted his time when he should have focused on getting the loan. Without the money, his farm was all washed up. Hell, he'd have trouble even feeding himself through the winter. After keeping his promise to his father for a dozen long years, he'd thrown it all away.

Idly sweeping the walk in front of the store, Becky Simmons watched Jesse mount his horse, his lean build molded into the saddle as he lifted the reins. Other storekeepers went back to their customers. Tail between his legs, Simon Brolyn picked himself up and rode off in the other direction.

Jesse Colburn had always caught Becky's fancy, the raw strength in his hands, his virile good looks as attractive to her as a flame to a moth. Now that she'd seen how masterfully he'd dominated the new man in town, she was even more intrigued.

She'd heard snatches of the threat he'd made to Simon, and seen the uncharacteristic slump of his shoulders as he headed out of town. Thoughtfully, she flicked the broom straw over the sidewalk and shook it out in the street. Something was going on. She didn't have any idea what it was, but she intended to find out.

Chapter Thirteen

John Morgan looked exceedingly out of place at the head of the long dining table.

Dierdre had seen his private study, a large open-beamed affair overlooking his barns and the maze of livestock pens. A perfectly matched set of horns, spanning at least seven feet across, hung over the rock fireplace. Whiskey bottles lined the granite mantel and, like giant stepping stones, cowhides covered the polished wooden floors between the oversized leather sofa and chairs. The room, and everything in it, reeked of money and rawhide.

In distinct contrast was John Morgan, presiding over the formal dining room with each massive arm resting on a frilly lace antimacassar. Silhouetting his impressive head of silver hair and broad imposing shoulders, a puffy cloud of organza draped the window in faultless Victorian splendor.

Dierdre wondered who the mighty John Morgan had let furnish this room with such a womanly touch. His late wife? A woman he'd spoken of in shamelessly derogatory tones. Or his daughter Sarah? A female he treated with not much more respect.

Kerosene lanterns flanked each end of the imported marble-topped sideboard, casting a smoky glow upon the yellow walls and ten-foot-high ceiling. Under different circumstances, Dierdre could have appreciated the moody ambience of her historic surroundings. Yet seated at Morgan's right hand, playing the dutiful daughter and gracious hostess, she was biding her time until she could thoroughly search Sarah's room for her diary.

"It's these blamed small-time operators," Morgan was saying to their guest between bites of steak so well-done it resembled cooked shoe leather. "They've all read that idiot Brisbin's book about how to get rich on the plains. Anyone with more than two nickels to rub together is moving in and grabbing up a plot of land. Bringing in herds of Texas cattle and running them on the open range. They'll drive down the price of beef and bankrupt us all."

"That's why you're wise to diversify now," their guest answered. Seated to her right, he exuded the same autocratic air as Morgan. Dierdre wondered what had been so important about her being here to entertain him.

"Lovely meal, Miss Morgan," the man said. "It beats the food at Mamie's Boardinghouse hands down—especially when her niece, Becky Simmons, does the cooking. You've certainly outdone yourself."

Their guest was well-groomed and courteous, but something about his smile made her uneasy. Maybe it was the smooth way he'd just complimented her at another's expense. "I can't take the credit, sir," Dierdre said. "I didn't lift a finger."

"As well you shouldn't. But you must call me Simon. Have you forgotten?"

"S-Simon. Of course not." So this was Simon, the man Sarah wrote about marrying, possibly the father of her child. Dierdre swallowed and ducked her head so he wouldn't see the shock in her face. She pushed a serpentine train of fried potatoes across her plate, suddenly too nervous to eat. How would she ever carry off the ruse with him?

"It's always a pleasure to be invited into your father's home. When I told my sister about the delicious quail you served on my last visit, she asked for your recipe."

Dierdre's fork slipped, scraping the plate as it derailed a few greasy potatoes from the procession. "Oh, yes. The quail." Back home, her culinary skills made eating-out a necessity. "I'm afraid I couldn't do that dish justice," she said truthfully, "but I'm sure the cook would be glad to share her cooking tips."

"How generous of you." Simon smiled charmingly, as if she'd just bestowed a grand favor.

"Now, Brolyn, you were saying," Morgan interrupted impatiently.

Simon reached out and patted Dierdre's hand. "I'm afraid business comes first, my dear."

She watched him adjust the length of his sleeve until a half-inch of snowy white shirt cuff showed before he turned his full attention back to Morgan. He was attractive enough, but she'd seen slick riverboat gamblers use the same maneuver in movies and that put her off.

He had an air of self-assurance about him—perhaps even recklessness—that would have served him well selling junk bonds on Wall Street. Some women found those traits appealing. Judging from her diary, Sarah obviously had.

Dierdre was less trusting. Having lived in the city that never sleeps might have been partly responsible. Having traveled to a time zone that measured time changes in years, not hours, had done little to alter her suspicious nature.

"Diversification during these times of prosperity is the only safeguard for the future," he said.

He spoke with authority, but he lacked Jesse's strong chin, or his powerful body honed by hard work. Maybe she was being old-fashioned, but she much preferred the quiet strength and dependability she sensed in Jesse Colburn.

She blotted her greasy fried potatoes with her napkin, and ruefully shook her head. She was some judge of character. The minute things had heated up, her "dependable" Jesse had abandoned her, leaving her to face John Morgan alone.

"You'll have the latest in self-regulating wind-mills," Brolyn said. "They adjust to the speed and direction of the wind. A dozen will bring you up all the water your stock will ever need."

Morgan guffawed. "Good thing about wind is, it's free and Nebraska's got plenty of it."

"Isn't that the truth," Dierdre concurred. As far as she could tell, the wind here never stopped blowing.

Morgan frowned at her. "Just hand me another biscuit."

Biting her lip, she passed the bread basket. She needed to keep her mouth shut. She'd worried about how well she might carry off the charade, how she'd fill in the gaps of information that the real Sarah would know. Perhaps that wasn't going to be as hard as she'd feared. Neither Morgan nor Brolyn seemed inclined to include her in any worthwhile conversation.

"If I'm not needed, I believe I'll go to my room and freshen up." *And search for the diary*. She folded her oily napkin next to her plate and pushed back her chair.

Morgan glared at her. "Nonsense. You'll stay and help entertain our guest. He's run out of roast-ing ears."

Obviously, her entertaining duties extended only as far as keeping the men's plates full of food. She smiled stiffly and passed the corn to Simon.

"And you haven't had any beef steak," Morgan chided her.

"No, I haven't." For health reasons, she rarely

131

ate red meat, but having never heard of choles- terol or low-fat diets, Sarah would probably have had no such misgivings.

Reluctantly, Dierdre stabbed and lifted one of the less-well-done pieces onto her plate. She took a dainty bite and chewed, prepared to dislike it.

Swallowing, she cut off another piece, pretend- ing to savor it this time. She didn't have to fake it. The steak was the most flavorful and tender she'd ever tasted. Morgan was controlling and egocen- tric, but he knew how to raise prime beef.

While the men carried on a conversation that pointedly excluded her, Dierdre nibbled a sliced carrot, waiting for them to finish eating. The car- rot was overcooked and smothered in butter, but its natural flavor was intensely sweet.

Intrigued, Dierdre took another bite of potatoes. She'd never thought of a potato as having much flavor but, again, she detected a natural sweetness.

Jesse's cooking had a strong sweet taste too, she thought wryly, but that had been from the sor- ghum he'd hidden in almost everything he'd made her.

She finished the rest of her carrots, a vegetable she rarely ate. She could see why the Europeans had derided early American settlers for their un- distinguished approach to cooking, but the pro- duce itself tasted wonderful. Unless Sarah's taste buds were a whole lot more sensitive than hers, the flavor of food had drastically changed through the years. And not for the better.

She tried to remember when she'd last tasted a

really sweet ear of corn or juicy, ripe wedge of watermelon. Had it been when she'd lived at home in upstate New York? It had to have been at least twenty years—maybe more.

As a historian, she was aware that modern food was far more processed than in the 1800's, but she'd never considered how that might affect its intrinsic taste. Fruits and vegetables that had once been allowed to ripen naturally were picked green. Farmers depended on chemical fertilizers to push production from depleted soils.

She finished the last piece of meat on her plate and leaned back in her chair. Modern technology—with its growth-stimulating hormones, additives and pen-fed animals—had its place, but in some ways it obviously couldn't compete with good old-fashioned nature.

Not unlike conception. She smiled to herself. Without artificial insemination, she might never have conceived, but she would have preferred the advantages of the old-fashioned way, provided she'd had a worthy husband.

Not that she'd even gotten past the kissing stage with anyone lately. Or had even wanted to. Except for Jesse. With just a simple kiss, he'd made her forget she didn't belong in his arms.

Swept up in the excitement of his embrace, she'd even wondered what making love to him would be like. As she recalled the heat of the moment, her pulse leapt disconcertingly.

Heart pounding, she realized the dangerous detour her mind had taken. Colburn might have had his good points, but he was still a nineteenth-century male with definite ideas about a woman's place. She should be glad he'd disappeared before she made a fool of herself and created a bigger mess of Sarah's life.

Dierdre forced herself to concentrate on the table conversation. Even though she was expected to be seen and not heard, it was better than daydreaming about Jesse.

Brolyn was still talking ranching. "The windmills will help draw the water to your herd. The improved steel plows, seed drills and new threshers you ordered will give you a jump on the other cattlemen when beef prices go south."

Plows. Seed drills. Threshers. Dierdre sat up straighter. She'd figured Brolyn had meant diversifying into better-quality breeds of cattle—not into farming.

"As soon as the equipment arrives, I'll plant a section of wheat." Morgan dragged his biscuit through a rivulet of beef juice and used it to crowd some carrots onto his fork.

"The new combine harvester just invented will allow you to expand your planted acreage to ten times that next year," Brolyn said. "All I need is a release on the bank draft and your equipment can be shipped."

Dierdre quickly did the math. If she remembered correctly, a section was 640 acres. A square mile. Brolyn was talking about farming ten square miles. During the time she'd authenticated books for Sam, she'd read numerous pioneer accounts from this region. Farming in the heart of the Sand Hills eventually proved a disappointing experiment. Even after the Kincaid Act of 1904, which enlarged the size of each homestead from 160 to 640 acres, most new settlers had left within a decade, forced out by the environment.

"My bank drafts require two signatures," Morgan was saying. "I'll send word to the bank president first thing in the morning."

"You're recommending agriculture here on a large scale?" Dierdre asked Simon, unable to restrain herself any longer.

"Sarah, pass the beans to Mr. Brolyn."

Dierdre spooned up some string beans laced with ham and offered the bowl to Brolyn. She could understand if Morgan was going to buy new tools to cultivate and harvest hay for his stock, but to divert his resources and plunge headlong into farming the Sand Hills would be disastrous.

"What about the problems with erosion?" she asked. The Sand Hills were essentially 20,000 square miles of sand dunes stabilized by grass.

Brolyn took the dish with both hands, his long, tapered fingers grazing hers. "Now, you mustn't worry your little head about such details."

Morgan growled. "Simon's right. Leave matters alone which you know nothing about."

Dierdre bit back a retort. The last thing she needed was to mouth off and blow her cover.

"Until now," Brolyn told Morgan, "ranchers had no options left if they were hard-hit by an early blizzard, diseased calves or rustling. Fortunately, with the recent improvements in farming technology, the risk can be spread out, guaranteeing success."

"Not if the land is ill-suited for commercial farming," she blurted out.

Simon stopped, a forkful of beans halfway to his mouth. Morgan looked at her as if he'd never really seen her before.

Now that she had John Morgan's full attention, Dierdre wished she'd kept her mouth shut. This was Sarah's fight, and given Morgan's lack of respect for his daughter's viewpoint, one she couldn't possibly hope to win.

"Where did you hear those ideas?" Simon asked.

You don't want to know. "Here and there," she said.

"Where exactly?"

Mostly *there.* "I believe I have a unique perspective on the situation." *To put it mildly.* Although no one would believe her, she had the wisdom of the past hundred years of history on her side.

Morgan shrugged as only a frustrated father could. He turned to Brolyn. "When I came back from Ogallala, she'd moved onto the homestead. Now, if that don't just beat all, I don't know what does."

Dierdre finished her beans, but they'd lost their flavor. John Morgan was close-minded, prejudiced and chauvinistic. It would serve him right to lose everything because of his stubborn pride, but she didn't want to leave Sarah to such a bleak future.

"For one thing, droughts make farming the Sand Hills impractical," she countered. "Unlike the rich bottom land fed by the Platte River, the sandy soil and shortage of water here will doom commercial farming on a wide scale.

"To keep pace with progress and survive the severe blizzards, ranchers are going to have to change the way they do business. You need to improve management techniques and fence in the natural meadows. Not become a farmer."

"What's gotten into you?" Morgan demanded. "Young ladies who want to marry well must restrict themselves to more ladylike conversational topics."

Simon wiped his mouth fastidiously with a linen napkin, but he couldn't hide the muscle twitch nervously pulling at the side of his mouth. "For someone with such strong views, perhaps you should research your facts. If you did, you'd know that plowing the virgin land increases rainfall. Cultivated fields absorb and store rainwater. Putting the plow to the land leads to more trees, which creates more rain."

"That's a theory supported by town builders and real estate speculators trying to lure prospective settlers to Nebraska. There's no proof." And there never would be.

"As cultivation has increased, so has rainfall. After severe droughts, the rain increased in the late 1870's—a fact which coincides with expanding farming. How do you explain that?"

"A purely anecdotal observation," Dierdre argued. "Not something upon which to base an important business decision. What ranchers must do is improve their stock, import Hereford and Angus cattle, and fence off their herds to prevent indiscriminate breeding."

Simon glanced at Morgan and coughed.

"Land's sake, Sarah. Mr. Brolyn is a guest in our home and an authority on changing weather conditions. Everyone in Ogallala was talking about his research. Does this have to do with you getting it into your head that you could homestead?"

"Women have done it."

Morgan shook his head. "Those women are unnatural."

"Because they didn't need a man to fulfill their dreams?" Given the choice, she would have gladly ordered up a loving husband and father for her baby. But since that wasn't possible, she'd done the next best thing. If she'd waited for the perfect man, she'd never have gotten pregnant.

"Women were created to bear children so a man could pass down his land to his heirs."

"Is that all I am to you? Breeding stock?"

"That's enough!" Morgan turned to Brolyn. "My daughter's obviously going to require the protection of a strong-willed man. When she marries, I'll present her husband with the largest dowry in the state. She'll make a man rich in his own right."

Simon glanced at her as if he were appraising one of his new and improved threshers, and was ready to take it for a test-drive. "She's a prize no matter what endowment she might bring to the marriage."

"You should take special notice, girl. You could do a lot worse. Mr. Brolyn has made quite a name for himself among the local ranchers. He's even lectured at the University of Nebraska," Morgan said. "Make a man a fine son-in-law."

Already an old maid at twenty-five, Sarah was ripe for Morgan's matchmaking. Dierdre just wasn't sure Simon was the right match. "Who said I'm planning on marrying at all?"

Morgan slapped his meaty palms on the table, an already ruddy complexion turning redder. "It's bad enough you tried to move into the homestead, but you can't mean you're queer, too?"

Dierdre watched a vein pop out on the side of Morgan's neck. She knew she didn't belong in this century, but all things considered she'd thought she was blending in quite well. She conceded she might unknowingly have exhibited an odd quirk or two, but she hardly considered herself . . .

"*Queer?*" A laugh caught in her throat. "You mean as in *sexual preference?*"

"Sarah! I've taught you better than to use such language. Your mother may have filled your head with all kinds of nonsense, but I won't allow it."

Jowls quivering, he clenched and reclenched his jaw, as if choking on his own anger, "It's high time you settled down to start a family. Since you're apparently not inclined to choose a mate for yourself, I'm more than capable of doing it for you. Consider yourself forewarned."

Morgan rose and moved toward his study. "I could use a cigar and a good stiff drink," he said to Brolyn.

"Me too, sir." Brolyn stood up and cast her the same long-suffering expression as her father.

"We'll take our coffee in half an hour. Perhaps you'll have come to your senses by then," Morgan said, leaving Dierdre silently fuming.

During family conversations when she'd been growing up, no one had ever been left out—no one's opinion was deemed more valid than another's. They discussed a variety of subjects: politics, economics and all aspects of American history.

She hadn't always appreciated those sheltered days around the dinner table, she realized. A stinging burned her eyes. The weekends and after school had been rambunctious times of horseplay for her brothers as they traipsed in and out of the house, creating mischief rambling on their upstate New York property. Less so for Dierdre, who was usually confined to the house because of her health, her nose stuck in *Ivanhoe* or the *Little House* classics, trying to imagine her own adventures. Still, even inside under her mother's attentive supervision, she'd enjoyed a warm blanket of closeness and affection.

Nothing like how John Morgan had raised his daughter. He treated her as if she were a commodity to be traded, a fertile womb to give him heirs. Morgan didn't deserve a daughter like Sarah. He didn't deserve any children at all.

Sarah should have been nurtured and treasured, just for being alive. That's how Dierdre planned to raise her child.

A coldness permeated the formal dining room, unrelieved by the warmth of the exquisite Victorian decor or the roaring fireplace in the study. Chilled to the bone, Dierdre clutched herself, trying to ward off the sudden emptiness she felt inside. She longed to be with her unborn baby, ached to feel its movement within her body. She'd wanted to fully experience every moment of the pregnancy, but she'd already missed out on too much.

The only thing that had made the separation bearable had been Jesse. From the first heart-wrenching day when he'd informed her that she'd lost the baby, she'd felt a certain warmth from him. She'd sensed his anguish when he'd scolded her for joking about dying. Then, just when she'd begun to appreciate what it was like to depend on someone else, he'd abandoned her, leaving her feeling more alone than ever.

Shivering against a bitter chill no fire could warm, she decided she'd had enough. Determined to return to her child, she got up and slipped down the hall unnoticed. She had to find the diary. She knew of no other way to escape Sarah's barren hell—and her own.

Jesse Colburn wearily unsaddled Sage and turned the animal into the corral with its usual portion of hay and a pitchfork full of alfalfa as a treat. He had nothing to celebrate, and hadn't for as long as he could remember. Yet after the week he'd had, he planned to break out the bottle of whiskey he kept in the barn. It seemed selfish to splurge on himself and not pamper his horses.

"Lucy, did you wait up for me?" he called as he reentered the barn. A joyful whinny from the back stall answered him as he moved through the dusty shadows.

Of course she had. That was the difference between animals and people. You knew where you stood with animals. They didn't tell you one thing and then do the other.

"How's my favorite girl?"

The black pony nudged his pocket for the candy he always brought her and he tickled her chin. "I'm all out, darlin', but I've got something almost as good."

With a tuneless whistle, he added alfalfa to her hay and checked to make sure she had enough water and fresh straw. Then he reached onto the shelf behind the bag balm and retrieved a whiskey bottle. It was three-fourths gone and had gathered at least six months of dust.

He flopped onto a pile of straw in Lucy's stall and took a long, deep pull, shaking his head as the white lightning crawled inexorably down his throat. It tasted like turpentine. He forced down another mouthful or so, finding it tasted marginally better.

While Lucy ate, he found the familiar sound of her slow, rhythmic chewing a comfort. He'd missed the sounds and smells of his farm. But what he regretted most was having had to pen up Lucy night and day while he'd been away. Because of her blindness, he didn't like leaving her outside unprotected when he was in town.

"I'm home to stay this time," he said as much to himself as to the pony. "I won't leave you alone like this again."

Lucy had belonged to his mother. When she'd died, he'd vowed to take good care of everything she'd left behind—the land, the crops and her horse. Since he'd found Sarah by the side of the road, he hadn't even had time to take Lucy for a ride. Some job he was doing keeping his promises.

He forced down another mouthful of liquor, and noticed that this time it didn't taste half bad. No matter how hard he worked on the farm, he thought as he waited for the whiskey's kick, there didn't seem to be enough of him to go around. It would be even worse if he had a family to provide for. Just a few days taking care of Sarah had shown him that.

He should be thankful for the valuable lesson she'd taught him. He wasn't cut out for nursing. He was better alone.

"No," he said to Lucy. "Life with Sarah Morgan would never work out. We're too different from each other."

He took another swig. He *wasn't* hurt that Sarah had gone back with her father—he'd known she would. It was the best thing for her. There was too much water under the bridge between the Colburns and the Morgans. At least he didn't have to worry over her anymore.

He took another deep pull, wiping his mouth with his sleeve. Now there was some mighty fine tasting whiskey. Settling back into the hay, he crossed one leg over the other and eased his hat down a notch.

For all her strange ideas, though, Sarah had grown into an exciting woman. He'd never forget the way she'd reacted when he'd kissed her. He'd imagined what it might be like plenty of times since that one time in grade school, but he hadn't ever expected to get the chance again.

He could still feel her warm lips working against his mouth, taking his breath away like a fast jigger of good bourbon. She'd leaned into him, letting him know she didn't want him to stop. He'd have bet she was as hungry for him as he was for her. If he hadn't called a halt when he did, he might have tumbled under her spell and never gotten hold of himself again.

Feeding the warm buzz in his head, he upended the bottle and drained it dry. Sarah was back at home now, safe and sound. He was still broke. Nothing had changed.

A mournful flurry of wind whistled through the rafters, raining down dirt and leaves and feathers. Jesse pulled his hat down over his eyes even further. Why had he ever worried about Sarah? If he wanted something to fret over, he didn't have to look past his own front door.

Jesse started to take another drink, then noticed

the bottle was empty. With an oath, he tossed it over the top of the stall. It landed unsatisfyingly in one piece in the soft dirt.

Nothing had changed and likely never would. Except that even half-drunk, he couldn't stop thinking about her.

Chapter Fourteen

Dierdre lit a lantern at the stair landing and entered the first room she came to, wincing as the door creaked open. If she was in the wrong room, she didn't want anyone downstairs to know it. When her movements drew no notice from below, she held the lantern out before her as if it were a protective amulet, dispelling the darkness in a narrow arc around her. As the light passed over the face of a baby, she gasped.

She approached the four-poster mahogany bed, heart pounding until she realized that the baby was actually a beautiful doll with lifelike features and impossibly perfect porcelain skin. Below the green velvet sleeves and skirt of its lovely Victorian dress, the doll had exquisitely shaped hands and tiny black boots. Painted brunette curls peeked out from under a stiff lacy bonnet. Her lips were permanently pursed into a saucy, rose-colored bow.

Dierdre sat on the bed's pink and white patchwork quilt, almost reverently touching the doll's delicately curved glass fingers. The doll must have belonged to Sarah. With its brown hair and eyes, the doll might even have resembled Sarah as a child.

After her mother's death, had the young Sarah cradled the baby doll in her arms, pretending to comfort it when she had no one to comfort her?

Unexpectedly, a lump swelled in Dierdre's throat. She'd known she would discover bits and pieces of Sarah's life when she searched her room, but she hadn't expected to be so moved by them. She ran her thumb over the doll's smooth chin. If she ever got back to her baby, she'd make sure her child never had to suffer in the way Sarah must have.

Loud laughter wafted up the stairwell from below, accompanied by a long-winded speech. From the snippets of slurred conversation, Morgan and Brolyn had apparently already found quite a bit to toast. She hoped their schemes didn't include any plans for her.

Feeling an overwhelming urgency, Dierdre turned up the wick on the lantern. She began her search with the drawers and standing wardrobe. Most of Sarah's attire consisted of exquisite party gowns and fashionable wool dresses with matching coats. Quite a contrast to the lovely but simple dress she was wearing—the blue print Jesse had given her to wear.

Among Sarah's possessions, Dierdre noticed that there were no mementos or jewelry. Sarah had a pot of rouge that looked untouched, and a neat row of toiletry bottles for her hair and skin. Except for the doll, everything seemed terribly impersonal.

Lifting the hem of its skirt out of the way, she knelt to look under the bed, but it was swept clean. She'd already searched the soddie in vain. Where would Sarah hide a record of her deepest—and darkest—secrets?

Glancing around the room, she tried to put herself in Sarah's place. Naive and controlled by her father, she wouldn't trust just any place to hide her confessions. She might have a cubbyhole under the floorboards, or perhaps a niche in the attic covered by cobwebs and dirt. Yet somehow, Dierdre couldn't imagine Sarah going to such lengths of secrecy. The picture she held of the pioneer woman was far more innocent. Her gaze fell upon the doll once more.

On impulse, she picked it up. Something rigid seemed to add extra padding to the back of the doll's outfit. Dierdre bet it wasn't a corset. She eagerly turned it over, loosening the dress enough that from between the layers of starchy petticoats fell a leather-bound book.

Dierdre carefully lifted the book, holding it by its edges as she might a priceless first edition. It had been well-handled, but looked fairly new. The sheets were ivory-colored, unyellowed with age. She could have been holding a primer or an artist's sketch book, but Dierdre knew better. Except for the effects of the passage of time, this book and Sarah's journal in the future were identical.

Drying the oils from her hands the best she could, she opened the jacket. Inside, Sarah's childlike script with its occasional fanciful swirls covered the pages.

She flipped to the last entry, the fateful day Sarah had tried to visit her friend Becky, the same day she lost the baby. Dierdre anxiously turned the page. The rest of the journal was blank.

A chill snaked up her spine. There had been at least fifty more pages when she'd leafed through the diary in the future. What had happened to the remainder of the entries she'd seen? Were the pages only empty because those events hadn't happened yet?

The starkness of the empty pages evoked other— even more disconcerting—questions. Would Sarah ever return and make the entries? Or was Dierdre sentenced to live out the rest of Sarah's altered future?

Unwilling to explore that frightening possibility, Dierdre took a deep breath, trying to compose herself. If her having read the diary had opened a window in time once, maybe she could recreate it again.

Fingers shaking, she turned back to the beginning and began reading. When a creak in the hallway outside her room distracted her, she looked up and saw a glint of light in the shadows.

"Who's there?" she called out. She listened for an answer or another noise to reassure her that all was well. The lonely halls were silent.

Through the crack in the bedroom door, Simon watched Sarah freeze for a moment. He remained motionless until she went back to reading. He liked the way the light fell across her breasts. He could see that her shape had filled out since the last time he'd been here. Even in that dowdy dress.

At supper she'd played right into his hands. She'd broken her usual silence. Went on about women's rights until he'd thought Johnny Morgan was going to keel over from apoplexy.

When he first met Morgan's only child, he knew right off she'd taken a fancy to him. And why shouldn't she? She was just used to local cowpokes and losers like that Jesse Colburn at the bank.

Yet tonight, there was something different about her—something besides her shapelier figure. She'd seemed almost oblivious to his charms. He frowned. She'd actually contradicted him. Tried to make him look bad in front of her father. The Sarah he knew would have never done that.

He wished he knew what she was so intently reading. Perhaps a lewd novel which she concealed from her father? Simon chuckled to himself. That would make things interesting.

Or did the biddy keep a diary? He knew that pouring out their feelings on paper appealed to the romantic inclinations of some women. He considered such gross self-absorption a waste of time in a woman. He'd have to look at the diary and judge for himself.

He prided himself in knowing his opponents' every weakness. Whatever Sarah's secrets, he meant to find out what they were. He crept back down the stairs.

Chapter Fifteen

I can't imagine what I ever saw in Simon Brolyn.

Had I lived in these modern times, I doubt I would have given him a second look. He was rude and overbearing. I didn't recognize the subtle signs of his true nature at first, possibly because of my father's similar—but more obvious—disposition. Not all men behave in such a manner today. Or so Samuel Vanderbrief says.

Mr. Vanderbrief tells me that some men are undergoing a discovery of themselves as they struggle to find balance between their masculine and feminine sides. I can't imagine Mr. V ever having such a conflict. He is strong and confident. Yet beneath his rather rigid outer appearance, I find him gentle, patient and unselfish.

Thinking I am Dierdre Brown, he is forever bring-

ing late nineteenth-century books to my room for
leisure reading during my physician-imposed con-
finement. Wearing special cotton gloves which he
gave me, I faithfully read each manuscript, making
observations about the quality of the paper, or the
authenticity of the contents. Although I am no
expert, my unique situation does give me a certain
advantage.

We have even had several interesting discussions
about the political climate of the times, in which I
am extremely well-versed, having sat through numerous dinner parties with dignitary friends of my
father. To finally be allowed the freedom of speech
about various such matters has been quite exhilarating. I am pleased that the child growing within
me will be raised in such a progressive society.

At my request, Mr. V has promised that on his
next visit he will bring a collection of journals from
the pioneers in the Sand Hills. I eagerly look forward
to that occasion. I have little interest in returning to
my homeland, but I am curious to discover what
course its future held.

And, of course, I long to see Mr. Vanderbrief
again.

Chapter Sixteen

Dierdre thought Simon would never leave. After she'd helped the cook heat the coffee and serve it, her father had insisted she wait up until their guest departed. The evening dragged on until John Morgan had too much to drink and fell asleep on the couch. Refusing to call in one of the ranch hands, Simon had helped Morgan upstairs to his room himself. Only now, with the cadence of Simon's heels fading away on the front porch, did she have the opportunity to run back upstairs and study the diary. It had been the longest hour of her life.

As she entered Sarah's bedroom, Dierdre heard the nasty crack of reins—once and then twice—followed by the sound of horse hooves as Simon rode away. The graciousness he'd shown the inebriated Morgan obviously hadn't extended to his own horse. In her time, his equivalent would be a flashy-dressing attorney or investment broker revving his Porsche outside his date's brownstone, laying down a patch of rubber as he cut off a city bus.

Good riddance, she thought as she sat down on the bed and ran her hand under the pillow where she'd hidden the journal. Sarah was entitled to her own opinions about men, but that didn't mean Dierdre had to share her tastes.

Not immediately locating the journal, she moved the doll and the pillow, but it was no longer where she'd hidden it. Disbelieving, she pulled back the quilt and the sheets, exposing nothing but mattress ticking. That she knew of, none of the servants had had the opportunity to come into her room in the past hour. They'd stayed below, available to cater to Morgan's every whim. And John Morgan had been unable to find the stairs, let alone the diary. That left Simon Brolyn. Perhaps he had taken it when he helped Morgan to bed. Had he caused the creak outside of her room earlier?

Dierdre collapsed onto the bed, body shaking, nerves strained to the breaking point. Now that she'd finally gotten hold of the journal, how could she have let Simon steal it right under her nose? As far as she knew, the diary was her only link with Sarah—her one tenuous connection with the future and her baby.

In the lonely sound of wind rustling through the

cottonwood trees, she felt her window in time slam shut. Whatever would she do without that diary?

"Mr. Brolyn, your affairs are all in order."

Lindsey Seymour felt the first bead of perspiration trickle down his neck. A courier had been waiting with a message for him when he opened the bank. John Morgan wanted Brolyn paid immediately. Morgan hadn't had to add that he wanted Seymour to ensure that Brolyn left happy.

"I'm sorry for any inconvenience you may have been caused," he wheedled. "I can open an account for you and deposit the funds in it today."

"Now, having the money in your bank might be good for you," Brolyn said, with a hint of a smile. "But that's not going to help me wire it to pay for Mr. Morgan's new farm equipment."

"I can handle that transaction for you." Lindsey sat as tall as he dared, given his recent flare-up of hemorrhoids. "It's all part of the service we offer to preferred customers."

"Thank you. No."

"It's no trouble. I can run over to the telegraph office myself. Save you the walk." Besides, his backside felt better when he was moving around.

"You've been more than helpful," Brolyn said, looking at his watch. "But I'll be taking care of it on my way out of town."

"Leaving so soon?"

"Just for a few days. And only as soon as you give me my money," he added, the smile gone.

"Of course." Lindsey Seymour felt the rings of perspiration growing under his arms. He'd have to bathe and change his shirt again.

"Too bad you'll miss tonight's festivities." He pulled down the shade and opened the small safe in his office. He took out the money and counted it out for Brolyn's benefit.

Brolyn put the bills in a large saddlebag. "Church baptism or camp meeting?"

"Dance," Lindsey said proudly. "The camp meetings were last month."

"Why would I want to stay for a dance?"

Lindsey suffered a painful twinge and shifted in his chair. That new salve wasn't helping a darn bit. He smiled bravely. "Music. Food. The ranchers always get together to swap stories. And of course the prettiest girls in town will be there."

"Is that a fact?" Brolyn paused at the door. "Do you consider Miss Morgan pretty?"

Lindsey swallowed, his mouth as dry as a wad of cotton. "It isn't my place to say. But if you're asking if she'll be there, most likely she will. Her father likes her to represent the Morgan Ranch at such functions." Lindsey nodded and held his breath. Morgan wasn't an easy man to please, but it was a necessity if he wanted to keep his job.

"Well, I may just have to postpone my journey at that. Good day, Mr. Seymour. Give my regards to your boss."

Lindsey moved the shade aside just enough so he could peek out the window. With long, confident strides, Brolyn headed in the opposite direction of the telegraph office. When he got to the Longhorn Gambling Establishment and Saloon, he plunged through the swinging double doors, his saddlebag over his shoulder.

Sighing, Lindsey settled back in his overstuffed chair. He'd dodged more than one bullet recently where Morgan was concerned. He'd placated Simon Brolyn today. And he'd lucked into delaying the loan to Jesse Colburn after the previous day's incident. If he hadn't, he might already be looking for another job.

He unfolded Morgan's note and reread the last sentence.

Under no circumstances are you to approve a loan to Jesse Colburn.

How had Morgan found out about the application so quickly? He'd only been back in town a day. Maybe he'd heard about Colburn's altercation with Simon Brolyn, too.

Lindsey shrugged and stood up. No matter. He'd done the right thing. He deserved an extra hour to go home and pamper himself with a bath. Perhaps the General Store had gotten in his favorite talcum powder.

Night had fallen long and hard for Dierdre. As she lay in bed hours later, she tried to figure out why Simon would want the journal and how to get it back from him.

As a suitor alone, Simon might have had reasons for wanting to spy on Sarah Morgan. He could be checking up on her just to find out how she really felt about him, or maybe he suspected she'd been unfaithful. Dierdre prayed Sarah hadn't confided any secrets in the diary that she didn't want Simon to discover.

Whatever the reason behind its disappearance, the loss of the diary could be as much a disaster for Sarah as for Dierdre. She had to get it back. She just hoped it wasn't too late.

After rushing through breakfast, Dierdre looked for a ride to Mamie's Boardinghouse where Simon was staying. John Morgan had left at daybreak, so she sought out Mason, the only other man she knew on the ranch.

"I need to go into town," she said when she found him. She'd rather not have had to depend on anyone but herself to get around, but her equestrian lesson with Jesse had highlighted some definite flaws in her riding technique.

"Your daddy ain't gonna like you running off again now that you're home." Mason swirled something black and disgusting around in his mouth and deposited a stream of it into the dirt near where she was standing. Dierdre jerked her skirts aside, inhaling the strong fragrance of tobacco juice wafting above the even more unpleasant barnyard odors.

"I was hoping that if you had supplies to pick up in town you could drive me." She didn't know how else one would ask for a lift. She was used to hailing taxis, not hay wagons.

"He won't stand by while you ignore his orders.

Victoria Bruce

He won't let you make a fool out of him," Mason warned.

"Well, he won't have to let me," she pointed out. "He's managing fine without my help."

Mason made a hacking sound that could have been laughter or a death rattle. "He's used to getting his own way. Just because you're his daughter won't make things any easier for you."

Then it is about time someone stands up to John Morgan, Dierdre thought. Unfortunately, it would have to be someone else. She couldn't afford to make any more waves. Morgan's next move would probably be to put her under house arrest, so she held her tongue.

"Why do you want to go?" He launched another impressive arc of juice, which splattered farther away this time.

Survival, she wanted to say.

"I'm looking for a husband," she lied. "It's time I settled down and got married. But I don't want my father to know." She nearly choked on the gross fabrication.

Mason's weathered face cracked into a hundred happy creases. "Well, why didn't you say so? John's little talk last night must have done some good."

"How did you know about that?"

"I didn't eavesdrop, if that's what you mean."

"My father confides in you?"

Mason shrugged. "We've been friends a long time."

"Then you know he's not giving me much

·160

choice." Even for Sarah's sake, she couldn't hide the bitterness in her voice.

Mason found something of apparent interest on the horizon. She followed his gaze, saw nothing peculiar, and knew he'd said all he was going to for the moment.

"I'll need to get a few things before we leave," Dierdre said.

She went into the house and packed a bag with enough of Sarah's clothes to last a week. She even put in the pot of rouge and some lavender toilet water. It might take every trick she could conjure up to get the diary.

When she returned, Mason eyed the bulging suitcase. "I'll be spending a week with Becky," she said. He seemed to accept her explanation. Wordlessly, he helped her into a wagon he'd hitched to a pair of horses.

The road was rough, rutted from the rains. The wagon bounced in and out of furrows as deep as the rows plowed into the adjacent field. As they passed over a rut wide enough to swallow a wagon wheel, she realized how terrified Sarah must have felt on her way to see Becky that last day. Stranded and bleeding, she likely would have died had it not been for Jesse.

I might have died, she amended.

She looked down the road, anxious to leave that unsettling image behind, but the haunting feeling wouldn't go away. Mason must have sensed it, for he overcame his reticence to speak. "Your father means well," he said softly.

Dierdre glanced over, surprised.

"He's worried about you," he added.

"Worried that I won't do just what he says." If Sarah had felt she could talk to her father, she might not have ended up half-dead on a lonely road.

"He's just afraid . . ." Mason trailed off and she was concerned he might close up again.

"Afraid of what?" she urged. She couldn't imagine the mighty John Morgan afraid of anything.

The wind stilled until the only other sounds she could hear were the clip-clop of the horses and the creaks and groans of the wagon. Mason seemed far away, wrapped up in his own thoughts. Finally, he cleared his throat.

"He doesn't want to lose you like he lost your mother."

She was dumbfounded. Did Mason live in another reality than the one she'd observed? "He treats her memory like she was worthless," Dierdre cried.

Mason sadly shook his head, his hat shadowing his deeply etched face. "It's not my place to interfere, but I guess I know him as well as anyone. He just wants to hang on because—"

"Because he's greedy and selfish."

Mason whistled a few plaintive bars of a song through his teeth before continuing. "He wasn't always like that. He tried his darndest to give your mother the same comforts she had back East. Before Miss Elizabeth got sick, he had big parties and invited everyone for miles around. He saw the land as a sacred gift."

"And now that he's accumulated so much of that land, he believes he's God."

Mason smiled at her from under the brim of his hat. "He's not a bad man."

"And you would know?"

Mason nodded. "I would know."

Dierdre felt a glimmer of hope. She wanted to believe him. She'd feel easier if she knew Sarah might return to a *loving* home, but she'd settle for *safe*.

She studied Mason's weathered hands patiently working the reins. Could she trust him? Sarah's father did, but that was different. Mason had made his position clear. He was loyal to John Morgan. Loyal to a fault, she suspected. Morgan probably didn't deserve Mason any more than he'd deserved Sarah and her mother.

"Your mother never challenged your father's authority," Mason said as if reading her mind. He kept his gaze trained on the road. "But I always thought she had a rebellious streak. Maybe you inherited it from her."

Dierdre felt the spark of hope burn a little brighter. She hoped so. Given this harsh environment, Sarah needed all the fire she could get.

Chapter Seventeen

Jesse heard the wagon long before it came into view. He'd been trying to repair the fence next to the road for the better part of the morning. He'd cussed that pompous ass, John Morgan, sworn at his ungrateful cattle, and wasted a few unwanted thoughts on Sarah. He was feeling generally out of sorts and ornery as a bear.

As the horses drew closer, Jesse noticed that one of the objects of his irritation was riding on the buckboard, her head held high. Given the fact that Sarah had high-tailed it home as fast as a settler staking out his claim during a land grab, Jesse expected her to demonstrate at least some measure of humility. Yet, despite her fervent declaration that she wouldn't knuckle under, she showed no hint of embarrassment over moving back home.

She'd changed out of the dress he'd given her and into something far nicer. For someone who'd so recently embraced the unique possibilities of homesteading, the snug-fitting outfit and matching hat were more suited for meeting royalty than hoeing the garden. It made no difference that she'd shed his mother's favorite dress for one the same shade of robin's egg blue. Like the Morgan she was, she'd used him. Worse, he'd allowed it.

As she passed, Jesse watched for some sign of remorse, but she glared at him with those big brown eyes as if he'd wronged *her*.

Mason touched the brim of his hat and Jesse nodded. "Think the weather will hold?" Mason asked.

In a pig's eye. Nebraska weather was as unpredictable as a woman's moods. If you waited a couple of hours, either would change. Jesse gave the standard reply. "Hard to tell."

"Don't work too hard then," Mason said.

He soon might not have a choice. He could work from now until doomsday and just be one step ahead of a drought or grasshoppers or Morgan's cattle; but without money, he couldn't hang on much longer. Jesse drove a post into the earth and added post-hole digging to his list of grievances.

While Sarah was off in town, probably ignoring the local cowboys so she could dance up a storm with that no-account dandy, Simon Brolyn, he'd be warming a can of beans over the fire and nursing his blisters.

As hard as he tried to put her out of his mind,

he kept imagining that weasel holding her close, putting his hands on her, feeding her compliments like candy. The thought tied his stomach in knots. He drove the post-hole digger into the ground, brought up dirt and slammed it down again, hollowing deeper, his arms aching.

He should go just to watch her make a spectacle of herself, if he didn't have so much to do. He stretched out a roll of barbed wire and pulled it tight. It was a good thing he'd laid some up last year when he could afford it. He had about five more hours of work before he'd be out of wire.

When he finished, he should do something more for himself than cook a can of beans. Maybe he'd even go into town. He couldn't remember the last time he'd taken time off just to loaf around. Becky *had* been after him to save her a dance.

He wiped the sweat from under his hatband and fastened the strand of wire to the post. He deserved to take one night off to enjoy himself. No one could argue that he hadn't earned it.

Dierdre looked at the Prairie Bend storefronts and hitching posts and water troughs in amazement. It wasn't as if she hadn't studied such towns. She'd spent days poring over old photographs yellowed to a pleasant sepia. Yet the pictures didn't do justice to the rustic look and feel of the actual buildings.

A shop boasting a wooden barber's pole and the gilt letters "Tonsorial Parlour" on the window made her glad she'd already given up her tonsils and adenoids—until she realized her tonsil-less body was in the future.

She didn't have to read the sign to the Longhorn Gambling Establishment and Saloon to recognize the honky-tonk music of the player piano or the swinging doors of a saloon. Captivated by the sight of an old-time barroom, she peered inside as they passed by it, catching a glimpse of a woman wearing a startling tail of feathers in her elaborately coiled hair, and a most revealing fuchsia dress on her lush body. A dance hall girl!

Dierdre had lived for reruns of *Gunsmoke*. Feeling as if she'd stumbled onto a convincing Hollywood set, Dierdre craned her neck. Two cowboys entered the saloon and the doors swung back and forth behind them.

"Did you see that?" she asked excitedly, turning to Mason.

"Don't believe I did," he mumbled, appearing especially attentive to the road.

Dierdre shook her head, trying to hide her enthusiasm for Mason's sake. Whether it was on Main Street in the Old West—or on television and the Internet—keeping inappropriate viewing from tender eyes was a universally thankless task.

Farther down the road were tamer sights. Mamie's Boardinghouse, a yellow two-story building with well-tended flowers in its faded green flower boxes, looked the example of respectability. As did the Prairie Bend General Store. A blonde with braids looped over her ears glanced out the window, staring wide-eyed between the butter churns and brooms lining the walk in front.

"Becky looks surprised to see you."

"Uh, do you think so?" Dierdre waved at the woman, trying to cover her nervousness. If anyone would be difficult to fool, it would be Sarah's best friend.

Mason got down from the wagon and offered his hand to steady her. "Your father will be back tonight," he said, following her into the store with her bag. "If he hears you've gone off and done anything crazy, he'll snatch you back to the ranch so fast your head will spin."

"I have no doubt about that." She could only hope John Morgan wouldn't hear about what she was about to do. She smiled at Becky, who had come out and seemed to be listening intently to their conversation.

"Better go now," he said. "I've got a plow to pick up at the blacksmith's."

"It looks like you've come for the night," Becky said after he'd left. She lifted the heavy leather and tapestry suitcase and put it down again. "Or longer."

"Only if you'll have me," Dierdre said tentatively.

"Of course. When you didn't come before, I thought I'd die of boredom. The only diversion I had all week was when Jesse Colburn came in for supplies."

Dierdre's heart took up an unfamiliar rhythm. "Really?"

"Come sit down. I'll tell you all about it."

Becky took her by the hand and led her to some chairs huddled around a pot-belly stove. With the clement weather, there was no need for a fire, but Dierdre imagined how nice one would feel this winter. That is, if she were still there.

"Well, you realize Jesse's trying to get that loan from the bank."

"No, why?"

"Everyone knows he failed to produce a crop this year after a herd of your father's broke through his fence."

He'd never mentioned it. "Can't Jesse fall back on his cattle for income?" Dierdre asked.

"What's a handful of milk cows got to do with it?" Becky asked sharply. "He raises wheat and corn."

Jesse was a *farmer*? Dierdre had been so pre-occupied with her own problems, she hadn't even asked him what he did for a living. Given the difficulty and ultimate impossibility of farming this region of the Sand Hills, she'd just assumed he must be a rancher.

"Jesse likes to keep things to himself," Becky went on, her excitement building once more. "But the day I was expecting you, I saw him meet with the bank president. It didn't take long to figure out what he was there for."

A couple glanced in the store window and Becky looked annoyed. When they walked on by, she continued. "Then he stopped by the store. I waited on him. He was very polite as usual. Next day, he

169

returns. Says he needs sorghum and cornmeal. The entire time I've worked here, he has never ordered either item. When I asked for the money, he didn't have it. I offered to try to work things out with him," she said, closing her light blue eyes briefly as if savoring the memory.

Becky's face suddenly hardened and her eyes snapped open. "In spite of my willingness to help, he insisted he had to get back to his chores. He was only a few dollars over his credit limit, but he gave me no choice. I had to make him leave his gun as security. Have you ever heard of anything so strange?"

"You took the poor man's gun?" Dierdre hadn't exactly felt comfortable with Jesse wearing a sidearm, but she'd never suspected he'd given it up for her. "What if he needs it for protection?"

Becky's eyelids narrowed. "Sarah Morgan. Are you questioning my actions? And why the sudden concern for Jesse Colburn? He's lived next to your ranch for as long as I can remember and you've never shown him the least bit of interest."

"But, Becky. To take the man's weapon for a one-gallon jar of sorghum?"

"How do you know it was one gallon?" Becky asked suspiciously.

Dierdre swallowed. She knew because she'd seen the jar. Jesse had faithfully fed her from it, first by the spoonful and then laced in her food. If she'd known what he'd sacrificed to get it for her, she would have tried to appreciate it more.

"I hardly know Jesse," she said truthfully. She

170

hoped her cheeks weren't as flushed as they felt. "W-what I meant was, a pistol for a small amount of food doesn't seem a very fair trade."

"I gave him options," she said heatedly. "That's the one he chose."

Dierdre bit her lip, but Becky went on, apparently still not satisfied. "He mentioned helping you get your wagon out of the mud."

"Just what any neighbor would do."

"Except he's not just any neighbor. Your father's had it in for him for years."

"I didn't come here to talk about Jesse Colburn," Dierdre said. She'd already raised Becky's suspicions enough where he was concerned. "I need your help."

"I thought so. You just don't seem yourself. Tell me what's wrong." Becky patted her hand.

Dierdre hated to deceive her, but she could see no other solution. "I'm in love," she said, playing a hunch.

Becky's face fell. "With who?"

"Simon Brolyn."

Becky's long, narrow face brightened considerably. "Well, it's about time. I began to think you'd never succumb to his charms."

"I wouldn't have . . ." Dierdre protested.

"But you looked into his eyes . . ." Becky pressed her hands to her bosom.

Actually, I looked under Sarah's pillow, Dierdre retorted in her mind.

"Found what you'd been missing . . ."

Found the diary was missing.

171

". . . and fell madly in love."

And just plain got mad.

"It's so romantic," Becky said dreamily.

"Except there's one little problem." Yeah, and if she discounted the whole time-travel thing, she was virtually carefree.

"I'm listening."

"It's very delicate. I don't know quite how to put it."

"You're doing fine," Becky prompted.

Dierdre debated what character flaw would most likely sway Becky's sympathies enough to help her, without ruining Sarah's reputation. Using what she knew of Becky so far, she took a chance.

"I think Simon's affections may belong to someone else."

"No. It's not possible. He's been courting you for months."

"Which makes his behavior even more disconcerting."

"That's understandable. *If* it were true. Which I'm sure it's not. What evidence do you have that he's been . . . indiscreet?"

"Just a feeling," Dierdre said.

"It's probably nothing."

"Except . . ." She wondered how much of the truth to tell her. "There have been rumors."

"There are always rumors. You have to ignore them. Women will talk. It doesn't mean anything." Without pausing to take a breath, Becky eagerly leaned forward. "What kind of rumors?"

"It's been said that he keeps a journal," Dierdre said reluctantly.

"Oh." Becky's enthusiasm faltered. "That's hardly cause for alarm. I hear he's doing research on the increasing rainfall. He may only be recording his findings."

"Perhaps. But, don't you see? If I could read the journal for myself, I'd be privy to his thoughts—without letting him know I do not yet fully trust him. Perhaps then I could put my doubts aside and do the right thing."

"You mean marriage."

Dierdre nodded.

Appearing to mull this over, Becky smiled, a conspiratorial gleam in her wide-set eyes. "How do you propose to proceed?"

Dierdre gazed at the boardinghouse across the street. "Maybe I could get into his room."

Becky gasped. "You know Aunt Mamie doesn't allow women above the first floor. She's very strict about appearances."

"Then I'll have to pick the time very carefully."

"When no one's around?"

Bingo. "On second thought," Dierdre said, tapping her chin, "I can't ask you to be involved. It's just not right. This is my problem. The less you know, the better." She lowered her voice. "That way if I discover something *awful*, you won't be burdened with the knowledge."

Becky reached out and grabbed her hand. "Sarah, I'm your best friend. It's the least I can do."

"No. This really should be private. What if I uncover an old girlfriend, or even a hidden mistress? I couldn't ask you to share such a horrible secret."

"But I know the habits of my aunt and her boarders better than anyone else. I see everyone who comes and goes from right here. You need my help." She squeezed Dierdre's hand until it hurt.

Dierdre waited as long as her throbbing fingers would permit before pulling free. "All right. If you insist." She subtly shook out the pain in her hand. "You must promise though, should I uncover any blemish in Simon's background, you'll keep it in the strictest confidence."

"Absolutely," Becky agreed, too quickly. "You can count on me. In fact, I have an idea how you can solve this business tonight. My aunt said that Simon has changed his mind and will be staying in town so he can go to the dance. It lasts until midnight."

"How do I get into his room without being seen?"

"The house will be empty. My aunt will be at the dance." She grinned. "Being normal single men, all the boarders will be there, too."

Dierdre grinned back. No movies. No TV. A Saturday night dance was probably the only show in town. "Okay," she said, whispering in Becky's ear. "Here's what we're going to do."

Fiddle, banjo and harmonica music spilled from the livery stable, an oversized barn with a hayloft. The scent of oiled leather, sweet-smelling hay, and kerosene smoke mingled in the magical night air. If Dierdre hadn't been on a mission of the utmost importance, she would have been tempted to dance the night away.

Keeping time with music, hatted ranchers and cowboys pushed their skirted partners counter-clockwise around the room in a slow-moving oval. In the open stalls along each wall, braces of women crocheted on bailed haystacks, while children frolicked and the men discussed the usual topics of weather, cattle prices and the railroad.

Becky nodded toward a table piled with bread and pies, and Dierdre noticed Simon Brolyn sipping something that looked like apple cider from a pint jar. An attractive woman bumped his arm, sloshing the liquid over the rim. Apparently trying to use the incident to her best advantage, she struck up a conversation, batting her eyes and throwing everything she owned at him.

Obviously, she didn't know the "rules," based on the theory that men were hunters. The hypothesis went that men needed to hunt their "prey" in order to be pleased with what they caught. When a woman circumvented that process, she interfered with the natural order of things. A man looking for a quick fling might be temporarily interested, but the chemistry wouldn't be there for the long term.

To Dierdre, the analogy of hunters and prey seemed especially applicable in her new still-untamed, not-quite-civilized surroundings. Sure enough, despite the woman's beatific smile,

Simon tipped his hat and moved away.

"You see," Becky mouthed. "He's not interested in anyone but you."

For a man whose faithfulness Dierdre had put in question, he certainly wasn't cooperating. Maybe he did love Sarah. She'd have to be careful not to ruin what they had together.

He noticed her then and put down his drink. He crossed the room, eyes on no one else. He was either charmed by Sarah Morgan, or he was an awfully good actor.

"I was hoping you'd be here tonight. I just found out about this little shindig today—otherwise, I would have been out of town. Would you care to dance?"

Dierdre had planned for this moment, only to realize she didn't know the steps to the odd, shuffling dance. "I think I'll sit this one out," she said. "We can talk, though."

"As you wish. Would you like to step outside for some air?" He smiled so benignly Dierdre had to remind herself he'd stolen the diary.

"Thank you, no. Becky and I just got here. The walk from the boardinghouse was quite refreshing."

"About last night." He guided her by the elbow to a less crowded corner. "You said some unusual things over supper. I was quite surprised at your candor. In fact, you seem to have had a change of heart since I saw you several months ago."

"About what?" She'd given him any number of topics on which to trip her up. Incensed at the lack

Thrill to the most sensual, adventure-filled Romances on the market today...

FROM ◆ LOVE SPELL BOOKS

As a home subscriber to the Love Spell Romance Book Club, you'll enjoy the best in today's BRAND-NEW Time Travel, Futuristic, Legendary Lovers, Perfect Heroes and other genre romance fiction. For five years, Love Spell has brought you the award-winning, high-quality authors you know and love to read. Each Love Spell romance will sweep you away to a world of high adventure...and intimate romance. Discover for yourself all the passion and excitement millions of readers thrill to each and every month.

Save $5.00 Each Time You Buy!

Get Two Books Totally
F R E E —
An $11.48 Value!

▼ Tear Here and Mail Your FREE Book Card Today! ▼

PLEASE RUSH
MY TWO FREE
BOOKS TO ME
RIGHT AWAY!

Love Spell Romance Book Club
P.O. Box 6613
Edison, NJ 08818-6613

AFFIX
STAMP
HERE

of respect Sarah received, she'd obviously said too much. Now all she could do was try to repair the damage she'd done and not make any more blunders.

"My proposal. I was hoping for an answer tonight."

Dierdre's jaw dropped. She'd prepared for their encounter as carefully as possible, but she hadn't anticipated this.

"Surely you haven't forgotten what we meant to each other since I've been gone?" he pressed.

That *would* seem a major oversight on her part, she thought—especially if he'd fathered Sarah's baby. She frantically looked around, hoping she could catch Becky's attention and call her over. Unfortunately, Sarah's friend was listening to the band, her back turned. Dierdre was on her own.

"I find the relationships between men and women so confusing," she said, quoting a line she remembered reading in Sarah's diary. "Must I really give you an answer so soon?"

He laughed, but she wasn't sure he was all that amused. "Soon? It's been months, darling. If I haven't made the seriousness of my intentions clear, I'll have to remedy that." He moved closer.

Resisting the urge to step out of his reach, she studied him, trying to see him through Sarah's eyes. Her pioneer counterpart's experiences were vastly different from her own. Dierdre had been sheltered, but nothing like Sarah who'd been isolated on a ranch in the sparsely populated Sand

Hills with only parties and visits to girlfriends in town for stimulation.

Maybe if she'd been raised that way, she'd be attracted to Simon's charm and intellect, too. "So, do you want to settle down?" she asked.

"Naturally."

"Live on the Morgan Ranch?"

"Until we find the right piece of land for me to continue my research."

"What about babies?" Unmarried and frightened, Sarah had already lost one baby. She deserved a husband who not only loved her, but would appreciate and love their children.

"When the time is right."

"And when would that be?"

"When I'm secure with our financial position."

"And you're not now?"

Simon's mouth tightened and his forehead wrinkled into a frown, dipping the brim of his hat. "I have no desire to depend on your father's wealth. I'm determined to give us the same luxuries you're accustomed to, but it will be by my own efforts."

"So you don't want my dowry?" Dierdre watched for his reaction.

A look of irritation chased across Simon's face, but he shook his head. "It's not necessary. As I told your father, you're a prize regardless of what else you bring into marriage."

"So you'd forgo the dowry?"

If Simon thought her interviewing him this way was strange, he gave no indication. His frown relaxed, replaced by a broad smile. "Is that what's worrying you? You think I don't love you?"

The music changed to a spirited rendition of "Turkey in the Straw" and she had to speak up to be heard. "There's a reason I must know for sure."

She'd become quite protective of Sarah. If her prayers were answered, Sarah was safeguarding her baby in the future and she was determined to do right by her. Since Dierdre had the experience of a century's worth of women to fall back on, it would be a shame not to take advantage of it.

He glanced at her appraisingly. "I've been trying to figure out what's different about you lately. You seem to have rounded out in all the right places."

Dierdre hoped Simon knew that true love wasn't based on appearances. His assessment of her physical assets made her feel like a horse on the auction block having its teeth examined.

"And your cheeks seem fuller."

"I hadn't noticed," she said absently. How could she? She'd never seen Sarah's face before last week. She caught Becky's attention and gave her the signal.

"You remind me of someone."

"That happens sometimes, doesn't it?" Becky was making her way across the room. Dierdre smiled and nodded at her.

"I know." He snapped his fingers. "You remind me of my sister . . ."

"How sweet."

"When she was carrying her first child."

The song ended and in the ensuing moment of silence, Dierdre's smile froze.

"Sarah, you've monopolized Mr. Brolyn all evening," Becky said. Sliding between them, she squeezed Dierdre's hand and waited for her next cue.

Dierdre's mind raced. Simon had mentioned the changes in her before. She'd assumed it had more to do with her personality than her looks. Did Simon suspect that Sarah had been pregnant? If so, had he taken the diary to confirm his suspicions?

". . . some of us came to dance," Becky was saying.

Simon watched her intently. If he wasn't the baby's father, Dierdre thought, his misgivings could ruin whatever chance Sarah had to escape her father's control. But if he was capable of taking the diary, he might be capable of a lot worse.

"Sarah, you can't let this man go to waste," Becky said impatiently. "We're short of male partners. Just let me borrow him for the next set, I promise I'll return him in one piece."

"I really don't think this is the time—" Simon protested.

"No, no. By all means go," Dierdre said, belatedly following the plan. "You don't mind do you, Simon? As a favor to me. Becky doesn't often have an offer to dance."

Becky glared at her behind Simon's back, reminding her that wasn't part of the script—even if it were perhaps true.

"That's unfortunate," Simon began, "but I hardly see . . ."

Dierdre shrugged an unspoken apology to Becky. "What I mean is, her aunt Mamie is very strict about appearances—especially where single men are concerned."

She'd never met the old girl, but Becky had told her as much that afternoon. "Since you're a friend of mine, I'm sure she'll make an exception."

Before Simon could mount a more concerted argument, Dierdre linked Becky's arm with his. "I noticed a friend of my mother's I haven't seen in years. I should pay my respects. Have a good time."

With that, she slipped through the bystanders, milling at the front door until she heard the music start up again. To the tune of a plaintive waltz, she fled out into the night in search of the diary.

From the shadows beneath a trio of trees outside the livery stables, Jesse watched Sarah tilt her head back to talk to Simon. Even through the dust motes kicked up in the barn, her honey brown curls shone, reflecting the flickering light.

He'd expected Brolyn to be strutting his stuff around the dance floor like a bantam rooster in front of the henhouse. Instead, Sarah had let him trap her in a corner, and Jesse didn't like it.

His father had taught him you could tell the truth about a man by the look in his eye. Well, he didn't like the way Brolyn looked. And he didn't like the way he looked at Sarah.

Jesse told himself he had no designs on her himself. She was a Morgan, and nothing could change that. After the ease with which she'd changed her tune, he'd be a fool to keep on worrying about her.

Although he did miss having her to talk to—even if she had strange ideas sometimes. Recalling the days they'd spent together, he felt a troublesome longing begin to build, scratching and scraping at his insides until it was hard to draw a deep breath.

Jesse leaned against the cottonwood tree, letting the hard bark dig into his spine. That was better. Just as he was getting his breath back, he saw Sarah hurry out the door directly toward him.

Dierdre glanced over her shoulder. Simon wore a disgruntled expression as he awkwardly pushed Becky around the room, his lead so strong that Becky's shorter steps had him stepping on her toes. Thank goodness she herself hadn't agreed to dance with him, Dierdre thought, as she hurried on. It was bad enough Becky had gotten stuck with the tiresome chore.

Someone stepped out of the shadows. "Leaving so soon?"

"Oh! Jesse, you scared me. I didn't see you. No, I'm just taking some fresh air." The night was warm and inviting, but she had much more serious pursuits than stopping to make small talk.

"Headed for the boardinghouse?" he asked, moving into the light.

"Uh, no. The dust was just getting a little thick inside."

"Sneaking off for a secret meeting with Brolyn?" he continued. His eyes were hidden by the shadows from his hat, but his voice sounded uncharacteristically gruff. If he hadn't run off on her days before, she would have thought he was jealous.

"Of course not. What kind of girl do you think I am?" She bit her lip, hoping he didn't try to answer that. What else was Jesse to think? He knew about Sarah's miscarriage. "I only wanted to catch my breath."

"But you weren't dancing. With Simon, or anyone else."

"I'll dance later," she said, anxious to get away. "Now if you'll excuse me. . . ."

"Why not right now?" Jesse challenged.

"Why not right now what?"

"One dance. Just for old time's sake. It won't mean anything."

Precious seconds were ticking past. Inadvertently, she glanced down the empty street in the direction of the boardinghouse, and Jesse frowned.

"Oh, all right," she said. "But just one song." A simple waltz to satisfy his suspicions was harmless. If he danced anything like Simon, that would be all she could handle anyway.

The band was playing a dance she knew how to do. She helpfully raised her arms in the correct position in case he didn't. She had no time to waste.

183

Victoria Bruce

Ignoring her coaching, Jesse took her hand and led her under the darkened canopy of trees, the firmness of his touch brooking no argument. When he turned to face her, he placed a steadying hand firmly at her waist and drew her nearer.

The span between them wasn't at all immodest, especially by modern standards, but Dierdre noticed that the distance was significantly less than that of many of the partners inside. He pulled her even closer and began to dance, his work-roughened hand enveloping hers. She felt the strength in his muscles, bestowed by a lifetime of hard work, coupled with the grace of a man who knew his body and its aptitudes.

In sharp contrast to the stylized pose of ballroom waltzers, or the restraint of a city-bred gentleman sharing a casual twirl, Jesse held her with an intensity she'd never felt before, his arm cradling her as if he'd never let her go.

She cautioned herself not to let Jesse's powerful grasp affect her. She'd allowed him to distract her once before when she should have been concentrating on getting the diary. If she'd demanded he take her to the ranch instead of going off with him to the creek, she might have found the answers in the diary and already be back home.

All she had to do was think back to the pain she'd felt when Jesse had left her to face John Morgan alone. Even though she suspected he'd done it for her own good, the emptiness that spread through her was all the reminder she needed that she was better off relying on no one but herself.

184

"You can't marry Simon Brolyn," he whispered.

He tightened the grip at her waist, and any thought that didn't include him flew out of her head. Feeling suddenly light-headed, as if her heart couldn't pump enough oxygen to her brain, she closed her eyes.

"How did you know he'd asked me?" she said. "I only just found out myself."

"I put two and two together." Jesse's breath feathered the skin on her neck. "And you can't marry him."

"Why not?"

Jesse stopped swaying for a moment, but Dierdre felt as if she were still moving with him in time to the music. The slow, sad strains of the waltz wafted sensuously through the trees.

"Because . . ." He began to move again, and the hardness of his hipbone dug deliciously into her side.

"Why not?" she repeated softly, looking up at him, her eyes adjusting to the darkness.

"You can't marry him because . . ."

Because I want to marry you, a voice said in her head. She'd imagined hearing those very words since she was small.

"I wouldn't tell you this if I didn't like you," he began. His reluctance to speak his feelings was as sweet and tender as a nervous schoolboy on his first date.

"You're doing fine," she prompted. "You were saying that I can't marry Simon because . . ."

"He's not the right man for you."

185

She felt a warm surge of feelings in the region of her heart. She could tell he felt protective of her, but she hadn't been sure his feelings went any deeper.

"How do you know?" Her knees felt weak, but she seemed to be moving and swaying effortlessly, buoyed by Jesse's strong arms. Her pulse raced on as she waited for his explanation.

"If you thought about it, you could figure it out."

Dierdre's mouth went dry. She'd done her best to watch out for Sarah's best interests, but suddenly she didn't want him to be talking about Sarah. She wanted him to be talking about his feelings for *her*.

"I've lost years of memories and clues," she urged. "You'll have to help me."

Jesse could see the silhouette of her upturned face, backlit by the lights from the barn. She was the most beautiful woman in Prairie Bend. The delicate scent of the lavender water she wore was intoxicating. As if just overnight, she'd grown from a sensitive child into a spirited woman. Even if she had gone home, dammit, he still felt as protective of her as the first day he'd laid eyes on her. That was the reason he couldn't get her out of his mind. He didn't want her making a mistake. Yet he couldn't tell her that she couldn't marry Simon because he didn't like the way the man looked at her. She'd think him mad as a hatter.

She deserved someone who could give her all the things she was used to—and more. Though he'd resented the fancy clothes and her father's vast holdings, he had to admit that she wasn't to blame for any of it. If given a choice, naturally she'd gravitate to what she was used to. It was better than toiling and dying in poverty as his mother had.

"I just don't like the man."

Brolyn could probably give her all the things she needed—he wouldn't deny that. But that still didn't change the way he felt. And he didn't trust anyone who beat his horse.

"If he's not the right one for me, then who is?"

He shrugged. "I wouldn't know. But surely there's enough rich cattlemen to pick from locally—most who'd be obliging enough to marry into the Morgan family."

Sarah missed a step. "So I should choose someone whether he loves me or not?"

"Love isn't really necessary as long as he's able to give you adequate protection."

"Which you think I need."

"Looks like it from where I sit."

"Because of my relationship with Simon?"

"That. And other things," he said. He didn't mention the pregnancy.

"Like my considering homesteading the soddie?"

"I knew you'd never stay at the soddie. That was only a matter of convenience for you until your troubles blew over."

"I noticed that once my . . . father returned, you didn't stay around to 'protect' me," she retorted.

He stiffened, angry at her implication that he'd

played the coward. "From your own father? I wasn't aware that you wanted or needed saving from him."

"I think when things got too hot, you decided it was easier to let me face my father alone."

He shook his head. "It wasn't my battle. I may hate John Morgan, but I'm not going to use his daughter to fight him. The decision was yours to make."

"So why the concern for me now?"

Dierdre watched his face soften in the shadows and wondered if she meant more to him than he cared to admit. But before he could answer, the music stopped and a rowdy cry spilled out of the barn.

"The band is taking a break," he said, dropping his hands to his side. "Here comes your beau."

She glanced over her shoulder. Sure enough, Simon was outside looking around. Becky was anxiously pointing at them, her mouth sealed in an unattractive frown.

Damn. She'd wasted her opportunity to search Simon's room for the diary. In Jesse's arms, she'd nearly forgotten everything but her own name. Why didn't he mind his own business instead of treating her like a child?

"I'd like to stay," he told her, "but my one dance is over and I have nothing left to say to Brolyn."

"I think you *should* go," she agreed, but when he walked away, she watched him the whole time.

"What were you doing out here dancing with Jesse Colburn?" Becky demanded, glowering at

Dierdre. "You were supposed to be checking Simon's room. Isn't one man enough for you?"

Dierdre suspected that Jesse would be more than enough man for any woman. As she studied Becky's pinched face, she wondered if her friend's annoyance could be jealousy rather than genuine concern. Perhaps she'd been wrong to take Becky into her confidence.

Simon joined them, his polished features twisted into a snarl. "There's no future in socializing with a poor dirt farmer like Jesse Colburn," he said.

"No future at all," Dierdre agreed, laughing mirthlessly at the private joke.

Dierdre looked from Simon's suspicious glare to Becky's brittle face. Their hostility dashed what little was left of the warm, sensual feeling she'd experienced in Jesse's arms.

But it was better this way, she told herself. If Jesse had stayed, she might have admitted Simon wasn't right for Sarah. He certainly wasn't the right man for Dierdre Brown.

Simon had nothing to fear. Dierdre had never lost her heart to a man, in the past or the future. And one dance with Jesse Colburn wasn't going to change that.

Chapter Eighteen

Dierdre woke up the next morning in the room she shared with Becky. The woman had already neatly made the other narrow cot crowded into the tiny space. From the silence in the communal dining room beyond her bedroom door, Dierdre figured she must have missed breakfast, as well as the clearing of dishes, and the exodus to Sunday services. If the majority of boarders had decided to continue last night's courting from across the aisles in the white steepled church at the end of the street, it was the perfect opportunity to search Simon's room—provided he'd gone out for the day, too.

She hurriedly put on last night's dress. The faint fragrance of lavender seemed to follow her as she walked to the door, reminding her of dancing with

Jesse. She reached for the door, the sweet scent of being held in his arms wafting around her. She turned the knob, but the door would not open. The solid wood door had a double lock—probably another of Aunt Mamie's precautions against the evils of the men who resided on the second floor.

Dierdre tried again. Must be stuck, she thought. That happened in her historic old apartment all the time. She tugged harder.

Suddenly, a key turned in the lock and the door flew open, sending her off balance. Becky stood tight-lipped in the doorway, last night's precision-tooled braids a static-charged mess. It was as if a sleepless night and a Nebraska windstorm had conspired together to create the ultimate bad-hair day for Becky. Somehow, Dierdre didn't think she'd spent the morning in worship.

Becky stepped back, revealing John Morgan dressed in his black regalia. Face red with rage, he strode into the tiny room and slammed the door.

"What the hell have you done to disgrace me now?"

Now what? She'd lost an ideal chance to get into Simon's room last night. She didn't need any more obstacles—especially from Sarah's father. She didn't know how much longer her patience would last before she told him what she thought of him.

"I'm not aware of anything I've done wrong. You'll have to be more specific."

"You've been with a man." He made it sound dirty and despicable. "Who is he?"

Victoria Bruce

Dierdre shook her head. She couldn't have told him if she'd wanted to. Because Sarah had written "Marriage to Simon is inevitable," she'd assumed he was Sarah's lover, the father of her dead baby. Even if she'd known Sarah's secret, she wouldn't have shared it with John Morgan.

"You're in the family way."

"No."

"Your temperament is changed. You've been acting as flighty as your mother did while she was carrying you."

Dierdre gritted her teeth. Men always blamed everything on hormones. "Just because I'm willing to stand up for myself doesn't mean I'm pregnant."

"That's exactly what I'm talking about. You never sassed back before. And you never used words like that before. He was right about you."

"Who was right?"

"Simon Brolyn. He recognized that something was different. Said you'd probably deny it. He's offered to make an honest woman out of you."

"He's claiming responsibility?" Dierdre asked.

"Of course not. He's just a respectable man who wants to do right by you to save the Morgan honor."

"But I'm not with child." Jesse had told her Sarah had lost the baby. Only he and the doctor knew for sure, but that was more information than she was prepared to tell Morgan.

"You give me no choice," he growled. "No grandchild of mine will be born a bastard. You'll be married in the church on Wednesday."

Windmills In Time

"I won't do it. I'm not going to have a child, and even if I were, there's no way you can force me to marry Simon."

His eyes grew dark, the pupils shrinking to tiny pinpoints. "You'll go through with it all right. Or you'll stay in this room until you see the wisdom of marrying."

Dierdre gasped. Up until now, she'd considered Morgan a nuisance. But a claustrophobic sensation suddenly overcame her, intensified by the small room. Morgan was a powerful man. Even if he couldn't force her to do anything she didn't want to do, he could make her life miserable.

"Do I at least get to choose what to wear?" she asked, pretending to go along.

"Of course." He sounded a bit relieved. "You can put whatever you need on account with Becky."

"I couldn't possibly buy my dress already made," she improvised. "I'll need a seamstress working around the clock to design just the perfect gown."

Morgan sighed and pulled a wad of bills out of his pocket. "Buy whatever you want, but you'll have to do it from this room. Be ready for an eleven-o'clock service."

"Have Mason waiting out front an hour early with our best carriage," she said. "I can't permit the groom to see me in my wedding dress before the ceremony."

"Why not? What difference does it make? Oh, never mind. Just be there." Morgan left her, locking the door behind him.

She heard his steps move away from the door,

the rumble of his voice as he talked to Becky and her aunt. She grabbed the doorknob and shook it in disgust. It was locked up tighter than Grant's Tomb. Of course, Grant had died *before* they'd entombed him, she thought, giving the door a solid kick. Something slid down the wall in the dining room and crashed to the floor.

"That's enough, Sarah," he said. "Don't think you'll get any aid escaping before your wedding."

She could hear him counting out money, maybe for the damage she'd done or to keep her locked up.

"Don't you ever forgive?" she asked him through the door.

"Never."

"Then you're going to die a very lonely old man," she said.

She heard him sigh.

"See you at the church on Wednesday," he said through the door, and then she heard another door slam. She knew that now she was alone.

"Anybody home?" a voice called from the barnyard.

Jesse took off his hat and wiped the sweat from his brow before putting it back on. "Over here, Mr. Dickens."

"Some weather we're having," Ben Dickens said, wrapping the reins around the wagon brake and stepping down. "Gonna have an Indian autumn if I don't miss my guess."

"Looks like it." Jesse set down the pail of slop

for the pigs. Wiping his hands on his jeans, he went to the wagon to help Kitty. Her brood of six tumbled out the back like puppies waking up from a dog pile.

"Mind if we stop for water?" she asked.

"You're always welcome. You know that."

Kitty had been friends with his mother. After her death, she and Ben always found one excuse or another to stop by after their monthly trips to town. Kitty had wanted to take him in at fourteen, but he'd made his decision to go it alone. Even if it meant not having a family, he couldn't allow his father's land to be sold. It had been his father's dream, to work the soil and create with his own hands. But that had been a long time ago. And now, even if he had the nerve, he couldn't tell Kitty he didn't need watching over anymore—it wouldn't do any good.

"Kids were getting kinda antsy," she said.

"You don't say." While Ben watered his horses, a game of tag broke out and soon the yard was filled with the sound of children's laughter. Ben Jr., the youngest, was an easy mark, but he bravely ran after first one sibling and then another. In his effort to tag someone, he forgot to watch where he was going.

Before Jesse could stop him, he tripped over the slop bucket and landed face first in the pigs' supper. The other children were silent. Then one by one, they began to laugh.

Blinking out from beneath a layer of sour milk and rotten potato peels, Ben held his dripping arms away from his already-drenched clothing.

Kitty shook her head. "That boy has two left feet," she said, starting toward Ben Jr.

"I'll take care of him," Jesse said. "Go on inside and help yourself to some coffee. Come on, Benny. Let's get you cleaned up." The four-year-old obediently followed him to the horse trough. "Peel off those clothes first and climb in."

The child handed him his shirt. Though none of them matched, the buttons had been carefully sewn on with twine. Next came the pants. The knees and seat had been neatly patched.

"I'll wash these out. You crawl in the tank."

He had his hands full just taking care of the land and his animals, Jesse thought. How anyone with six kids ever managed, he didn't know.

He rinsed out the clothes and hung them on the fence. In the stiff afternoon wind, they'd probably be dry before Ben. When he returned with some soap and a towel, he heard a sniffle. He suspected that somewhere beneath the scraps of food, embarrassed tears ran down the little boy's cheeks.

"I need someone to help me feed Lucy. I don't suppose you'd have the time today?"

Another sniffle. "Really?" His voice was shaky and yet so sincere it nearly broke Jesse's heart.

"You bet. If you want to."

"Sure I do." The child wiped his nose with the back of his hand.

"Now dunk your head under the water," Jesse instructed.

Closing his eyes and holding his nose, Benny lay

back in the trough, his expression as serious as a repentant sinner taking the plunge at the baptismal fount. He came up with a shout. "That's cold."

"Here, quick rub this soap all over."

Benny took the soap, but he was shivering so hard he couldn't maneuver the bar past the exposed skin on his arms. Jesse soaped up a corner of the towel and quickly worked it over the child's arms and legs and through his hair.

"Rinse once more and you're done."

Benny obeyed and sat back up, engulfed by the large trough, his longish brown hair hanging in spiky strands over his big brown eyes. Jesse combed the hair back from Benny's forehead. If his own brother had lived, he'd have known more about how one went about giving children baths.

And if Sarah's child had survived, Jesse thought, the baby would probably have had Sarah's brown hair and eyes.

"Jesse," Benny asked. "How come you don't have kids of your own?"

"Don't need any. Not as long as you come by to visit me. Now stand up." Jesse dried off the child and wrapped him up in the towel.

"How would you like to wear one of my shirts until your clothes dry? I guess you're getting old enough."

Benny's solemn expression cracked into a shy smile. "I'm six." He held up four fingers.

"You're four." Jesse said, picking him up. "But that's pretty big. As soon as you warm up, you can help me in the barn."

Without Ben to be "it," a new game had erupted among the children marked by squeals and counting backwards. "Joshua Dickens. You're peekin'. I'm telling Ma."

"How do you know I'm peekin'?"

"I saw you."

"If you had your eyes shut like you was supposed to, you wouldn't have seen me."

The games changed each time the kids visited, but the gist of the children's squabbles stayed the same. Jesse grinned and carried Benny into the kitchen where Ben and Kitty sat talking. A cup of hot coffee sat at his usual place at the table. He got Benny his heaviest flannel shirt and slipped the boy's thin arms through it. The shirt hung off his tiny shoulders and pooled on the floor at his feet. Jesse sat Benny on his knee.

"My shirt's not a bad fit. You'll grow into it in no time."

"I guess you've heard the news?" Kitty asked.

Jesse rubbed the towel over Benny's head, ruffling his fingers through the boy's wet hair. "Depends," he said.

"About Sarah Morgan."

The room grew impossibly still. He slowly worked the towel around Benny's tiny ears and neck. "Can't say that I have."

"She's getting married. Met a handsome man with money, they say. College-educated. What was his name, dear?"

"I was busy loading supplies." Ben Sr. seemed disinclined to pursue the conversation.

"Sampson Bowie, I think."

"Simon Brolyn," her husband corrected.

"See, you were too listening."

Ben grunted and Kitty beamed at Jesse. "I heard from Becky that the ceremony is tomorrow at eleven. A small wedding. Just a few close friends of the family."

"If John Morgan has any friends left." Ben hid behind his cup of coffee.

"Yes, well. He used to be liked as much as anyone around. He just hasn't been the same since Elizabeth got sick. Losing his woman can do something to a man." She turned to Jesse. "Do you know this Mr. Brolyn?"

"We've met," he bit out.

So she'd ignored everything he'd said. Danced cheek-to-cheek with him, then ran right back to Simon's arms. Jesse took a drink of coffee, clutching the tin cup until the sharp bent handle dug into his hand.

"I hope she'll be happy," Kitty was saying. "She deserves it after growing up without a mother."

The coffee left a bitter taste in his mouth. At this time tomorrow, Sarah would be Mrs. Simon Brolyn.

"It's a mite sudden, though. Folks have been talking. Married life is hard enough without rushing into it."

Jesse imagined Simon taking her in his arms. Unfastening the collar of her dress. Slipping off her clothes. Pinching her tender skin.

He looked up at Kitty and saw her watching him

199

closely. "Something wrong, Jess? You look a little peaked."

"I'm fine. I'll see if Benny's clothes are dry yet," he said, slamming out the door.

He couldn't think about Sarah being with Simon. He'd tried to make excuses for her taking a lover, realizing that a smooth-talker like Brolyn could sweep an innocent girl off her feet. But now she'd chosen Simon—even after Jesse had warned her. He'd done his best to protect her from herself. What she did from here on out was none of his business.

He wasn't going to let himself get sucked into what the Morgans did. They always came out on top. He had no doubt—this time would be no different.

Yet try as he might, he couldn't shed the image of Brolyn mistreating his horse.

Chapter Nineteen

Wednesday morning, Dierdre secreted the money John Morgan had given her into the hem of the dress she was wearing. The amount wouldn't purchase a pair of decent seats at a Broadway musical, but it was enough to buy her way out of Prairie Bend. This was one wedding where the person left standing at the altar would be the groom.

Until things blew over, the bride's stand-in would be on the closest thing to a stage out of town. Pretending to prepare for her honeymoon, she'd borrowed a few things from Becky that she'd need for the road, but she hadn't spent a penny of her escape money. Now that her wedding day had arrived, it was time to put the main part of her plan into action.

Since she was apparently a pariah until properly

married off, she'd been alone the majority of the past two days. Becky had slept in her aunt's room, and only came in to see Dierdre when her aunt was conveniently nearby. The room's single window had been nailed shut. Even if she were to break one of the glass panes, the opening would be too small for her to slip through.

As she reviewed her plans to hijack the wedding carriage out of town, she found the noise of shopkeepers greeting customers, boarders slamming doors, and hurrying boots echoing off the boardwalk, unwanted distractions. After living on the wide-open prairie, she'd grown used to the subdued and peaceful sounds of nature.

Over the background noise, she thought she heard someone walk through the dining room. "Becky, is that you?" she called.

A shuffling sound moved toward her door. "I'm not supposed to talk to you until after the ceremony," Becky whispered, her voice muffled.

"That's okay. I just need you to bring me a headache powder. I have a migraine."

"I really can't. Aunt Mamie's gone to have her hair set. And she strictly forbade me to open this door unless she was present. It's for your own good," she added.

"Hmmm." Dierdre had expected Becky's response. She'd shift to Plan B. "Then could you have Simon come down? I have a confession to make. The weight of it must be making my head throb."

"Simon's upstairs getting ready. He sent for a

barber and a tub of hot water an hour ago. You can tell me, though." Becky moved closer to the door and Dierdre smiled.

"I know that. You're my best friend. Maybe I just can't think straight because of the migraine. But this is something I can only discuss with Simon. He may not even want to marry me when I tell him."

Through the door, she heard Becky gasp. "I'll get the powder. A bride naturally has jitters on her wedding day. You really are doing the right thing marrying him."

Dierdre pulled down the shade and extinguished the light. Attired in one of Becky's dresses, she climbed under the covers.

A few minutes later, she heard Becky tentatively open the door.

"Oh-h," Dierdre moaned from the bed, throwing her arm over her eyes. "Come in and close the door. The light's too bright."

The door closed.

"Can you measure the powder out for me? I don't trust myself to do it right."

"You really shouldn't fret so," Becky said. "Mr. Brolyn is a wonderful man. I didn't tell you this, but there was a fight one day in front of the bank."

Dierdre peeked out through squinted eyelids, hoping her guise as a migraine sufferer was convincing. Becky opened the tin and carefully mixed a spoonful of the powder in a glass of water.

"Jesse Colburn came storming out of the bank, and for no reason at all, punched Mr. Brolyn in the mouth. Knocked him into the street and dirtied his nice clothes. I've never seen that man exhibit such a temper."

From beneath the shield of her arm, Dierdre could see Becky's face flush with excitement as she recalled the incident.

"It was altogether frightening," she continued. "Mr. Brolyn's fortunate he didn't receive great bodily harm."

"Simon did nothing to provoke Jesse? You're quite sure?"

"Nothing at all. I was standing right in front of the store where I could see everything. Simon didn't even retaliate against Jesse. So, you can see, Simon really is the best choice. You wouldn't want someone who couldn't control his emotions."

Dierdre smiled to herself. If anyone knew how to control his emotions, it was Jesse—to a fault. There had to be more to the incident than Becky knew or was telling. "Your headache remedy is ready," Becky said, replacing the lid on the tin. She held out the glass to Dierdre.

"Uh, just put it on the table. I can't bear to move my head."

"But I just went to all the trouble of making it for you."

"And I'm grateful. I'll drink it in a moment."

Becky set it down with a bang. "You should be thankful anyone will marry you at all," she said. "If news gets out that you're in the family way, your reputation will be ruined."

Windmills In Time

"Has my father been spreading that?" Dierdre asked.

"Your father's the last one who would want anyone to know. I-I just figured it out for myself," she insisted, avoiding Dierdre's gaze. "The least you could have done was tell me."

"I couldn't tell you. Because it's not true."

"Then why are you here?"

"It's all a misunderstanding. I don't want to marry anyone right now. If you wanted to, you could help me get away until I can straighten things out."

"No, I couldn't," Becky said quickly, turning for the door. "This is for your own good. There aren't that many available men in Prairie Bend. You don't want to end up an old maid."

And she didn't want to make vows that she wouldn't be around to keep. Dierdre threw back the covers and jumped Becky from behind, pulling back her arms with a move she'd seen on a cop show. "Don't utter a sound," she hissed. "Or I'll have to"—Dierdre searched for a threat that would frighten her into submission"—bop you."

A member of the James gang she'd never make.

She wasn't sure how "bop" translated into 1887 pioneer-ese, but Becky must have gotten the message. She continued to struggle, but she did it as quietly as possible.

For her size, Becky was remarkable strong. She put up a valiant fight, but Dierdre was driven by forces that went far deeper than the fear of ending up an old maid. She looped a belt through the

205

crook of Becky's elbows and pulled it tight.

"I'm sorry to have to do this," Dierdre said, fastening Becky to the bed frame with a second belt. "But I don't want anyone thinking you aided and abetted my escape. It's for your own good," she added.

Becky glared at her with pure rage. Apparently, she didn't accept the trite adage as wholeheartedly now that she was on the receiving end.

"I'd rather not gag you, but I think that's taking politeness too far. I will let you choose the color of scarf. How about this one?" Dierdre held up a plaid design. "No. Don't answer. I'd hate to have to bop you. Wool is probably too scratchy. How about this lace affair?"

Becky nodded and Dierdre did the honors.

"I hope you won't be prisoner here too long. I can tell you it's a little claustrophobic."

Dierdre glanced out the window. Mason was parked outside. "Have to go. My carriage awaits."

She'd never been on the lam before, but she hoped she was catching on fast. She slapped one of Becky's most concealing straw hats on her head and tied the ribbons under her chin. Grabbing her suitcase, she walked out the door. A skeleton key was in the lock.

She locked the door behind her, dropping the key into her pocket.

When Mason saw her, his look of pleasure gave way to one of surprise as he looked at her feet.

Dierdre glanced down, realizing her mistake. In

her hurry, she hadn't noticed that the hemline, which must have proved quite discreet on Becky's smaller frame, exposed her clunky shoes and socks, and worst of all, the nineteenth-century's harbinger of sin, the dreaded ankle.

"Must have shrunk," she said, trying to pull Becky's dress down over her petticoats. "I'll change at the church,"

She smiled and let the perplexed man hand her into the carriage. "Can you get the rest of my things? My trousseau, you know."

She blushed. Not because she had any delusions that she'd be using the imaginary trousseau any time soon, but because from what she'd learned about Mason, he had taught young Sarah how to ride and was maybe even closer to her than her father. Breaking a trust of such long standing wasn't something she did lightly. He'd protected Sarah just as he tried to protect John Morgan.

Mason paused at the boardinghouse door. Dierdre waggled two fingers at him, praying Becky hadn't gotten loose yet. As soon as he stepped inside, she picked up the reins, ready to flee as fast as she could. Perhaps she could have chosen a safer mode of transportation, she realized as a yapping dog chased a rabbit in front of the horses and her wish for expediency was granted. The horses bolted and she was off. Ready or not.

At that moment Jesse Colburn drove his wagon past the church where Sarah planned to be married. He was early, the place was still deserted, but then he didn't plan on going to the ceremony. From his vantage point, he could see all the way down Main Street to where one of Morgan's buggies was stopped in front of Mamie's Boardinghouse.

In fact, the carriage was already heading toward the church. Probably part of the wedding party, he thought grimly. As he looked closer, he recognized the driver, Becky Simmons, by her dress and the broad hat she wore pulled over her face. She leaned out over the front of the rapidly approaching buggy, yanked so far forward by the galloping horses he thought she'd surely fall, but she caught herself and pulled back, her feet flying up in the air, only her grip on the reins keeping her from toppling over backwards.

Swiftly picking up speed, the carriage careened precariously through the streets. Customers and clerks ran from every store to see what the commotion was about. Mamie's Boardinghouse emptied out like ants racing from spilled water. Simon Brolyn rushed out the door, his face covered in lather.

Dress blown up over her head, Becky shot by a procession of riders led by none other than John Morgan and K. P. Stringer, the most pious reverend for miles around.

With the buggy headed straight for Jesse at breakneck speed, he jerked Sage off the road, barely avoiding a collision as the blinded woman pulled her skirts away from her eyes. Her bonnet blew off as she sped by, exposing her short brown hair, shorn in ragged layers.

He knew that head of hair. He'd cut the burrs out of it himself. In horror, Jesse watched Sarah Morgan struggle to gain her balance as her buggy tore past the church and out of town, drawn by a team of runaway horses.

Chapter Twenty

Trees flew past like the blurred figures of commuters waiting for a subway car to stop, only for Dierdre there was no conductor aboard.

She'd never been more scared. Even waking up in the past—which had given her more than her share of anxious and heartrending moments—couldn't compare with the immediate danger of being at the helm of a team of runaway horses. She had no control over the reins. Her balance at any given moment was precarious at best. Fortunately, she'd managed to pull her skirt down from over her eyes.

If only she'd learned about handling a horse before she decided to use them for her getaway. It was the past's equivalent of knowing the bus schedule in Manhattan or the quickest way to travel crosstown in the afternoon. If she got out of this alive, she'd learn how to ride a horse, she promised. She'd take carriage rides through Central Park. She'd pay special attention to the drivers' techniques. Like Hercules, she'd muck out stalls.

No. She probably wouldn't do that. But she'd do the rest, she vowed. If only she survived.

Ahead, she saw a deep ditch across the road, rushing toward her with lightning speed. She wished she were still blinded by petticoats and gingham.

The fast-approaching rut with its trickle of run-off water grew in her mind to the width and depth of the Red Sea. She'd taught Sunday school for two years and knew the songs by heart. Although that might count for something, she very much doubted the sea would part for her.

Mere yards away from her latest plague, one wheel hit a pothole of equally immense proportions to the impending wall of water. The carriage tipped sharply, flinging her bag from the wagon as if it had been launched by a catapult. Pitched sideways, she clawed for a handhold, feeling the friction burning of leather reins sliding through her grasp. Just when she was sure the wagon would roll, she lost her balance.

Time slowed.

She flew through the air. Rather than her life passing before her, she remembered all the admonitions of safety her mother had pounded into her head.

Victoria Bruce

Don't overexert. Don't take chances. Look before crossing the street. With one impulsive decision, she'd broken them all. In her defense, though, she realized how hard it was to look before crossing the street when you're airborne.

She somersaulted in the air, landing unceremoniously on the ground, atop her tapestry suitcase, with a loud plop. The carriage righted itself. The horse stopped to graze in the field. The birds in a nearby tree kept on singing.

It was a miracle.

She had survived. For once, she'd broken all the rules, went against her upbringing, and didn't have a seizure, concussion or broken bone to show for it. Just a mild rope burn from where she'd held onto the reins too long.

The adrenaline rush was exhilarating. She felt incredibly alive. Even cocky. She had come through the ordeal without anyone's help. At least, no one *human*, she amended, remembering her last promise.

She looked around her at the dip in the washed-out road. So that's where they'd gotten the term *last-ditch*, she thought, beginning to laugh. Her laughter brought hallucinatory applause. She'd avoided a shotgun wedding and was still alive to tell the tale. As the imagined accolades grew louder, the birds stopped singing. The ground reverberated beneath her. A dust devil sprang up from the direction she'd just come. The applause became thundering hooves. Her cocky grin collapsed as Jesse Colburn rode over the rise with half the town behind him.

Jesse spotted the empty buggy next to a gully in the road. His heart pounding against his chest, he pulled his wagon up alongside Sarah's buggy and jumped off before it had stopped. Fearing the worst, he ran to the edge of the wash.

Sarah sat in the ditch on her crushed suitcase, her bonnet strings tangled around her neck, the too-short sleeves of Becky's mustard-yellow dress exposing her dirt-streaked arms. Lord, sitting there in one piece, as calmly as a passenger waiting for the next stage, Sarah Morgan was as beautiful a sight as Jesse had ever seen.

"Are you hurt?" he asked, leaping into the wash with her. He took her by the shoulders and gently helped her up.

"Only my pride," she answered with a small smile.

Somehow he bet that was still intact, too.

Like a war party circling the wagons, the townspeople surrounded them, stirring up a gritty-tasting flurry of dust. "What in heaven's name do you think you're doing?" Sarah's father demanded as he rode up.

"Just out for a drive," Sarah answered him coolly.

"The ride's over. You better get your behind up out of there. It's eleven o'clock. The parson's here to marry you and Simon Brolyn." Morgan closed the lid of his watch with a loud snap and motioned to K. P. Stringer. With the sober demeanor befitting a funeral, the parson dismounted and stepped forward, wearing a long black frock, a tall black hat, his Bible folded against his chest.

Jesse crawled out of the gully and kneeled down, extending his arm to Sarah. As she took his hand, he looked into her big brown eyes, and realized that he couldn't let her father bully her into marrying Simon. In fact, he wasn't going to let Simon marry her under any circumstances. She didn't want Simon, or she wouldn't have been fleeing from him on her wedding day, disguised in Becky's clothes. If she'd go to these lengths to escape, she deserved his protection.

He helped her up. The warmth of her palm in his felt so familiar, so right. "She's not marrying Simon," Jesse told John Morgan. When she squeezed his hand, he knew he was doing the right thing.

"The hell you say," Morgan boomed. "Step away from her."

"No, sir. She can't marry Simon . . ." He was tired of seeing her ruin her life. Simon didn't know how to take care of her.

Sarah smiled.

". . . because she's marrying me."

Sarah dropped his hand like it was a hot potato.

"Over my dead body," Morgan roared.

"We don't want it coming to that, sir, but I'm marrying her." He knew how to take care of her better than anyone else. If he had to marry her to protect her, that's what he'd do.

"Now, wait just a minute. Don't I have a say here?" Dierdre stamped her foot, showing a substantial amount of ankle. The skirt was too short by a few critical inches, Jesse noticed. Glancing upward, he found that the bodice was immodestly tight. He'd seen Becky wear the dress on numerous occasions, but she'd never filled it out the way Sarah did.

He forced his gaze to her face and found her watching him as if she could read his mind. Embarrassed, he leaned over and whispered in her ear. "I suspect going through two grooms in one day won't help your chances of a respectable marriage after today, but I'll be damned if I'm going to let you marry that snake. He's dangerous."

"And you're not?" She lifted her determined chin, innocently bringing her lips uncomfortably close to his.

He did feel a little unpredictable. This near, he could see that the hair he'd cut was growing fast, forming little wispy curls at her neck and along the angle of her jaw. Unexpectedly, he inhaled her hair's sweet lavender fragrance and wished he could run his fingers through the strands, extracting moans from her, this time of pleasure instead of pain.

Sarah stepped back, holding her palms up in front of her. "I don't intend to marry anyone today."

Jesse linked his hand around her wrist and pulled her aside, leaving John Morgan sputtering on his horse and the crowd growing restless. "I'm trying to save you here," he said. "How about giving me some trust?"

Dierdre wanted to, but she couldn't speak for Sarah. "You don't even know who I really am," she said, tugging on her arm.

"And you do?"

Dierdre had no argument there. As far as Jesse knew, she'd lost her memory.

"You can marry Simon, or you can marry me," he hissed at her, ignoring the raised eyebrows of Sarah's father. "He might have money to buy you nice things, but he's not going to treat you the way you deserve—not like I will. You're going to have to trust me on this."

Dierdre looked into his eyes and found a blaze of emotion which she'd never seen him unleash before. She quit struggling. The man was trying to help her, just like when he'd rubbed her strained back, fed her sorghum-laced cakes, and carried her into the soddie so she wouldn't have to step on any more stickers. Every time she'd really needed him, he'd been there for her. But she couldn't marry him. She had to go back to the future. And she couldn't marry Sarah to him. As far as she knew, Sarah still wanted Simon.

"Simon Brolyn's no good for you," Jesse said evenly.

Dierdre glanced over at Simon, who was heatedly talking to John Morgan, his lip curled into a petulant sneer. She didn't want to interfere in Sarah's love life any more than she already had, but she was inclined to believe Jesse.

"When we were little," Jesse said, "we made a pact that we could tell each other anything. I'm telling you now, if you agree to marry me, you won't regret it."

Something deep inside Dierdre told her to trust him. It had been so long since she'd really counted on anyone but herself. She'd struggled to stay independent, certain it would be far less painful than what Jesse was offering. But here was this gorgeous hunk of flesh standing in front of her, ready to go to the mat for her.

"When my father came for me . . . you left without a word." Her voice sounded less like a woman's and more like a frightened little girl, waiting in the dark for someone who would never return. "You'd have to promise never to leave me like that again."

"You have my word," he said.

She wanted to believe him. She didn't know what was right for Sarah, but as she gazed into his clear blue eyes, she felt something changing beneath her carefully constructed defenses. She did trust him, she realized. Tacitly, she'd entrusted him with her life and she'd do it again.

It was all happening so fast. Not wanting to examine her decision too closely, she leaned into his gentle pressure on her wrist. Tall and strong, Jesse effortlessly pulled her into the crook of his arm. In the heat of his embrace, the rest of her doubts retreated. Together, they faced John Morgan.

"Sarah's agreed to marry me," Jesse said.

The crowd was rubbernecking like a boat full of

conventioneers trying to get their money's worth on the budget tour of New York harbor. Morgan waved the nosy onlookers away. "Simon Brolyn has offered marriage to protect Sarah's good name—and the Morgan reputation. If you want to do what's best for Sarah, you'll leave quietly."

"Simon's not fit to own a horse, let alone take a bride," Jesse said.

"Now see here." Hearing his suitability questioned, Simon forced his way closer, ready to defend his claim. "I'm just trying to do right by her," he said. "Make her an honest woman."

"Sarah's already honest," Jesse declared. "And I won't allow you or anyone else to claim otherwise."

Dierdre felt her knees go weak, and he hugged her closer. Apparently, Simon thought better of pushing his luck with Jesse, for he seemed to shrink within his suit before her eyes. He closed his gaping mouth and retreated into the crowd.

"It's me that's got a confession to make," Jesse said to Morgan. "I've spent the night with Sarah."

"You're telling me *you're* the fox who got into the hen house?" Morgan's eyes bulged in apparent disbelief. "Sarah's mother could trace her roots all the way back to the Mayflower. You can't trace roots further than a failed wheat crop. I should shoot you where you stand."

"That'll be enough of that talk," the preacher warned. "This man's owning up to his mistakes. Even God wouldn't deny him forgiveness."

"No child of mine is going to bring a bastard into this world," Morgan spit out.

"A child should be with its father," the preacher insisted.

Dierdre spoke up. "There's no baby."

"Get on with it," someone yelled.

Morgan's horse pranced nervously, and he quickly brought it under control. "You just want my money," he charged.

"No, sir, I don't expect any," Jesse said. "I'll find a way to provide for her. And she won't have to do what my mother did. You do remember Annie, don't you? After my stepfather died, she had to plow the fields into her ninth month."

Jesse hadn't said two words to her about his mother. As she watched him confront Morgan, she noticed a new level of strength and confidence in the tilt of Jesse's chin, the set of his jaw.

Surprisingly, Morgan was the first to drop his gaze. "You'll get no dowry," he said gruffly.

"That's fine with me," Jesse said. "Now that we've got that out of the way, let's get on with it, Parson. I've got a 'failed' wheat field to plow under."

Chapter Twenty-one

"Dearly beloved . . ." the minister said in a deep tremulous voice.

The limb above the preacher's head swayed and creaked. Instead of a protective bower for sharing sacred wedding vows, the solitary elm reminded Dierdre more of a hanging tree.

"We are gathered together . . ."

Dierdre looked around at those who had "gathered." One of Morgan's men spit a black gooey wad into the weeds and adjusted his gun holster. Another balanced his hat on the tip of his finger. She watched him finesse the brim of his felt hat—permanent sweat rings for a hatband—back and forth, adjusting for the fluctuating wind. Not exactly the kind of wedding party who would check the gift register at Saks Fifth Avenue.

". . . in the sight of God."

"Is this legal?" she blurted out. Surely one needed to apply for a marriage license in 1887 Nebraska. Maybe no one had remembered to do it.

The preacher frowned, his mouth pulling so tight that a tiny scar on his cheek turned white. He reminded her of Clint Eastwood in one of those spaghetti westerns where he was trying to make up for a mistake in his past. "Deacon Eastwood" gave her a curt nod and continued.

Dierdre still had her doubts, but she bit her tongue. She didn't want to ruin Sarah's wedding day—even though Sarah wasn't here to enjoy it.

The wind picked up and the bonnet hanging from tangled ribbons around her neck flapped unceremoniously across her back. Grimacing, she plopped Becky's hat back on her head, covering the spikes of short hair which were poking out all over her head.

All of her life, Dierdre had dreamed about the fine wedding she'd have. It would be on the rolling lawn of her parents' house. Caterers would hover in the background waiting to serve food under the snowy white canopy stretched across the yard. She'd have a string quartet playing chamber music.

Her dream collided with reality. The only music she heard was the distant lowing of a cow.

"Do you, Jesse Samuel Colburn, take Sarah Morgan to have and to hold . . ."

Dierdre glanced over at Jesse, her heart pounding in an uncomfortable rhythm. She hadn't even known his middle name. Her mother's warning echoed in her head. *Don't trust strangers*.

At the appropriate pause, Jesse said "I do" in a strong, firm voice. "And do you, Sarah Elizabeth Morgan, take Jesse Samuel Colburn to have and to hold, in sickness and in health."

Jesse had seen Sarah in sickness and knew for a fact she could be stubborn and querulous. And beautiful. He wiped a dirt smudge off her cheek, remembering how lovely she'd looked even when covered in mud.

". . . to honor and obey . . ."

"Obey?" Sarah's head swiveled toward the parson. "I hope you don't expect me to promise that unless it's in the groom's vows too."

"Fine by me," Jesse whispered. He doubted the new Sarah would obey him or anybody else. In fact, she probably wouldn't sleep until she found a way to get the marriage annulled. Once she got her father calmed down and folks realized she wasn't with child, she and her intact dowry would be prime marrying material again. He prayed Simon Brolyn would be gone before then.

"I don't like relying on anyone for anything," she added.

As far as he could see, she depended on her father for everything. "You'll get used to it," he said wryly.

". . . 'til death do you part?"

"You did promise you wouldn't leave me," she said in a strained voice.

His heart slammed against his chest. He didn't

figure she'd take her vows to him in earnest. "Yes, I promised."

"Then I do," she said to the minister.

"If any man here can show just cause . . ."

Jesse glanced over the crowd. Brolyn apparently hadn't waited to congratulate the bride. Belated guests, Becky Simmons and her aunt Mamie had just arrived in a wagon driven by Mason.

Braids pulled unevenly to each side, Becky stood up in the back of the buckboard, craning her neck in his direction. She took in the scene: he and Sarah, the parson. Her bloodless face cracked into a look of shock and disbelief. They'd never know whether she thought she had just cause to stop the wedding or not, for she fainted dead away. No less surprised, Aunt Mamie left her lying in the wagon in a heap.

The parson let out a sigh of relief. "Then by the power vested in me by the State of Nebraska, I pronounce you man and wife."

"Shouldn't that be *husband* and wife?" Sarah protested.

"You may now kiss the bride."

Jesse leaned down and covered her mouth with his, effectively cutting off any further objections. He'd wanted to do this for days—ever since the dance. He just hadn't known he was going to have to marry her to get the opportunity.

She stiffened in his grasp. Without relinquishing the sweet taste of her mouth, he immediately relaxed the grip on her arms. Caught off balance, she swayed and he gently steadied her. Unexpectedly, her lips opened beneath his, sparking a heat from deep inside, a hungry warmth that made him forget the fifty witnesses looking on. Her hat tumbled from her head as Sarah arched up to meet his lips. He deepened the kiss until the earth could have moved beneath his feet and he wouldn't have noticed.

When she finally pulled away, she stared at him in apparent confusion. Still affixed by yellow ribbons around her throat, the bonnet floated and twisted in the breeze. The wind whipped her dress around her full hips, pressing a crease in the space between her legs. Feeling a sudden hardening in his groin, he discreetly covered it with his hat and hoped no one had noticed.

"I'll be keeping an eye on you, boy," Morgan said, his wedding present more a threat than a gift.

The parson was first to shake Jesse's hand. Amid congratulations varying from contrived to arguably sincere, Jesse watched Morgan and his henchmen mount up to leave.

Using his hat as a fan, Mason revived Becky. As he turned the wagon around, Becky looked back at Jesse, her pale blue stare cold as ice.

His gaze on Sarah's soft lush lips, Jesse barely noticed the other girl. According to the *Farmer's Almanac*, he should begin plowing soon. Weather permitting, he'd never missed the recommended hours for plowing and planting—not even the time he'd been laid up from eating some bad pork.

He studied the flush put in Sarah's cheeks by their kiss, and the ache in his groin intensified. A man didn't get married every day, he told himself. The blasted plowing could wait.

"That was very heroic of you, Jesse," Dierdre admitted after the crowd dispersed. Given the bleak alternative of living out the rest of her life with her dictatorial father, Sarah was probably far better off married to Jesse. And she had his promise that he'd never leave the woman.

"Maybe I misjudged you before," she said magnanimously. "Although you needn't have put quite so much effort into the 'you may now kiss the bride' part."

"Who said it was any effort?" he asked with a grin. A flicker of desire smoldered in his eyes.

She caught her breath, seeing the unhampered flare of emotion in his eyes. "Now, wait a minute. This was all just an act to keep my reputation intact. Wasn't it?"

"No. That was your first husband-to-be who wanted to marry you to save your reputation. Or so he claimed. I just didn't want you marrying that lout." He hitched his horse to the wagon. "Shall we go home?"

She planted her feet. "I'm not going anywhere until you fully explain your motives."

He threw her ruined valise into the back of the wagon. "Well, I'd hoped to get home before dark so I can feed the animals. If we leave now—"

"Not those motives." She could feel her magnanimity wearing thin.

"A man who's been single as long as I have needs

a woman for all kinds of things." He grinned mercilessly.

A flush of heat shot through her cheeks. "But that's not what I had in mind when I married you." She'd only been trying to protect Sarah's best interests.

"You can't expect a husband to stay faithful to his wife without certain"—he placed his hands on her waist to help her onto the wagon—"you know."

He was standing so close she could feel the heat from his body. Sarah's husband—no, *her* husband—was expecting all the benefits of marriage? Oh Lord, she thought, scrambling into the wagon and out of his reach. What had she done?

"We haven't talked about where we'll live," he said, crawling up beside her. "I'd prefer to stay at my house. Make feeding the animals and working the fields more convenient."

"You're absolutely right. I'm not abandoning the homestead, but you should live at your farm where you're needed."

"I promised never to leave you," he said. "Remember? That's what you said you wanted."

He flicked the reins and the wagon began to move, intensifying the panicky sensation of things closing in on her. The wagon hit a bump, throwing her sideways into Jesse, and he instinctively reached out and put his arm protectively around her.

"You can't mean to deny me on my wedding night?" he asked.

She shrugged off his hold on her and grabbed onto the seat with both hands. "And you can't mean to force me against my will?"

"No," he said softly, amused by her loss of composure. "That wouldn't be any fun at all."

The fun, he thought, would be in trying to change her mind.

Chapter Twenty-two

Dierdre followed Jesse into the soddie, wondering how she'd gotten herself into this mess. Two weeks ago, her biggest concern had been how to have a child without a husband. And now, ironically, her major problem was how to keep her husband from getting her with child.

Prolonging the inevitable moment when it was time to go to bed, she fussed around the soddie, sweeping the dirt floor until Jesse told her to quit stirring up dust. Then she shook out the bed linens. He lifted an eyebrow as if suggesting she had something romantic in mind. He seemed to enjoy her discomfort.

Lounging back in a kitchen chair, he read the *Farmer's Almanac* by the kerosene lantern, a booted foot crossed over his knee. If it hadn't actually felt homey compared to living alone in Manhattan—with the bookstore cat, Sebastian, as her only overnight visitor—she would have kicked him out.

It was just for one night, she told herself. Tomorrow, she'd work out another plan for getting the diary. Hopefully, she'd soon be on her way back home.

She knew better than to think this living arrangement would last for long. She'd seen a thing or two in old movies about two people unwillingly sharing the same hotel room. They usually ended up hanging sheets between two beds. *And longing for each other in the dark.*

Dierdre shook her head, determined that wouldn't be her. She had only one goal in mind: to get back to her baby. Now that she'd escaped from Morgan's jail, nothing handsome Jesse Colburn did was going to distract her.

She wouldn't hang up sheets. That only made the forbidden more inviting. She'd have to think of something more foolproof.

As if reading her mind, Jesse spoke up. "About ready for bed, honey?"

"Just about," she said, smiling sweetly. "You can come in when I call."

Jesse's grin slid off his face in a look of surprise. Dierdre wished she could have captured it on film.

She got up and went into the bedroom, closing the door firmly behind her. Living on her own in New York City, she'd learned a thing or two about survival. She'd show him that women weren't the helpless creatures he likely believed they were.

A few long minutes later, Jesse heard her call his name. He glanced at the closed door, wondering what she was up to. First, she'd treated him as welcome as a polecat, and now she was inviting him into her bed. He hesitated.

"I'm not done with this passage. I'll be along when I'm through."

Dierdre gritted her teeth. He was just being stubborn. How could she show him how little control he had over her when he wouldn't even take the bait? She opened the door and whispered to him from the darkness of her room. "Don't stay up too late." Her voice dripped honey.

Jesse slammed the almanac shut and sat up straight. His boot banged against the table, nearly upsetting the lantern. He mumbled something.

"What did you say, dear?" Pure and innocent, her voice floated from the bedroom as if it had been carried on a cloud.

He'd expected a hard-fought range war with Sarah putting up fences which he would eagerly try to tear down. He'd been prepared to hound her relentlessly.

"I don't need much sleep," he said, staring at the partially open door.

"Me neither," she sighed from the other room.

Jesse's hand twitched and he jammed it in his pocket. Had she decided to take her wedding vows to heart? He swallowed, remembering how inviting she'd looked with her wedding dress wrapped around her long legs.

"It is kind of cold, though. Must be the dampness in the walls. Wish I had a bed warmer."

Like a thirsty horse drawn to water, Jesse picked up the lantern and crossed the room, lured by the seductive words. He pushed the door open wide and stepped into the bedroom. He took a deep breath, expecting the subtle scent of lavender. From within the darkness, a pungent odor assaulted his sense of smell. *What the hell . . .*

"Horse liniment!" He thought he heard a snicker, but the sound was lost among the rustle of bedclothes. "What'd you do? Take a bath in it?"

"Just a little back spasm. Nothing to worry about. I thought I'd use the liniment as a preventive measure."

"To prevent what?" he cried. "Mold from growing on food in the next county?"

He lifted the lantern, but Sarah was shielded by the shadows. Still, as the source of the odor, her location was painfully obvious. As his eyes adjusted to the darkness, he smiled and shook his head. She was using the liniment to put him off.

"I didn't want to trouble you," she said. "You've already done enough."

Apparently not. If he was going to top this, he'd have to go one better. "I'd gladly have helped if you'd asked," he said generously. He shifted his weight from one foot to the other. Maybe it was his imagination, but the heat from the liniment seemed to be warming the room.

Or maybe it was just burning his eyes.

He set the lantern on the nightstand. Except for the sound of his own breathing, the room was silent. He pictured her trying to reach around to her back, rubbing the ointment onto her smooth silky skin . . .

"It's no trouble, Sarah. Next time you just ask."

He blew out the kerosene lantern with a sigh. He'd never slept with a woman without touching her. He didn't know if he could. Even one who smelled like a gimpy horse.

He walked to the bed and sat down on the edge. His weight caused her body to roll toward the middle until he could feel her soft curves touching him. She squirmed away, obviously trying to stay on her side of the bed.

Jesse undressed down to his undershirt and jeans and climbed in under the covers. Almost immediately, he felt her lose a few inches of ground. He smiled and stretched out, fingers laced under his head. In the narrow bed, he accidentally trapped a lock of her hair under his elbow. She jerked her head, pulling the strands out of his reach.

"No good night kiss?" he said.

She complained about her back, grumbled a hasty good night and turned onto her side, facing the wall.

Heat radiated from her body, reminding him that she was only inches away. He smiled and inhaled. The odor of liniment didn't seem so bad anymore. He must be getting used to it.

Or maybe she'd just destroyed his sense of smell.

Simon Brolyn rode his horse into the nearly deserted town of Prairie Bend. He was glad no one was around to witness his return. His wedding day had turned into a fiasco. And all because of that grasping opportunist, Jesse Colburn. He hated anyone who made him look bad. And now he'd let Colburn get away with it twice.

Simon was a proud man. He didn't have many earthly possessions, though no one ever would have guessed. He talked big, dressed well, and whenever he sold someone something, he made them think he was doing them a favor.

Last year he'd peddled wringer washers until some fool woman had her arm torn up in one and he'd been run out of town.

This year, he was an expert in farm equipment. He'd soaked Morgan for a fortune for equipment by telling him he needed to diversify into farming. If he'd been selling a new breed of cattle, he'd have told Morgan he should focus on diversifying his stock.

He'd planned on spending the night in Morgan's fancy house. Then Colburn had turned the tables on him, leaving him no choice but to spend another night in Mamie Simmons's ramshackle hotel.

He couldn't imagine what Sarah saw in Colburn. Becky had tried to warn him at the dance, but he'd underestimated Jesse's influence over her.

Simon jerked his horse to a halt in front of the boardinghouse and his horse gave a little buck. Simon jumped off and kicked the mare harshly in the flank. Putting fear into animals was the only way to control them. The nag didn't know her place. Just like that Morgan bitch. He'd show them both.

The streets were starting to fill up with people. The wedding must be over. He'd ask for supper in his room. He wanted to be nowhere in sight when folks came around asking questions.

As he wrapped the reins around the hitching post, a wagon pulled up beside him and he noticed a wan Becky lying in the back, her gaunt cheeks stretched over her jutting cheekbones in a most unattractive fashion.

"Thanks, Mason," her aunt was saying. "I know your allegiance is with John Morgan, but his ungrateful daughter didn't even acknowledge poor Becky's presence at her wedding. The whole affair was just shameful. And after all Becky's done for her."

"Miz Simmons," Simon said, "let me give you a hand with your niece. She's entirely too delicate a girl to be out in the sun without a hat."

Aunt Mamie brightened. "How kind of you to say so. I was just telling Mason. I've gladly raised her since my brother and his wife died. She's brought me nothing but joy. Not a selfish bone in her body."

"Sounds to me like she's not the only one who's selfless."

"Well, thank you," she said, preening. "Would you care to have supper with us in our private quarters tonight?"

"I'd be honored," he said, helping her down from the wagon.

"Give me some help here, man," he ordered Mason. Colburn might think he'd beaten him, Simon thought as they carried the limp but conscious form of Becky inside, but there was more than one way to skin a cat.

He might have lost the new Mrs. Colburn temporarily, but he wouldn't rest until he'd remedied the situation. The stakes were too high.

Chapter Twenty-three

When Dierdre awoke the following morning, the bed next to her was empty. She hadn't heard Jesse get up. He must have been very quiet, she decided, for she'd been extremely aware of his presence throughout the night. She'd only dozed fitfully—worrying about what she'd do if he suddenly decided to exercise his spousal "rights"—but he'd been the perfect gentleman.

Maybe he'd realized this marriage wasn't going to hold the benefits he'd supposed, and had arisen before daybreak and gone home. That certainly would make things easier for her, she reasoned.

On impulse, she ran her hand over the impressions in the sheets where he'd slept and found them still warm. *Jesse hadn't stolen away during the night.* He was apparently going through with his commitment to Sarah.

Dierdre crept to the door and peeked out. The kitchen was exactly as she'd left it last night—clean and bare. He'd left no sign that he'd been here or that he was ever coming back. He'd even taken his *Farmer's Almanac*.

The soddie felt suddenly empty—infinitely so—its four-foot-thick walls and small deep-set windows compounding the unlived-in feeling. A house should have laughter . . . and children.

Pulling her wrapper tightly around her, Dierdre reminded herself that none of that mattered now. She was living someone else's life while her own spun on beyond her control. The first order of the day's business was pumping water.

She padded into the kitchen to get the pail off the stove, but when she tried to lift it, she found the bucket full of water. It had been bone dry when she went to bed. Testing the temperature, she found it just right to wash up.

Jesse must have heated it. Pleased, she smiled. True, he didn't have two nickels to rub together, but if he treated Sarah this nicely when she returned from the future, maybe she'd fall in love with him.

And he with her.

Dierdre's smile slipped. She felt a kinship with Sarah and wished her the very best. Yet, the idea of Jesse loving Sarah didn't bring the satisfaction she thought it would.

It wasn't as if she wanted to stay or anything, she told herself as she used the water to clean up. She was still determined to find a way home.

Carrying the bucket of wash water outside, she recounted the factors that might have conspired to send her into the past. There was the pregnancy, discontinuing her anticonvulsant, and finding the diary. She couldn't do anything about the pregnancy or her medication, not while she was stuck in the past. Besides finding the diary, she was at a loss about what else she could do.

She poured the water over a patch of wild white daisies, and thoughtfully walked to the horse trough to refill the pail. Hearing the grinding of gears, she looked up at the windmill wheel rotating in the wind. The sunlight reflecting off the steel blades reminded her again of the strobe-like effect of the light in the bookstore. If the flashing lights triggered her seizure, and the seizure produced the right conditions for her to switch places with Sarah, maybe she could recreate the short-circuit in her brain with bright lights. Of course, she thought wryly, since she couldn't just flip a light switch, she'd have to depend on nature for help.

Abandoning her bucket, she studied the shiny blades to see what effect they'd have, but the sun's angle was wrong. She moved around the property, trying out different vantage points, until she found the best position from which to see the sun glinting off the spinning wheel. She sat on a patch of grass and stared at the windmill, concentrating on how much she wanted to be with her baby.

She kept up her vigil until the afternoon clouds finally obscured the sun. Disappointed, she went into the house to rethink her theory. Even if she could reproduce the identical strobe-like lighting as in the bookstore, unless Sarah had the same neurological disorder that she did, the flashing lights would have no influence.

Which meant she had no control over her situation, and all she could do was wait. Feeling completely frustrated, she whirled around, wishing she had the answer. At that moment, Jesse strode into the soddie, carrying an odd-shaped metal tub. Tiny blue flowers dotted the painted surface.

"Where do you want it?" he asked. "In here or in the bedroom?"

She'd been tied in knots, desperate to figure out a solution to her problem, but something about the way he'd asked her opinion—as if she were actually the mistress of the house—undermined her desires. The soddie wasn't much by mighty John Morgan's standards, hardly more than four walls in its current condition, but she could imagine the pride a woman homesteading her own place might feel.

"That depends on what it is," she said.

He lifted an eyebrow. "It's a bathtub. We can store it on the wall so you can use it near the stove. Or, if you're worried about privacy, we can put it in the bedroom."

Noticing how he'd used "we" as if they were doing the house thing together, she felt an odd flutter in her chest.

"Maybe you think I look strong as an ox," he said around a self-effacing grin, "but this is getting a mite heavy."

She glanced at the outline of his straining muscles. He was lean and taut like a finely wound watch. Her cheeks warmed and she pulled her gaze away from the arms that clutched her tub.

"Next to my side of the bed will be fine," she said hurriedly.

Realizing what she'd said, she felt the flush deepen. Given her sheltered upbringing, the fact that she and this virtual stranger had staked out "sides" of the bed seemed incredibly out of character.

Jesse carried the tub into the bedroom and placed it in the cramped space between the bed and the wall. With the sun nearly down and the soddie losing light fast, his presence dominated the small room. "I can heat some water for you."

If she'd thought she could ignore her new husband, he wasn't making it easy for her. She'd had a better chance of holding her own ground when he was bossing her around. "I couldn't ask you to do that. Tomorrow's soon enough."

"Oh, I don't know about that." He sniffed the air. "I've kinda got used to sleeping in the house instead of in the barn with the horses."

"Are you suggesting that I smell?" she asked, dropping her guard.

He shrugged. "If the shoe fits—"

"I took a spit bath just this morning," she protested. "Not that it's really any of your business."

"Maybe you should use something stronger than spit." He grinned, looking absolutely charming and devastatingly mischievous at the same time. He shook his head. "Now don't get all riled up. The tub is for your back muscles. So you won't have to use horse liniment."

"Oh," she said, mollified. "Th-that's very nice of you."

She'd planned to use the liniment ploy to hold her new husband at arm's length a few more days, but she hadn't been all that fond of the smell, either. Now she'd have to think of something else.

"It's probably not what you're used to," he added, "but it's the best I could do."

"No. It's beautiful," she said, running her hand over an enameled forget-me-not on the tub. Definitely not what she was used to, but for an avid historian, better. At least temporarily.

"It belonged to my mother," he said.

The quietly spoken words hung between them in the tiny room, Dierdre finding her defenses as impotent as the walls of sheets erected by hapless strangers in the movies. Against her will, Dierdre looked up at Jesse. She didn't want to get involved with his past. She didn't want to go there—didn't want to open that door. But he'd shared something special with her, and she wasn't sure she wanted to turn back, either.

"You rarely speak of her," she prompted, knowing she'd regret it.

"No, I don't." He struck a match and lit the kerosene lantern. The light cast a golden glow off the rich earthen walls. "I better start heating the water."

She should have been relieved that he'd changed the subject, but the feeling of emptiness returned. Even Jesse's humming as he prepared her bath did nothing to dispel her loneliness.

When he'd poured the last bucketful of water into the tub, he left, shutting the door behind him. Dierdre disrobed and dipped a toe into the heated water. It was perfect for a leisurely soak.

She stepped in and settled into the tub, a gasp of pleasure escaping her mouth as she felt the soothing warmth of the water envelop her in a wet rush. Legs dangling over the sides, she leaned back against the rim, using only her hair as a pillow.

There was no radio, only Jesse's intermittent humming for music. No bubble bath to scent the water, just the rich pungent fragrance of the prairie. Dierdre breathed deeply, letting the earthy scent of her surroundings fill her lungs. Mother Nature's bouquet was all around, a reminder of the life that had sprung from her belly.

As she relaxed, Dierdre could hear Jesse moving around in the other room. A mere two weeks ago, she'd looked out the window and seen the sun reflecting off the windmill for the first time. Now she was married, homesteading Sarah's place after a fashion, and still no closer to returning home.

She sighed and immersed herself deeper in the

tub. Closing her eyes, she suddenly felt an unexpected fluttering in her eyelids. She tried to grab the edge of the tub, but her hands wouldn't obey. As if she were in a long black tunnel, she felt herself drifting away.

"Help!" she cried. She heard the word escape her lips as if someone else had said it.

"Help me," she repeated, recognizing the symptoms of a seizure.

And then she saw a light at the end of a tunnel. She could see Sam's home, and someone standing precariously close to the edge of a balcony, her protruding abdomen silhouetted by moonlight.

Was that Sarah?

The woman turned, and Dierdre saw her own face. This was *her* and *her child*, she realized. She was leaving the nightmare of the past behind and returning to everything she'd ever wanted. She was going home where she belonged.

From afar, she heard a door spring open and she felt Jesse's hands close around her arms. She sensed the worry in him as she began her journey home.

"Sarah." She felt Jesse shake her. He was gentle at first, then more insistent. "Sarah, wake up."

Dierdre heard him, but she couldn't allow him to hold her back. She'd made a baby in the future. Her responsibility was with her child.

"You can't let me down now," Jesse said. "You came through hell and are getting stronger. I'm not going to lose you now. Morgan took one woman from me, but he'll not take you, too."

Hearing the pleading in his voice, she almost wished she wasn't leaving. But she didn't belong here. She was no country girl. She'd been sheltered and coddled her whole life. She needed to be in the future where women having babies had doctors and hospitals with modern technology.

Watching herself in the present, she recognized the glassy look that came over her eyes. A moment more and she'd be there, feeling the growing child within her.

"Try harder," he said.

She had to consciously resist the yearning in his voice or she'd be lost. He couldn't know what she'd have to give up to stay with him.

Hands lifted her up. She felt a cool sheet float over her body. Was she dead?

"Don't go," he said, his lips at her cheek.

Fighting his urgent pleading, she struggled to make out the fading image of Sarah and the baby. Since traveling into the past, Dierdre felt that a piece of her had been missing and she had to find it. Now, it was within her reach.

"Don't leave," he begged. "Don't leave me now."

The insistence in Jesse's voice was like an invisible cord that wouldn't let go. Against her will, her tenuous link with the future dissolved, and the outline of Jesse's body became more pronounced.

"I'm not going anywhere," she heard herself say through dry, parched lips. "Not yet."

He groaned and drew her to his chest. She could feel his beating heart through the sheet. Sweat ran down the crevice between her breasts. A cool film of perspiration broke out across her forehead. Her eyelids relaxed.

The spell was over. She'd lost her opportunity to go to the future for now. She couldn't understand what had triggered the episode—maybe something going on with Sarah—but she knew full well that Jesse's persistence had prevented her from leaving. She could still hear his anguish as he pledged never to let Morgan take another woman from him.

Jesse brushed her sticky hair off her brow. "With the wedding and your accident, so soon after losing the baby, you probably just overexerted. I'm going to make sure you get more rest."

"Another woman," she murmured, wondering who Morgan had taken from him.

"Oh, no," he said, mistaking her meaning. "There's no other woman."

"Who?" she croaked, trying to anchor herself somewhere, and escape the tormented dreams that followed a seizure.

"You can't think of that. There'll be plenty of time to discuss things when you're feeling better."

"But I want to know now. I need to know. What woman?" Her words slurring, she swallowed painfully, trying to make order of her scrambled thoughts.

Jesse watched her struggling to sit up. He moved her over until she was cradled next to him on the bed, her head on his chest. Maybe he should try to keep her awake. He'd heard that certain head injuries were dangerous if you allowed the patient to go to sleep.

Torn between leaving Sarah to fetch the doctor and staying so he could watch her, he decided he'd keep her awake as long as he could. He'd assess the situation in the morning.

"The other woman was my mother," he began softly. He wished Sarah had inquired about something else—anything else. "She was a beautiful woman. Not in the traditional sense, perhaps, but she had a strong heart and an even stronger will. She never wanted to be a farmer's wife. But because that's what my father wanted, she made it her life. After my father died, I took his place in the fields alongside her. Promised myself I'd do things the way Dad would have wanted to make the farm work—no matter what it took."

Looking down, he saw that Sarah's brow was smooth and untroubled, as if she were already asleep. If this spell was anything like the last, in the morning she wouldn't remember anything he'd said.

"That was back when I thought wanting something bad enough could make it happen. If that were true, though, Mother would never have died. I'd have gotten her the help she needed."

He brushed a lock of hair out of Sarah's eyes and felt her forehead for a temperature—something he'd hesitated to do before. But now he was her husband. He didn't know quite how he'd managed that, but here he was. And if he wanted to check his wife for fever, there was no one to tell him he shouldn't.

Sarah's forehead was cool and clammy. He ran his fingers over her temple and her cheek. No fever. Resting in the crook of his arm, she looked so peaceful he couldn't bear to disturb her. Or was it his own selfish needs he was thinking of? The comforting way having her body next to his made him feel?

He must be crazy. He couldn't even take care of his own spread and now he had a wife to worry about. What the hell was he going to do with her? When he'd thought he was losing her, he'd felt so alone that it scared him. He hadn't had those feelings since he was fourteen years old.

He'd thought he knew Sarah, never suspected that she'd be able to make him feel as if he couldn't live without her. But he'd been wrong. Laying his head on hers, he wondered what else he'd been wrong about.

Chapter Twenty-four

Last night while resting in my room, I became fascinated by the shimmering outline of the full moon through my window. I opened the door to the balcony to get a better view. As I gazed up into the clear night sky, I saw red and green arcs dancing in the moon's corona.

While watching the flashing lights, I imagined I was home again, in my own bed. Not the fancy carved mahogany bed I'd had in the new house, but the one I'd slept in as a child. Crudely carved from cedar, it reminded me that my father hadn't always been wealthy.

Strange as it seems, I wasn't alone. My neighbor, Jesse Colburn, lay next to me, holding me as tenderly as a child. I was unclothed, except for the rather drafty protection of one thin sheet.

Even though Jesse had his boots on, it appeared unseemly for him to be lying with me this way. Surely my father would have killed Colburn if he had found us together. At the very least, I wouldn't have been able to sit down for a week—no matter that I am twenty and five years and a fully grown woman.

What has happened since I left the past, I cannot guess. Had I not clung so tightly to my grip on my new life, I believe I surely would have slipped back into the past. More than ever, I realize there is nothing there for me. I thought I was in love, but I was foolish. Now my concern is for the baby growing in my belly.

The doctors tell me my imaginings occurred during another seizure, but their tests can't confirm it. I suspect they are puzzled, but I do know they fear for the baby's health. The physicians concur that the increased stress on my body from the pregnancy is partially responsible for the episodes. More seizures could harm the child.

They now encourage me to resume taking an anticonvulsant. Since the medication itself can injure the baby, they have started me on a low dose, seeing no other way to protect against future episodes.

Since I've been given another chance to be a mother, I'm determined to do all I can to ensure the safety of this child. Still, I worry that I may not be doing enough. I don't know what I'd do without Sam's support. If not for his concern and guidance, I might have already lost hope.

Or, as was once my way, gone running back to my father.

Chapter Twenty-five

Dierdre woke with a kink in her neck and a tongue that felt twice its normal size. She'd had the most confusing whirlwind of dreams. Jesse had peopled them all, except the ones that had taken place in the future. She'd imagined he'd taken her in his arms and held her all night long, her head on his shoulder.

Rubbing her neck, she seemed to recall the hushed breeze of his breath as he whispered to her. While she had hovered between wakefulness and sleep, he'd brushed the hair from her eyes and told her things he'd probably never told anyone. Things about his mother and dreams that had died along with the innocence of childhood.

She glanced at the bathtub he'd brought, and noticed he'd already thoughtfully emptied it for her. The memory of how he'd prepared her a hot bath warmed her. The only thing that would have made the picture complete was if her baby could be with her too.

Her baby. Dierdre sat straight up, despite the throbbing pain in her head. She'd had a chance to go home last night. Where she belonged. It hadn't been just a dream. She'd looked down at Sarah on the balcony and seen her having a seizure. As she'd suspected, the convulsion must have been the triggering mechanism that had caused her and Sarah's conscious minds to change places. Then at the last moment, she'd allowed Jesse's pleading to pull her back.

She'd missed her opportunity to return to her baby.

Shaking her aching head, Dierdre remembered how Jesse kept talking to her, all the while telling her to stay—begging her not to leave him. Something about not letting John Morgan take her from him as he'd taken his mother. Because of some misplaced sympathy toward him, had she forfeited her opportunity to return to her baby? Or had she simply allowed her physical attraction to him to distract her from everything she'd ever dreamed about? Where was the strength in that, the self-reliance she'd struggled so long to acquire?

She got out of bed and began dressing, trying to regain her center of balance apart from Jesse. She needed a way home that wasn't dependent on

Sarah having another seizure, she decided. As far as she knew, that left only the diary.

She had to find it. But then what about Jesse? she wondered, recalling how his soothing words had comforted her. He'd stood in the gap between the past and her future, holding her back. The longer she stayed, the more difficult leaving him might be.

Opening the armoire, she took out the blue dress. Her fingers lingered over its soft fabric, remembering the day he'd chosen it for her over the rough, brown muslin. He'd told her blue had been her favorite color.

Tossing the flowered print dress on the bed, Dierdre resolutely took out Becky's ugly mustard-colored gingham and put it on. If getting closer to Jesse meant she'd have a harder time returning to the future, then she needed to get the diary back as soon as possible. She'd devise a long-term strategy, too—just in case tracking down the journal took longer than she hoped. She had to make her plans now, she realized, before Jesse caused her to lose any more objectivity.

From the knoll separating his property from the Morgans', Jesse watched Sarah hanging laundry on a line stretched between two saplings. The sun was uncommonly warm for so late in the season. Like a fool, she'd forgotten to wear a hat. It was as if with her memory, she'd lost all common sense.

She wasn't the only one who'd taken leave of her

senses, though. He'd promised her he'd take care of her, but he had no wheat to plant—and no way to get any without selling off part of his family's land to Morgan. Still, just as he'd done in late summer for the past dozen years, he'd begun cultivating the fields for the September planting. As he worked, his mind had drifted back to Sarah so frequently—worrying that he shouldn't have left her alone—that he'd abandoned the fields that begged to be plowed, the rows he had tilled as crooked as a dog's hind leg.

Now watching her bend down to the wash pail, he admired the full curve of her skirt as it pulled across her hips. Arms gracefully moving in concert, she wrung the water out of his shirt and hung it on the makeshift line. He recognized the faded print of his mother's blue dress. Next, a pair of snowy white drawers. He smiled. He was her husband, yet the first view he'd had of her underclothing was seeing it dangling from a tree in broad daylight.

He wouldn't mind changing that.

She stooped to throw out the wash water and when she straightened, her hair—which had been growing out nicely—fell into soft waves that clung to her head like a shiny brown cap. With a raking swipe of her fingers, she combed it off her face and raised a hand to shade her eyes. She waved. She'd seen him.

Like a snooping schoolboy, he'd been caught spying on his own wife. With a flush of embarrassment working its way up his neck, he nudged Sage toward the soddie.

"I need to go to town," she said when he got within earshot. Her cheeks were pink from exposure to the sun.

"Can't it wait?" He wanted her to rest up before she rode that far. He wasn't ready for another scare like she'd given him last night.

"Not long."

"What do you need?" Whatever it was she wanted, he wished he could afford to get it for her, but he knew better.

"It's personal."

"Are you ill again?" He dismounted, a sick feeling in the pit of his stomach. He couldn't hope to know all the private things that could go wrong with a woman. If she was having complications from the miscarriage . . .

"No. Not really. I just have something I need to do."

He wished she'd trust him enough to tell him what it was, but he guessed that was too much to expect. They were still practically strangers.

"I could take you on Monday."

She nodded and smiled, and he felt as if he'd granted her the greatest of wishes. "I've got some money," she said.

Reaching down, she unrolled the hem of her skirt. It didn't matter to him that it had been Becky's dress and that it didn't fit. It was her wedding dress. A knot caught in his throat as he remembered how naturally beautiful she'd looked—

and how nervous he'd been when he said "I do."

She pulled a wad of bills out of a slit in the hem. "This fifty dollars should help with my expenses."

He stepped back. "I don't want your father's money."

"This doesn't belong to him. It belongs to me. And I want you to take it."

He hesitated, thinking how much he could use the cash. It wouldn't go far in getting ready for the long winter, but it would help get him through until the end of the month. Too bad he wouldn't have enough left over to buy Sarah something special.

Reluctantly, he took the money. He counted out half of it and gave the rest back to her.

"I don't like owing anyone," he said stiffly. "I'll pay you back."

She smiled. She probably didn't believe a word of it.

"I've got an idea. It's time I learned how to ride a horse. Learn again, I mean. How about you give me some riding lessons and we'll call it even?"

"I guess so," he said, "but I don't mind taking you to town when you want to go. I just can't do it before Monday."

He didn't want her traveling anywhere alone for a while. He just wanted her beside him in the wagon where he could make sure Brolyn couldn't get to her. And, truth be told, maybe he just wanted her near him.

"No, I'd rather know how to get around by myself. That way when I want to go somewhere I won't have to depend on you."

So she really didn't want to be with him. With her father out of the picture, she just needed his help. An odd sinking feeling coursed through him.

"You don't need *me* to teach you. Most of your father's ranch hands would probably fall all over themselves to help you."

"I don't think so," she said slowly.

"Mason would gladly work with you."

"I don't want Mason to realize that I don't remember how. He's sure to ask questions."

"What does it matter? You've got nothing to hide now. Your father already thinks you're in the family way." He started to lead Sage away.

"I'd rather have you," she said.

He turned, his heart pounding. "What?"

"I want you to teach me."

He forced his breathing to slow. He had to quit reading meaning into everything she said. "What makes you think I can teach you anything?"

She thought a moment. "Because you're patient."

He wasn't feeling patient. While watching her from afar . . . he'd dreamed of holding her near. He didn't know how many more nights he could keep from touching her. "Well, I suppose you'd do all right on Lucy. She's small and gentle."

Jesse led Sage to the horse tank before he promised Sarah anything else. It didn't matter what he wanted, he reminded himself. Sarah wasn't going to permanently change her ways because of him. She was still the same woman she'd always been— even if he wanted to believe she was different. He splashed fresh water on his face until the stinging cold brought him to his senses.

Being a bachelor for so many years had had its drawbacks, but it also had its advantages. The greatest benefit of living alone was that he hadn't known what he was missing. Straightening, his gaze went unerringly to Sarah.

Chapter Twenty-six

The next day, despite his best intentions to concentrate on farming, Jesse returned home to the soddie well before sundown. He began looking for Sarah before he even got over the knoll. When he didn't see her—or the telltale laundry on her line—he wondered whether this was the day she'd finally gone home. Surely she missed the comfort of her four-poster feather bed, he told himself. How could a corn-husk mattress compete with such luxury?

He'd almost convinced himself that she'd left, and that he didn't care, when he saw her down by the creek. Following the trail through the cottonwoods, he rode toward her, noticing she'd again forgotten her hat.

"Look what I found," she exclaimed when he

rode up. "We can steam these greens for supper."
She was industriously gathering mustard greens,
their tall yellow blossoms going to seed.

He stifled a grimace. Mustard greens weren't his
favorite. Even boiled hard and liberally doused in
vinegar, they tasted tough and bitter.

Sarah glanced at him for approval. When he
hesitated, she raised up, cradling her find in her
apron as protectively as a mother would a child.
"You do like them, don't you?" Her brown eyes
sparkled in the sunlight filtering through the trembling cottonwood leaves.

Suddenly the greens didn't sound so bad.
"Sure."

She rewarded him with a wide smile that intensified the glitter of gold in her eyes. "I think I'm
catching on to this homesteading thing," she said.
"While I was picking flowers, I discovered that the
ones with the pretty lavender-blue stars belong to
the onion family. The stems should taste good
with the greens . . . I think." Sarah fanned out the
corners of her apron to show him her treasures.

She'd collected bluebells, wild blue flax, blue
salvia and enough of the blue flowers she called
wild onions to cure a hundred colds. If picking
flowers in every shade of her favorite color was
any indication, she was well on her way to getting
her memory back. Her cheeks, which recently had
been pink and raw from exposure to the sun and
wind, had turned a healthy golden brown. She was
even more beautiful than the day he'd married
her.

She tilted her head back and looked at him inquiringly. "What brings you back so early? I thought you had to plow until dark."

"I planned to, but something came up." He got off his horse and let Sage loose to graze. An odd, queasy feeling gnawed at him and he shuffled his feet.

"Aw, heck," he said, jamming a hand into his pocket. He drew out a tiny velvet purse.

"When we got married, I didn't have a fancy ring to give you. And I couldn't afford to buy you a wedding present." He swallowed, the pounding in his chest making it hard to breath. As the sun dropped lower, the shade that had felt so good disappeared and the late afternoon rays beat down on the back of his neck.

Ignoring the uncomfortable, prickly sensation spreading from his neck into his face, he handed her the sack. "This is something that means a lot to me. It's not new, but I hope you like it."

Nervously waiting for her reaction, he watched Sarah catch the corners of her apron in the crook of her arm, and open the bag. She peeked inside, but he couldn't read her initial reaction. He knew she was used to much finer things than he could ever give her. He'd been foolish to hope his gift would please her.

Slowly Sarah took out the simple heart locket and held it to the light. She read the inscription aloud. "With love, J.C." She gazed up at him, the rich, earthy depths of her brown eyes doing strange things to him. "J.C. Those are your initials."

"Uh, yeah. Jesse Colburn."

"You had this inscribed?" She looked mystified, but she was still smiling.

"Me?" he asked, still caught up in the warmth of her eyes. "Uh, no." He snapped out of his momentary daze. "J.C. Those were my father's initials, too. He gave this locket to my mother on their wedding day."

"Oh," she said softly. Nodding, she caught her lip between her teeth and stared at it some more. He wished she'd say something else so he could tell what she was thinking.

"If you don't like it, you don't have to wear it."

"No. It's not that. The necklace is lovely. But it was your mother's. I don't know if I'd feel right about taking it."

"She'd want you to have it, if that's what you're worried about."

"How do you know?" Sarah pressed.

He studied the grass beneath his feet, trying to find the words. "Mama wanted you to be happy— what with you losing your own mother so young."

"Did we know each other? Your mother and I?"

"When you were little, my mother used to bring me over to visit. Mama always thought you were something special," he added.

Jesse watched a glistening appear in Sarah's eyes, making them even more beautiful. He wanted to kiss her, to chase away her tears, but he felt rooted to the spot.

Victoria Bruce

She slipped the locket back in the pouch and into her pocket. "I'll treasure it always," she said, smiling wistfully up at him.

His arms burned for her, but still he didn't close the gap between them. He'd rushed home to see her, telling himself he was just checking on her safety—yet all the time thinking how much he wanted to crush her to his chest, press her soft curves against his body. As his longing to hold her grew, the prairie wind blew hotter, drying out his mouth and stinging his eyes.

The breeze blew a strand of hair across her moist mouth. He stepped forward, brushing the lock of hair off her cheek. His finger glanced off her soft skin. She was his wife. He had a right to take her in his arms.

At his touch, she tilted her head back, but her thoughts were still unreadable. Whether she wanted him as much as he wanted her, he couldn't tell.

In the distance he heard a horse approaching. The staccato of pounding hooves echoed his rapidly beating heart. Reluctantly, he shifted his gaze from Sarah to the lone rider making his way toward them. Obeying his master's commands like a charger entering into battle, John Morgan's magnificent black stallion flew over the plains, tail outstretched, hooves eating up the ground.

From all appearances, Morgan was not here to pay a friendly call. Even Sarah must have been startled, for she dropped her apron, scattering the flowers and mustard greens at their feet.

"Let me handle this," Jesse said. Anticipating a nasty confrontation, he moved in front of her, putting his body between her and her father. Facing Morgan, Jesse shielded Sarah just as he'd always wanted to.

"You aren't with child," Morgan shouted to Sarah, even before he'd reined his horse to a stop. "You can give up this foolish idea about homesteading and come home."

"Good afternoon, Father," Sarah said, stepping to the side. "I've got a warm pot of coffee. Would you care for a cup?"

Morgan ignored her offer. "I talked to Dr. Mabe. That drunken old reprobate came by for a handout. Said he made a house call while I was in Ogallala. I asked him when the baby would be born and he said there would be no baby. That means you can come home. I'll get the marriage annulled."

The moment Jesse dreaded had arrived. He'd lose her now—just when he was realizing what he'd missed all those years of living alone.

"Do I have a say in this?" she asked.

"You're my daughter and I know what's best for you. You're coming home."

"Sarah is free to do as she likes, but I won't let you bully her," Jesse said.

"Who are you calling a bully?" Morgan snapped. "You stay out of this." He turned back to Sarah. "I don't know why you didn't tell me," Morgan continued. "It would have saved so much trouble. Climb on, girl, I'll send someone for your things."

He took his boot out of the stirrup to make room for her.

Jesse felt Sarah sway and reached out to steady her. She'd cave in now. He'd seen how Morgan handled people who tried to stand up to him. Like his mother.

Jesse hadn't known then about men driven by their own selfish greed. He pushed the painful thoughts aside.

"I did tell you I wasn't pregnant. Several times, remember? You wouldn't listen. I doubt you've ever listened to me."

"But Simon said—"

"And you believed him over me," Sarah broke in. "Your own daughter. What has he done that I haven't to deserve your trust?"

Morgan opened his mouth, but all he could do was sputter. His high-strung stallion spun around in a circle before Morgan calmed him. "What has trust got to do with it? It's a man's job to protect his daughter."

"Even if he's the one hurting her?" Sarah asked.

It took Morgan a moment to realize she was referring to him. His mouth snapped shut and his eyes grew dark with fury. Jesse watched the two face off in amazement. He could see where Sarah had inherited her riveting brown eyes.

"How am I hurting you?" John Morgan demanded.

"Your stock destroyed Jesse's crops and you haven't offered restitution. Since he's my husband, then that means it hurts me, too. The Herd

Law makes you liable for the damage."

"Not in these parts," Morgan countered. "Not as long as I've got any pull."

"Then maybe we should see about changing that," Sarah said evenly. "The law was written to protect the poor as well as the rich."

"You wouldn't sue your own father."

Determinedly, she crossed her arms. "I'll do whatever it takes to protect my land and my husband."

Morgan ignored her, his expression changing from anger to disbelief. "You're the man of the family. Can't you do something with her?"

Jesse shrugged and drew Sarah to his side. "I kinda like her the way she is," he said proudly. More surprising, he found that he meant it.

John Morgan shook his head. "Heaven help us."

"That's the best kind of help, sir," Jesse said.

Morgan reined his horse around to leave, then halted, studying Sarah as if he couldn't quite understand the transformation in her. "You've changed. If you're determined to stick it out here, young lady, don't expect any help from me. I won't spoon-feed you . . . but I won't stand in your way, either."

"Then that means your bank will reconsider my loan?" Jesse asked.

Morgan hesitated, as if considering all the angles. "With no guarantee you'll have a crop," he said, "you'll have to mortgage your land. Otherwise, I might be accused of showing favoritism."

"I doubt that's a character flaw you have to

worry about," Jesse said dryly. "You still want my farm? You going to take it from me if I miss a payment?"

Morgan glanced at Sarah. His face softened, the anger dissolving into an expression of reluctant respect. "Aw, hell no. Until I get an heir, I got all the land I need." He nodded at Jesse. "You try Seymour Lindsey again at the bank. No one gets anything by giving up too soon."

With that, he rode off, his retreating back as imperiously straight as ever.

"Did you hear that?" Sarah said when Morgan had gone. "You're going to get your loan. He as good as promised. You can talk to the bank when we go into town on Monday." She grabbed his hands and whirled around, pulling him with her.

He wanted to tell her that a lot could happen in two days, but her excitement was catching. For the first time in a long while, he felt as if there might be hope.

Still holding his hands, she laughed, dancing as they swung about in a circle like children playing ring-around-the-rosy.

Jesse glanced down at the ground where they trampled mustard greens beneath their feet. "Looks like there's going to be a change in plans for supper. And I was so looking forward to them."

Sarah caught his sarcasm and laughed. "I can always pick more."

"I don't suppose I could persuade you not to," he said, smiling.

"That depends. What are you offering?"

The countryside whirled around him in a blur.

He wanted her. He wanted to taste her, nibble on her chin and make love to her until he forgot his name and all the things that might stand in their way.

She grew dizzy first. Begging him to stop, she collapsed into the grass, her smile as innocent as when she'd sat next to him wearing ribbons and braids. She'd grown into quite a woman. He knelt beside her, drawing her against him until the heat of her body and the rays of sunshine on his back made him wonder if he'd flown too close to the sun.

His blood ran hot. His long-suppressed need ran hotter. When she circled his neck with her arms and pulled him down beside her, he feared he couldn't control his passion much longer.

"Jesse," she whispered, drawing his name out until the breeze grabbed it, blending it with the hushed rustling through the cottonwoods.

With the greatest restraint, he leaned toward her and placed a kiss on her soft, lush lips. Not content with such a fleeting touch, he surrendered to the yearning that was building inside and deepened the kiss. Her skin's heat and the sweetness of her mouth shook him to his core.

Trailing kisses across her cheek and down the angle of her jaw, he caught a whiff of lavender water, mingling with the fragrance of flower blossoms crushed by their entwined bodies. He followed the scent of lavender along her collarbone and lower, until the constraints of her dress impeded his exploration.

He untied the straps at the sides of her dress and lifted it over her head. Leaning her back into the cool, fragrant grass, he traced the faint scent of lavender from the hollow of her throat to the valley between her breasts. Heady with her fragrance, he reached under her camisole and cupped the curve of her breast, massaging its fullness.

"Want me to stop?" he asked, running his thumb gently over her nipple.

"Yes," she murmured. "Sometime tomorrow."

Jesse smiled to himself. She'd trusted him enough to choose him for her husband. Maybe she hadn't known what she wasn't getting into—he had no guarantee that she'd stick it out with him for even a month—but he'd show her he hadn't made an idle promise. He'd been telling the truth. He knew how to take care of her. It felt as if he'd been waiting for this moment his whole life.

Wanting to know her every taste, he impatiently removed her underclothing and flung it aside. He ran his tongue along the inner swell of her breast, curving up to her nipple. The dark-colored skin of her areola puckered at his touch, the nipple growing erect as he caught it between his teeth and gently sucked.

Arching up, she gazed on him with a look of desire that urged him to hurry. Freeing himself from the confines of his increasingly binding pants, he was struck by his lack of modesty, but she rose up to meet him so quickly their bodies came together in a frenzied furor.

He wanted to build her up slowly, but driven by her moans, he rode her as if the very devil were giving chase. Wild and raw, her need drove him to the edge of restraint, gripping him in its rhythm. He had thought himself to be over such animalistic urges, but his body moved as if controlled by unseen forces.

Her cries snatched what modicum of control he might have maintained, driving all thoughts but the hungry image of her from his mind. He was blinded by her beauty, possessed by the need to exorcise the inner demons that had held him captive so long.

"Yes," she cried, just when he could no longer hold back.

Blood pounding in his ears, Jesse felt an explosion as powerful as a gunshot. Lights exploded behind his closed eyelids like a crack of lightning. The sweetest pain rocked through him, pulsing warmth into his legs and head, expelling any previous notion of what making love to a woman was really all about.

Chapter Twenty-seven

Over the intermittent creaks of the wagon, Dierdre heard Jesse murmur encouragement to the horse. She noticed how effortlessly his long fingers worked the reins, how lightly he laid the traces across Sage's back as he guided him toward town. Nothing like the impatient frenzy with which they'd made love the day before.

Remembering her reckless abandon under the cottonwoods, Dierdre wondered whatever had come over her. She was about as opposite to an exhibitionist as one could get, never letting her sexual desires overrule her common sense. What if someone had come along and seen them?

Reaching into her pocket, she closed her hand around the heart-shaped locket he'd given her. She felt too much an impostor to wear it, but just having something that meant so much to him was a constant reminder of what they'd shared to-gether yesterday.

Jesse didn't seem to think less of her since then. If anything, he was more attentive. She was fairly certain, though, that with her restricted upbring-ing, Sarah would never understand their romp in the meadow. Dierdre stole a sidelong glance at Jesse. Wearing the suit she'd patched, he looked incredibly handsome.

Gazing at his profile, she realized she'd never sewn for anyone before, had never wanted to try. When she'd asked Jesse how he'd torn his jacket sleeve, he'd told her he'd gotten into a fight with someone in town over beating a lame horse. He'd shrugged it off, as if it made no difference to him, but the flash of anger in his eyes betrayed him. She would bet the other guy had more to show for the fight than a torn coat.

She'd felt the intensity of his passion when they'd made love—felt a reciprocal emotion in herself that only he had ever unleashed. Knowing that her response had something to do with trust, she realized how natural it felt to be here with him. But what about her baby in the future? And what if their lovemaking had conceived a new child?

Even though the future was logically the only place she belonged, getting closer to Jesse had made things harder—just as she knew it would. She'd allowed him into a part of her life she'd always kept guarded before. It felt good, though. And that was the problem.

"Can I drop you somewhere while I go to the bank?" he asked.

Thankful for the distraction, Dierdre pulled her gaze back to the road. The same feeling of wonder gripped her as it had the first time she'd seen Prairie Bend. Taking in every detail, she studied the vintage dress of the customers entering the lumber yard, the quaint storefront of the laundry and bathhouse, and the gilded lettering on the brick bank. She felt as if she were appearing in an old episode of *Gunsmoke* where all the actors were in costume, and all the sets were real.

"Where's the schoolhouse?" she asked.

"White, steepled building opposite the church. Thinking ahead to children already?" he asked, glancing at her out of the corner of his eye.

"No, of course not," she said, firmly. "What about the jail?" Every western town worth its salt had a jail.

"That would be around the corner from Mamie's Boardinghouse. Only one cell, but then we don't even have our own sheriff."

"Well, there's a job for you if you ever decide to give up farming." She'd said it in jest, but the sudden tension in Jesse's face made her wish she'd kept quiet. Maybe it wasn't right to try to change his future, but she hated to see Jesse lose his shirt trying to farm the land.

"You can let me off here at the General Store," she said quickly. "I need to see if I can patch things up with Becky." In Dierdre's eyes, Becky wasn't much of a friend to Sarah, but there didn't seem to be too many other women around that were of a similar age.

"Interesting choice of words," he said, stopping the wagon. He glanced at his awkwardly patched sleeve and grinned. If her handiwork was any indication of her ability to patch things up with Becky, she was in for trouble. Her stitches were abominable.

"You just wait, Jesse Colburn. All I need is practice."

He got out of the wagon and went around to help her—not unlike a beau on a first date. "Sounds good to me," he said, lifting her down. "I don't know how it could get any better, but if you insist. . . ."

After firmly planting her on solid ground, he continued to clasp her around the waist, his touch a reminder of how masterfully he'd stroked her in the grass.

This was far more than just a first date, she thought with a delicious shiver. This was her husband—their marriage no longer one of just convenience.

As she looked into Jesse's eyes, unable to divine the forces which had brought them together, she felt the air grow thick with longing as if the space between time had shrunk, and the time between space had ceased to exist for them.

She wondered if this was what it was like to . . .

A sound behind her startled Dierdre from her

straying thoughts. Turning, she pulled away from Jesse's grasp. "Becky, I didn't see you."

"I expect not," Becky said, a tight smile on her face.

Jesse touched the brim of his hat. "You're just the person my wife wants to see. She's been sewing up a storm." He winked at Dierdre and grinned.

"I think we can manage without your input," she said, elbowing him in the side.

"Then I'll see you ladies when I'm through at the bank." He tipped his hat and escaped before she could do further bodily damage.

"I'm a little rusty with a needle and thread," she explained to Becky. "But I'll improve with practice." She colored, remembering the kind of practicing Jesse had in mind.

"You always hated sewing. Has marriage changed you that much, Sarah? Or should I call you Mrs. Colburn?" Becky laughed, but the effort came out sounding tinny.

"Don't be silly," she said, returning the gingham dress and hat to Becky. "You'll call me Sarah, just like always. I would like to talk to you about it, though. Do you have a moment?"

Becky motioned to an empty bench in front of the store and they sat down. "About the day of the wedding," Dierdre began, "I'm sorry about having to tie you up. I didn't know what else to do. I couldn't let my father bully me into marrying Simon. Will you forgive me?"

"But you said you loved him," Becky said.

"That's true," Dierdre admitted, "but I didn't trust him.

"You didn't trust him," Becky hissed. "Yet you were so desperate for a father for your baby that you'd steal Jesse from me. What does that say about trust?"

Dierdre instinctively placed a protective hand over her flat belly and the hollow place that longed for a baby. "No, there's no baby. When I tied you up, my intention was only to get away. I didn't intend to marry Jesse—or anyone."

"Don't lie to me. If there isn't a baby, then why are you married? If you're going to get yourself in the family way to catch a man, you should at least have the decency to marry the father of your child."

"What do you know about that?"

"Enough to know that Jesse's not the father and you don't care a hill of beans about him."

"That's not true."

"Which part?"

"I'm not with child."

"And what about your feelings for Jesse?"

Becky was wrong there too, she realized. She did care for Jesse. A lot more than she wanted to admit.

"See, you can't even tell the truth when you're faced with it." Becky jumped up, her voice rising. "You court Simon Brolyn, get with child by someone else, and when Simon tries to protect your reputation, you turn on him and marry Jesse. But the proof is in the pudding, and when the baby's born, it won't look like Jesse. Simon told me all about you. Don't try to deny it."

Dierdre stood, knowing that something had unalterably shifted in Sarah's relationship with Becky. If their friendship was reparable, only time and Sarah herself would be able to heal it.

"I realize you're hurting," Dierdre said tersely, "but if you were a true friend, you wouldn't have helped to keep me locked up. It wasn't for my own good. It was for *your* own good. You only wanted to see me married off to Simon because you were afraid of losing Jesse."

Becky blanched. "Jesse doesn't love you. He doesn't care anything about you at all."

"I've cared about Sarah from the first time I saw her," Jesse said.

Becky whirled around, her face turning red when she realized Jesse had heard her. "You can't mean that. What has she got that I don't have? Is it because she's rich?"

Jesse frowned in disgust. "I've always tried to be nice, but I've never felt anything more than friendship for you."

"You're lying. You treated me better than anyone else has. I know you must care for me." Becky charged Jesse, fists pounding against his chest. Grabbing her arms, he held her at arm's length, holding on until the fight went out of her.

An old man wearing a graying apron limped out of the General Store. "Now we'll have none of that. Take your hands off her, young man."

Jesse let go and Becky stumbled, nearly collapsing. "Go on, git out of here," the old man said to him, dragging Becky inside like a wounded animal.

Wordlessly, Jesse took Dierdre's arm. She followed his lead, ignoring the stares of storekeepers and their customers. Humiliated, she heard none of the whispers and gossip going on all around her. Jesse's words were ringing too loudly in her brain. He'd cared about Sarah from the first time he'd seen her. Sarah, *not* Dierdre.

Dierdre had convinced herself she was marrying Jesse for Sarah's sake. But she suspected she had let her attraction to Jesse overrule her better judgment. Why else would she have so brazenly played the part of the wife? Did she really believe that making love in the grass with Sarah's husband had been in Sarah's best interests, too?

From the beginning, Jesse's kindness toward her had been because he thought she was Sarah. Although Dierdre had selfishly participated in the charade, as far as he knew, he'd made love to Sarah Morgan.

Dierdre had lowered her defenses with Jesse and made a mess of Sarah's life, but the masquerade was over. Jesse loved Sarah Morgan, not Dierdre Brown.

Becky watched Sarah drag Jesse into the hotel. Couldn't she wait until she got home to paw the poor man?

Sarah had deceived her in the worst way. Since third grade, she'd listened as Becky poured out her feelings for Jesse, pretending to be sympathetic. Becky had assumed that her secret was safe with Sarah. After all, they'd been best friends. Then, even though she could have had anyone she wanted, Sarah had selfishly snatched Jesse away from her.

She'd always suspected that Sarah could be extraordinarily cruel—it came from having all that money. And she knew Sarah didn't care about Jesse. She only cared about herself. First, she'd used and discarded Simon. Then, she'd thrown away her friendship with Becky. Sooner or later, Jesse would find out just how selfish the girl could be.

Becky took off her apron and folded it into a tidy square. If she had her way, he'd find out the truth about Sarah. The sooner, the better. . . .

"Why are we spending the night?" Dierdre asked, closing the shade of the hotel room window. "Didn't you get the loan?"

"Nope." Jesse yanked off a boot and dropped it on the floor. "Lindsey Seymour says he hasn't heard a word from John Morgan about my loan, but he's got a meeting with him at ten in the morning. I plan to be at the bank when he arrives."

"Speaking of the loan"—Dierdre frowned and tried to pick her words carefully—"there is something I'm concerned about. Not so much whether you'll get the loan money, but how you'll spend it."

He threw her a surprised stare. "Besides setting

aside enough for food and supplies, I'll repair some tools and buy seed, of course.

"I've been meaning to talk to you about that. Have you considered buying cattle with your money?"

When he didn't answer, she continued. "With the droughts and sandy soil, grasshoppers and wind, this land really isn't suited for commercial farming. The Sand Hills are much better for ranching."

"Is that so?" he ground out.

Dierdre didn't want to try to tell him his business—no one appreciated that—but warning him about the future was the least she could do for all he'd done to help her. She owed him that.

She'd approach him from a logic angle. "If you can look at this rationally, I think you'll see that the hard time you've been having working the land isn't going to get any better. The future for this territory is cattle. Not just random breeding, but fencing and specialization. The rancher who stays in business is going to have to enlist improved management techniques."

"Did your father ask you to tell me that?"

Dierdre turned to look at Jesse. His face was impassive and unforgiving. "No. Of course not. Why would you think so?"

"Because your father's been trying to get my family's plot for pasture land since I was knee high. I think it's mighty peculiar that now that we're married, you should tell me to give up farming to raise cattle. Makes me wonder whether

John Morgan wants me to branch out into ranching so he can take over when I fail."

"If you'd stop being so stubborn—just for a minute—you'd realize that I'm speaking the truth. Forget the bad blood between you and my father. This has nothing to with him. He doesn't understand what I'm talking about either, or he wouldn't be buying up farm machinery."

"He's buying farming equipment?"

"From Simon Brolyn," she said.

Jesse frowned, making his feelings about Simon clear. Dierdre rushed on. "There's something else I need to tell you," she said, trying not to watch him undress for bed. Lord, with his long, lean legs and narrow hips, he put thoughts in her head she shouldn't be having—not if she meant to leave this time with her conscience and peace of mind intact.

"All right. But are you going to sleep standing in front of the window all night? Or are you coming to bed?" He crawled under the covers.

"Okay," she said, reluctantly settling into bed as far away from him as possible. "But just to talk. This is important. It has to do with how I know farming won't work in this part of Nebraska."

"I'm listening. What's on your mind?"

She swallowed. "We need to talk." That was how couples in the movies always started out when one spouse had something awful to tell the other.

"You said that."

"I know. It's just that this is difficult to explain." It was Sarah he wanted, and she didn't feel right deceiving him anymore. She took a breath and let it out in a big sigh. "I'm not who you think I am."

"If it's about your past and the baby, you don't need to tell me. What you did before we were married is your business."

"No, it's not that." This was going to be even harder than she'd thought. How did she explain that she was from another time and place, that she'd married him under false pretenses?

"You've noticed that I'm not exactly like the Sarah you used to know." When he nodded, she continued. "I told you I lost my memory. That isn't strictly true. What little I knew of Sarah's life came from reading about it in her diary."

Jesse pushed up on an elbow and frowned. "If you're getting sick again, I'll try to get hold of the doctor. With all the excitement today, maybe you're having a relapse."

"I'm fine, really. In fact, I've never felt better. What I'm trying to tell you is that I come from a long way away. I don't belong here."

"Do you want out of our marriage?" he asked quietly.

The question rocked her. Jesse didn't turn away from her, but in his gaze she saw that he was poised to let her go if that's what it took to make her happy.

She'd never wanted to depend on anyone or anything, but now that he was prepared to give her up to make her happy, the lure of being on her own didn't hold the same appeal.

"No. It's not the marriage."

Considering the alternatives, she thought telling the truth now was the best thing for Sarah. What she didn't know how to do was explain that she'd temporarily taken Sarah's place.

"I know it was sudden," he continued, "but if you're not happy, you're free to go home anytime."

"It's not that either. I don't want to go home. Not to John Morgan's house anyway. Do you remember the night I grew faint in the bathtub?"

"You are sick again, aren't you?" He slapped his bent knee as if trying to punish himself. "I should have taken you to stay with Mrs. Dickens instead of subjecting you to the townsfolk so soon."

"Jesse. It's not your fault. You're the good guy here. What I'm trying to tell you has nothing to do with you. I should have told you in the beginning. As much as I'm tempted to stay here with you, there's someone else who needs me more."

"Is it Simon?" he asked too calmly.

"Oh, God, no."

That was something at least. Jesse snorted. "If it's your father you're referring to, I think he can manage on his own."

"Why does everything keep coming back to Morgan? What is it between you two?"

Jesse leaned back against the bed board and closed his eyes, feeling he'd merely dodged one bullet to be hit by another.

He'd thought she was working up to tell him it was over, that the accommodations of the only hotel in town he could afford were unsuitable—that the one thing worse than being ostracized by the entire town was living in a hovel with a man she didn't love.

Then she'd turned the tables on him, inquiring about a secret he'd kept for more than a decade. He'd never wanted to burden anyone with the memories he carried—especially not Sarah.

"If you want to keep it to yourself, I understand," she said.

"There's no reason to dredge up the past now. Nothing can change what happened."

"You might feel better if you talked about it."

Her invitation was tempting, like the promise of the first warm breeze of spring. He could almost imagine how much lighter he'd feel sharing the weight of the load with her. But then she might feel worse, so what would be the point? He shook his head. "Let's just forget about it."

"It's okay for you to think of yourself just this once. You don't have to protect me. I'm capable of handling whatever it is."

"I know, Sarah. If I'm trying to protect anyone, it's probably myself." He placed a kiss on the top of her head. "Now what is it you're so determined to tell me?"

She took a breath and let out a heavy sigh. "I haven't been truthful with you—even from the start. Today I realized that it's Sarah Morgan that you've always cared about, and I can't let you go on thinking I'm that person."

"So you've changed. Everyone grows up."

"It's more than that. Do you remember how,

when I didn't know about the simplest things, I said I lost my memory?"

He nodded and she went on. "I was lying. I didn't know about those things, because I'm not Sarah Morgan. My name is Dierdre Brown. And I live more than a hundred years in the future."

Chapter Twenty-eight

Jesse froze, his gaze fixed on his beautiful wife. "You're not joking?" he asked, completely stunned. "You really think you're someone besides Sarah Morgan?"

She nodded. "I know this sounds crazy, but just hear me out. I'm a historian and I work at a rare-book store in New York City. I got a shipment of personal accounts about pioneer life in the Midwest. I was especially taken with a diary by a twenty-five-year-old woman named Sarah Morgan. She wrote enough to let me know that she was unmarried and pregnant, with nowhere to turn.

"While I was reading her diary, I felt a special link with Sarah. You see, for over a year I'd been trying to become pregnant by artificial insemination."

"Artificial what?" Jesse asked.

She smiled. "That's a newfangled way for women who have trouble getting pregnant to have babies. Except for being a sperm donor, a man really isn't necessary. It's not the kind of situation I would have chosen for bringing a child into the world, but I told myself I could make it work."

"I told you I don't care what happened before our marriage," Jesse said hoarsely. "You don't need to concoct a story to explain your behavior."

"It's more than just a story. Our being together before was a lie—because I didn't tell you the truth. What I'm telling you now is fact. You can imagine why I waited so long, knowing you'd think me a liar or crazy."

Jesse leaned back against the headboard, the pressure building in his head. In his opinion, Sarah didn't seem crazy, but she had just admitted that she'd lied to him. Was she trying to escape from the marriage gracefully? If so, that made her crazy . . . like a *fox*.

"While I was reading Sarah's final entry in the diary," Dierdre continued, "I finally got the good news that the procedure had worked. I was pregnant."

Her eyes lit up. "I'd put so much of my hopes for the future into having a child. I must have thought it would solve all my problems. Only thing was, maybe because of the additional strain of the baby, I had a seizure—a convulsion—the first one

I'd had since I was a child. I blacked out and when I awoke, I was a hundred years in the past and you were calling me Sarah Morgan."

"If what you say is true, then where's the real Sarah Morgan?" he asked, a sick feeling bubbling up inside.

She shook her head. "I don't know for sure. I think we may have switched places. I seem to remember having strange dreams like this when I was small. After that, the doctors put me on medication and the dreams went away."

This was the woman he'd held in his arms, and vowed he'd care for. He'd promised her that if she'd only trust him, she'd never be sorry. As she'd gazed into his eyes, considering his offer, he'd thought he'd seen a change there. When he'd sealed their wedding vows with a kiss, he'd hoped she'd chosen him of her own free will. Afterwards, he'd told himself she'd find a way to get the marriage annulled—that was how he'd prepared himself in case she ever left him. From the rotten way he felt, his preparation had been totally inadequate.

"So you'll be leaving soon?" he asked, dreading her answer.

She thought for a moment as if still working out her plan. "It's possible. That's not something I can predict."

His gaze dropped to her bare neck. "Is this why you never wore the locket I gave you?" He thought he saw a glistening in her eye as she nodded.

"Since I may not have a chance to say goodbye,

I guess I should thank you now for all you've done—just in case there isn't time later."

"No need," he said gruffly. Rolling away from her, he blew out the light and lay back down in the darkness, not liking how alone he felt.

Maintaining a respectable distance between them, Dierdre curled up on her side facing him, watching the rise and fall of his chest. Despite the coolness of the sheets, heat radiated off his long, lean body. Reminded how easily he'd warmed her with his embrace, she wanted to reach out and touch him, but she couldn't turn back now.

He hadn't believed her, and she really hadn't expected him to. Trust wasn't an emotion of which Jesse had a surplus, but no amount of trust could bridge that fathomless gap between reality and her experience with time-travel. Which was why she had to right history before it was too late.

She needed to give Sarah the chance to make her own decisions, her own mistakes. She should have known that before she married Jesse, but maybe it wasn't too late. If Sarah could see Jesse through Dierdre's eyes, she'd have a hard time not falling in love with him.

Rolling onto her back, Dierdre squeezed her eyes shut, admitting she wasn't any less susceptible than Sarah. More than ever, she had to get back home . . . before she let him steal her heart.

The next morning, Dierdre crept up the back stairs of Mamie's Boardinghouse, crouching in the shadows outside Simon's room, determined to stay out of sight until she was sure the hallway was clear. Only a few minutes before, Jesse had left for the bank.

Stealthily, she moved down the hallway, hugging the wall until she found Simon's room. She listened for evidence of movement inside, but the only sound she heard was the wild beating of her heart. She took a breath and eased the skeleton key into the lock. The key turned with a grating noise that to her acutely tuned ears seemed to fill the narrow hall.

She waited, fully expecting Simon to yank open the door and demand to know what she was doing breaking in like a thief in the night. But when her advances brought no such outbursts, she turned the knob and went in, quietly closing the door behind her.

Ignoring the tall, lumpy bed, which seemed to fill the room, she began systematically searching the dresser drawers, rifling through Simon's precisely folded clothes as carefully as possible. The heavy scent of bay rum hung everywhere.

When she finished and still was no closer to finding the diary, she lifted his valise to the bed and unfastened the latches. His case was stuffed with promissory notes to a variety of people, as well as a number of loan papers. It appeared that he owed many people a great deal of money.

She picked up a note to the Longhorn Gambling Establishment & Saloon in the sum of two thousand dollars. How could he afford such lavish spending on a salesman's commissions? Was this what Simon had been doing with all the money he'd obtained from Morgan?

Shutting Simon's secrets back into the valise, Dierdre moved on to the last possible hiding place, the bed. On hands and knees, she checked under it, but unfortunately found nothing but a layer of dust on the hardwood floor. So that was it then. She'd waited too long to recover the journal. He'd already disposed of it.

As she gathered her courage to step out into the hall, she thought of one last place to look. She slid her hand under the pillow and felt the hard binding of a book. Her already rapid heart rate increasing with anticipation, she drew out Sarah's journal.

The possibilities of what lay within its covers set her hands shaking. Having finally reclaimed what she'd worked so hard for, she heard the soft, unmistakable click of the door opening.

"Have you grown tired of married life so soon?" Simon asked, grinning at her from the doorway.

"I came back for my diary," she answered, wondering if she could run past him and escape into the hall. Noticing the pistol strapped to his hip, she hesitated. That split second of indecision was her downfall. He strode into the room and shut the door, standing in front of it like the palace guard.

"So you say." He crossed his arms, his gaze drifting over her breasts and hips. "I think you missed what we had together."

"And what exactly was that?" she asked with more bravado than she felt.

"I was courting you." He relaxed fractionally, still watching her. "Surely I made my intentions clear. I wasted enough evenings drinking with your father. The taste and smoothness of his Tennessee bourbon helped. I, for one, appreciate fine quality where I find it . . ." He eyed her suggestively. "No matter how long it's aged." He winked, unduly pleased at his little joke.

"I have what I came for. I'm leaving now." She took a step toward the door, but he only smiled and shadowed her movement, bringing them closer together.

What had Sarah ever seen in him? Dierdre wondered. Had she looked beyond the veneer of his polished good looks and tailored dress, or had she naively fallen for his puffed-up intellect and salesman's charm?

"If you'd like, we can start up where we left off."

"Your advances are no longer welcome," Dierdre said, backing up. "I got the only thing I came for."

She stepped around him and reached for the doorknob, but Simon grabbed the journal and blocked her way again before she could open the door.

"Your diary made for interesting reading," he said, leafing through the pages. "I've always wondered what women really were thinking. Let's see what you wrote about me."

He began reading aloud. " 'I fear I do not understand the strange instincts of men, and how a woman might prevent provoking them. If my mother were here, I think she would explain even the most intimate aspects of human nature to me. Although I can't remember her, I sense that she had an open mind about things which are most often kept secret between a man and a woman.' Very titillating. I'd be glad to take over your education where your mother left off," he said, glancing up.

Dierdre could feel desire rolling off Simon in waves. She'd have to make her move soon. She refused to let him keep her trapped here against her will any longer than necessary.

He continued. " 'I fear I have made a terrible mistake from which there is no return. It started out quite beautifully as many dreams do, but it ended in a wretched nightmare for which I can only blame myself.' "

Dierdre stiffened. She'd thought nothing of the immorality of reading Sarah's diary, just as she'd studied countless others. But hearing Sarah's words in Brolyn's mouth seemed a horrible invasion of her privacy.

" 'If the outcome of my erring should result in a . . .' "

Dierdre lunged for the diary, unwilling to allow one more word to be read aloud.

"So you want it rough," Simon responded, pulling her to him. "Just like before."

He threw down the journal and jerked her close.

"Of course not. And what do you mean *before*?"

she demanded, pushing at his chest with all her might. Dierdre discovered that trying to shove him away was like ramming into a locked door. He grabbed her wrists and crossed her arms painfully at the small of her back.

"You remember. A little tussle on the front porch while Daddy was passed out in front of the fire. The perfect picture of a loving family."

What if Sarah hadn't cared for Simon at all? What if she'd felt compelled to marry him because he'd had his way with her? Dierdre struggled to free herself, but he only gripped her tighter, cutting off the blood flow to her hands.

"You raped Sarah," she shouted, the truth of her words sinking home as she uttered them.

"You were there," he said, the wild glint in his eyes intensifying. "Sure, it got a little out of hand, but don't tell me you didn't enjoy it." Dierdre tried to scream, but he forced her head back, muffling her cries for help with his mouth.

Realizing what a bad situation she was in and how helpless Sarah must have felt, Dierdre began to panic. She'd lived in a city with one of the highest rates of crime in the country and never come close to being physically attacked. The dangers a woman alone faced in the Old West suddenly crystallized with excruciating clarity.

She wrested her mouth from his painful embrace. Drawing a shallow breath, she shouted for help, but he clamped a hand over her mouth.

"You know you want it. If it wasn't for your

money, no one would give an old maid like you a second look."

Dierdre tried to bite down on his fingers, but he merely tightened his grip. She freed an arm from his animalistic embrace and tried to punch him with it, but her blow merely glanced off. Locking his arm around her neck, he brought her lips toward his. She struggled to shake his grasp on her neck by turning her head back and forth, but the attempt only seemed to further stoke the excitement burning in Brolyn's gaze.

She tried to knee him in the groin, but her long skirts were tangled around her legs, making it impossible. She felt helpless, her anger no match for Simon's strength.

He nibbled at her neck. His teeth felt like the tiny incisors of a dozen nasty rodents. Then he reached under her skirt and grabbed a handful of underclothing. She fought back, pulling away for a moment until he caught her again. She could taste blood where she'd bitten her tongue.

Powerfully, he bent her back over the footboard, ripping off his shirt with one hand. God, this couldn't be happening. The footboard cut into her back. His weight pressed heavily upon her, arching her over the board until she thought her spine would break. Her strength, if not her will, was nearly gone.

He tried to tear off her underwear, but thankfully the sturdy homespun material remained intact. When he straightened up to try again, Dierdre grabbed his gun and twisted away. "Don't move a muscle," she said, holding the gun on him.

Perspiring and panting, Brolyn wiped the back of his hand across his reddened cheek. "You women are all alike," he snarled. "You act like you're God's gift to men, then pretend you're too good for us."

"I said don't move or I'll make sure you never have the opportunity, or the equipment, to rape again." She lowered the barrel of the weapon just far enough below his belt to make her point.

Obediently, Simon slowly raised his hands in submission. She didn't want to compound Sarah's problems by blowing Simon away, but she was tempted. Instead, she snatched the diary off the floor and backed out the door, hiding Simon's gun in the folds of her skirt as she turned and fled down the back stairs. With any luck, she'd get across the street to their hotel room before Jesse returned from the bank.

From the front staircase, Jesse watched Sarah run out of a room and down the hall the other way, her hair as disheveled as her clothing.

Simon Brolyn leaned out the door, naked to the waist. "Come back when you have more time," he called after her.

He looked Jesse's way. "Oh, it's you," he said. "Did you really think she'd be satisfied with a poor sodbuster like you when she could have a real man?" He laughed and slammed the door.

Seeing Sarah leaving Simon's bedroom, Jesse felt poleaxed. Was this why Sarah had really wanted to come to town? To see her lover? Were Simon and John Morgan, and even Sarah, all working together to take his land?

After last night, Jesse had thought he couldn't feel any worse, but he now knew a whole new level of hurt. The loan money was burning a hole in his pocket, but money couldn't heal the sudden stab of betrayal.

When she'd asked him what the bad blood was between him and John Morgan, he'd been close to telling her things he'd never told anyone. What the hell had he been thinking? He'd known better than to trust a Morgan. How much more proof did he need?

Hiding in the shadows at the bottom of the stairs, Becky saw the stunned look of dismay on Jesse's face and slipped out the back way, smiling. Luckily, she'd seen Sarah sneak into the boarding-house and knew just where Jesse could find her.

He'd never take Sarah back now. It served the witch right.

Chapter Twenty-nine

Today Sam took me on a horse-drawn carriage ride in a wonderful place called Central Park. So quaint was the driver's attire and the carriage, had I not known that there were automobiles and buses whizzing along the city streets, I might have thought I had returned to my own time.

When we reached a pond, Sam paid the driver and we got out to walk among trees that are just beginning to turn for fall. I saw children fishing. The poles they used were quite different from the cane ones back home. But the smiles were the same. The sight produced such warm memories of a time when I must have been very little that I had second thoughts about all I'd left behind. I must have cared much more for my life than I believed, otherwise how could a reminder of past events evoke such a sweet, yet poignant, longing?

After we left Central Park, Sam had his driver take us to a fancy toy store. Although he claims he isn't comfortable around children, he nearly bought out the store before I could convince him that a newborn has no need for footballs or toy pianos.

Sam seems concerned that I don't remember much of Dierdre's life, but he has been very patient, hoping his ministrations will effect a cure. I don't know how restorative his attention might be for Dierdre, but for me, I am sure I have never felt better.

In fact, I am so happy and contented I have yet to find time to read the old pioneer journals he brought me. Although reading is a pursuit which used to occupy a great deal of my time, I find experiencing things for myself, with Sam as my guide, is now so much more inviting.

Chapter Thirty

Dierdre stood shaking in the doorway of her empty hotel room, Sarah's diary clutched to her chest. After fighting off Simon, she'd wanted nothing more than the solace of Jesse's strong, capable arms around her. The clerk had taken great relish in explaining that, after he'd delivered Mr. Colburn a note, her husband had hurriedly paid the bill and left.

No, he hadn't arranged for her transportation home, the man had gloated. No, he believed he'd seen Mr. Morgan just leave his bank for the ranch. Yes, she could pay to stay in the room for a few more days . . . as long as she entertained no male visitors.

Realizing how seriously Sarah's reputation had been tainted, Dierdre had stopped the clerk's haughty treatment of her by showing him the barrel of Simon's gun.

Yes, Mrs. Colburn, he'd gladly lock up the gun for her. Was there anything else—anything at all—that he could do for her?

Now, seeing the empty room where she and Jesse had spent their final night together, the last of her bravado fled, leaving her with an overwhelming feeling of abandonment. The pain was intense and startlingly familiar—even though she'd never lost anyone before. Her parents and brothers were all still living and she'd never been left.

Jesse had promised, but obviously her revelation last night had been more than he could accept. Despite the emotional anguish inundating her, she sat down at the writing table to do what she knew she must. She opened the diary to the first entry.

For the next hour, Dierdre read about the sheltered life Sarah had led, her inner longing to expand beyond what her station as a woman in the nineteenth century permitted. She covered the passages Simon had read aloud, empathizing with Sarah's confusion about male-female relationships and her self-blame regarding her pregnancy. Then Dierdre reached the entry made the fateful day Sarah had set out to visit Becky. She felt the building tension as she read Sarah's account about the worrisome pains she was experiencing.

Like rewatching a sad movie and hoping somehow the ending would turn out differently, Dierdre turned the page, but there was nothing more. The rest of the journal, which once had been filled with such innocently hopeful script that her own writing looked like chicken scratch in comparison, was still blank.

She was left with far too many unanswered questions. Had she tampered with Sarah's future so immutably that the girl could never return to finish her entries? Had she driven Jesse away, only to discover she was trapped in the past?

Sitting in near-darkness, Dierdre lit the lantern and pulled a shawl around her shoulders to ward off the cool air seeping through the cracks around the window. Fall was almost here. Funny she hadn't noticed the change in the weather before Jesse had left.

The bleakness of her present existence swept over her. Not knowing what else to do, she picked up a pen and began writing in the diary, recalling her days in the soddie, her normally awkward script oddly similar to the handwriting already in the journal.

Nebraska Sand Hills, 1887
Sitting in the relative shelter of a rare-book store in Manhattan, I could never have imagined the hardships of life in the Sand Hills during the 1880s. The wind blows endlessly, whistling through the cracks in the sod house until I finally search them out and fill them with mud and straw. Only the strongest of women can survive here.

Yet, looking out over the vast virgin prairie, I find

unspeakable beauty. On the seemingly rare occasions when there are clouds in the sky, lazy, shifting shadows march across the grassy plains, shading it with an array of changing colors. And if I look long enough, I can usually see the white tails of a herd of antelope. Blending into the hillside, the older fawns are harder to see, protected by the mottled spots that help hide them from their natural predators. I probably would not have noticed the herds— even though I've read many original accounts about them—except for the patient education by my nearest neighbor, Jesse Colburn.

He is by far the most handsome man I have ever seen. He sits tall astride his horse, his hat firmly planted on his head against the inevitable gust of wind. In this region, his farm is second in size only to John Morgan's ranch.

And he has left me.

I miss the company of prairie dogs, a hawk that is partial to the tree from which I hang my wash, and the nightly yipping chorus of coyotes. But most of all, I miss Jesse.

Now, more than ever, I am convinced that if I am ever to have a child of my own, I must return to the future. That is my only hope.

Three days later, after reading the entries in Sarah's journal until the pages were slick with wear, eating little and sleeping alone on the side of the bed where Jesse had lain, Dierdre closed the diary, exhausted.

She stared out the window as the relentless wind chased a lone tumbleweed down the street. A world away from Manhattan and the life she knew, yet she still burned with the desire to have a family.

It was the motivation behind the need that had changed.

During the past few days, she'd come to realize that her desire to have a child had been born out of wanting to create a bond that wouldn't die. Subconsciously, she'd sought something permanent that couldn't be snatched away from her. She knew now, as perhaps she'd always known, that no such thing existed. People were connected in mysterious ways, but there was no such thing as permanence. Like Jesse, people left. Like Sarah's unborn baby, children died. The only thing that mattered were the precious moments spent together.

She'd spent her life with her nose in a book, resenting her mother's overprotective ways, but then, when she'd had a chance to experience life firsthand, she'd spent most of her days cataloguing books in a temperature-controlled vault or in the sanctuary of the rare-book store.

Either way, she'd never really lived.

Ignoring the little girl inside her who'd wanted to know what it felt like to wash her clothes in a horse tank or grow her own food, she'd tried to satisfy the hunger vicariously through her research.

Now that she had the chance to do things on her own, she wasn't going to waste it. Finally ready to accept her new life, she sent word to Mason to come and take her home.

Chapter Thirty-one

Today, I took time to finally shuffle through the box of books Samuel most recently brought me and discovered my journal, written in my own hand in 1887. I cannot explain my shock in finding that the last entry, also penned in my script, must have been written by Dierdre Brown.

Her discourse about the difficulties of pioneer life set my curiosity at rest about what had happened to her, but her obvious unhappiness has disturbed me terribly.

Feeling so at home here—for the first time that I can remember—I selfishly hoped that, in my place, she would be just as happy as I am. I had begun to think of this baby as my own, come to love him from the depths of my soul.

Realizing I can in good conscience no longer as-

sume Dierdre's identity, I have discontinued the anticonvulsant without the doctors' knowledge. Daily, I pray my actions do not harm the baby. If I have made the wrong choice, I pray for forgiveness.

Chapter Thirty-two

The next day, Mason Diggs came to get her. With Sarah's diary in her pocket, Dierdre settled her bill, surprising the clerk by throwing Simon's gun in as a tip for his hospitality. Leaving him staring, his mouth gaping, she left the hotel, her back straight, shoulders squared.

"I've brought a message from your father," Mason said, helping her into the buggy.

But it's probably not repeatable, Dierdre thought.

"He's heard your man left you and he wants you to come home," he said, as he whistled to the horses.

"Is he asking me or telling me?"

Mason's wrinkled weathered face softened into

Victoria Bruce

a kindly smile. "He's telling you, but he's doing it politely."

Dierdre returned the smile. "I suppose that's an improvement then."

"Yes, ma'am, it is." He wound up his mouth, ready to launch a wad of tobacco juice into the wind. Instinctively Dierdre turned her head and swished her skirts out of danger, but thankfully Mason chose to resist the temptation.

"He'll be happy to hear I've decided to move home," Dierdre said.

Mason frowned and seemed intensely interested in the passing scenery. "I know it's not my place to interfere. And my speaking out this way isn't something that would make John Morgan happy," he admitted. "But I've known your papa all his life and I've known Jesse Colburn all his. And if I had to choose who to take you to, I guess I'd rather choose Jesse. I think you two belong together." From nervous habit, he winged a stream of black juice through the air and it landed safely on the side of the road.

"How can you say we belong together? There's been such hard feelings between our families." Sensing his loyalty to Morgan, Dierdre was stunned that Mason would encourage her to go to Jesse.

"'Tweren't always like that." He worried the pack of chew in his cheek, and Dierdre thought he'd said all he was going to on the subject.

"I don't remember it ever being any different," Dierdre said truthfully.

308

Mason cleared his throat. "That boy would have followed John Morgan to the ends of the earth . . . if he'd let him. He used to work at the ranch whenever he finished his own chores in time. He wasn't tall enough to mount a horse without standin' on a hay bale, but he'd beg us to let him work the cattle. He'd ride 'em, rope 'em, do tricks on the calves to make you laugh. Don't you remember? You used to watch him from your upstairs window, just after the new house was built." His voice dropped. "It was about the time your mama got sick."

"That was a long time ago," she said, wanting him to tell her more. "I don't remember it as well as you. What did I think of Jesse then?"

Mason glanced over, looking at her as if he couldn't believe she'd forgotten. "You thought of him like the big brother you never had. He watched out over you like a mother hen, treated you like you were spun gold."

Realizing how Jesse had brightened Sarah's childhood, she smiled. "And how did I treat him?"

"You worshiped him. Until your mother died. Then, after a while, you didn't have much to do with him anymore. You were almost seven then, and he was a year older."

"Liking someone when you're a child isn't the same as being married to them," she pointed out. "Besides, he doesn't trust me," she said, remembering how he'd withdrawn after she'd told him she was from the future. "And I can't say I blame him."

"He's proud. With you being a Morgan, it's not going to be easy for him to trust you."

"Why does he hate my father so?"

Mason looked at her in surprise, then shrugged. "I assumed you knew." When she shook her head, he ran a gnarled hand back and forth over his stubbly chin. The wind whistled a lonely tune across the plains, punctuated by the jangle of the horse's harnesses. Finally, Mason let out a big sigh. "I guess I've come this far, I might as well go all the way."

He shifted the wad of tobacco to the other cheek. "After your mother died, John Morgan disappeared like a bear hibernating for the winter. Oh, he still lived here, driving himself and the men into the ground. He pretty much left you on your own. I don't think he ever recovered from Elizabeth's death, but when he finally pulled himself together, he realized that he'd messed up where you were concerned. So he tried to court Jesse's mother, thinking that if Jesse and his mother came here to live, you'd be happy again. Jesse Colburn, Sr. had died about the same time as Elizabeth—worked himself to death on that fool farm if you ask me—and she was struggling to make ends meet.

"I don't rightly know what happened between your father and Jesse's mother. By that time, John was used to buying whatever he wanted. But he couldn't buy Annie. My guess is that she saw through him, knew he was desperate to set things right again for you, any way he knew how. He asked her to marry him and she turned him down flat."

Mason snorted. "Your daddy wasn't used to being put in his place. Despite his intentions to get you a mother and a brother, he fell in love with Annie."

Dierdre stared at him in amazement. She couldn't imagine John Morgan loving anyone except himself.

"He took her rejection badly—coming so soon after your mother's death. Jesse quit comin' around and your daddy wouldn't have anything to do with the Colburns. Eventually, Annie remarried. Fellow didn't have a pot to piss in . . . excuse me, Miss Sarah. I mean, he was real poor. But he was the genuine article and he tried real hard. He died when Jesse was fourteen. Jesse took over where he left off, trying to make something out of the farm."

A deep pang of sympathy shot through her. At an age when she'd been surrounded by her family, Jesse had been struggling to keep his family's farm going. He must have felt as if the weight of the world was on his shoulders.

"But that's hardly cause for a life-long feud," she said sadly.

Mason pulled up on the reins, guiding the horses around a deep rut. Looking into the distance, Dierdre could see her windmill over the next knoll, its shiny tower marking the fork in the road to the Morgan Ranch. In the opposite direction was Jesse's farm.

"It didn't end there," Mason explained. "The whole thing just seemed to keep festering inside your pa. He had big parties showing off how rich he'd become. During one party, I was out on the range with a sick bull, but I heard snatches enough when I got back to figure out what happened.

"It was about six months after his daddy died. Jesse showed up looking for help for his mother. She was having a baby and couldn't afford a doctor. Turns out, an important physician from Omaha was one of the guests. Your father turned Jesse away—I never knew whether John even learned the reason for his being there. When that boy tried to force his way in, some of the hands we'd hired for branding beat him up pretty bad. What I heard was when he came to and got himself home, his mother and the baby were dead."

"Oh, no," Dierdre murmured, her chest so tight it hurt to breathe.

Mason made a clucking noise of regret through his teeth. "Jesse blamed your father, of course. But most folks think he blamed himself even more."

No wonder he'd been so protective, fretting over whether she had a fever, making sure she ate. Not understanding the source of his profound concern, she'd been a difficult patient at best. Remembering the distress she'd caused Jesse as he'd tried to nurse her back to health, Dierdre fought back tears.

"I know Jesse never would have told you himself. He wouldn't have wanted to come between you and your daddy."

She took the heart-shaped locket out of her pocket and opened it. Two pairs of solemn eyes gazed up at her. Jesse's mother and father. Now she realized why the necklace had meant so much to him. Resolutely, she snapped the locket shut and slipped the necklace over her head.

"I need to talk to Jesse," she said fiercely.

"I was hopin' you might see things differently, but hear me out. Whatever losin' Annie did to Jesse, it did just that much more to your daddy. He won't admit it, but I know that's the main reason he's tried so hard all these years to buy out Jesse. Morgan can't stand the constant reminder of what an awful mistake he made."

Jesse hadn't been the only one with a heavy burden to carry. "You did the right thing telling me," she said.

Thirty minutes later, Dierdre walked up the path to a small wood frame house. Beside the door a rose bush tenaciously clung to its last yellow blooms. A blue faded curtain identical to the worn fabric in the dress Jesse had given her hung at the windows. Through the window she could see that the kitchen was plain and neat. A chair sat at the table, while two others hung from the wall unused.

She knocked on the door and when no one answered, she walked back down the path and toward the barn, hoping Jesse hadn't gone to town. Talking to him was the right thing, but she'd sent Mason back to the ranch, to keep her from chickening out. If Jesse wasn't around, she'd have a long walk home.

As she neared the barn, she heard Jesse's voice. His words were low and soothing as a lover's. With a twinge of jealousy, she peered inside the barn door. Compared to the heat building outside, the barn was cool and inviting. As her eyes grew accustomed to the reduced light, she noticed Jesse in the back stall. Quietly, she stepped inside, close enough to make out his words.

With his back to her, Jesse curried a small black horse. "You old thing, if I don't exercise you more you'll get fat." His voice was tender and she remembered when she'd last heard it. The night she'd lost the baby.

Jesse affectionately scratched behind the animal's ears and on its nose. When the horse turned to nuzzle Jesse's shirt, Dierdre noticed that it was blind, its eyes a milky white.

"You took good care of the place while I was gone," he said. His words were uttered as tenderly as a serenade. Dierdre wished he were speaking those words to her.

"I should never have left you alone this long," he said. "Can you forgive me?"

"Yes," Dierdre said softly.

Jesse kept brushing, sending puffs of dust curling into the air. "You'll have to do better than that if you want to sneak up on a fella and his horse. We heard the wagon a half mile away."

"Then you know Mason brought me."

"Yep. That mean you've moved back home with your father?"

"Not yet. I was on my way there when Mason told me about your mother."

When Jesse didn't respond, she continued. "It had to be awful losing her that way. I don't know how a child lives through something like that. I don't think I could. Maybe you'd feel better if you talked about it."

Jesse glanced over his shoulder. "What I've got to say won't change anything."

"In my time, we've come to understand that it's not good to keep things pent up inside. Sometimes the best way to heal the past is to face it."

Jesse leaned on the top rung of the corral. "I face it every day."

"But you've been facing it alone. You're not alone anymore."

"I thought you were leaving," he said.

"Not until we've talked this out." She paused. "He loved her, you know."

Arms still draped over the stall, Jesse stiffened, keeping the fence between them. "What did you say?"

"John Morgan was in love with your mother. Mason said that he started out trying to get a new mother and brother for Sarah, and ended up falling in love with Annie. When your mother refused to marry him, he wasn't just angry, he was hurt."

"I can't believe that."

"It doesn't excuse his behavior at the party or

since then, but it does make him seem more human."

"If he loved my mother, he sure didn't show it or he would have done whatever it took to protect her."

"That's what you would have done. But then, John Morgan's not the man you are."

Jesse looked into his wife's eyes and saw she meant what she said. He'd assumed he'd never be able to measure up by her standards. That eventually she would realize she'd made a mistake and return to her father. But she was telling him that in her estimation, which was the only one that counted to him, Morgan was the one who didn't measure up.

He clung to the thought, until memories of the past came rushing back, destroying the good feelings she'd evoked in him. "John Morgan played a part in it, but I didn't do enough to protect her, either," he said miserably.

"You were fourteen years old. You did everything you could."

He nodded.

"But you've been keeping it inside for so long, it has nowhere else to go." She walked over to him and put her hand on his shoulder. "You said that you and Sarah made a pact—that you could tell each other anything. I want you to tell me about this now."

Jesse glanced at her sharply, then looked down at the ground. "I told John Morgan my mother had been in labor for twenty-four hours and needed help."

Jesse felt the memory flood back. He was fourteen years old again, scared and shaken. He'd stayed with his mother as long as he could, but he knew something was terribly wrong—something that only a doctor could fix. He'd nearly collapsed with relief when Sarah's dad told him he had one of the most famous doctors in the country as a guest.

He shook his head, wrestling with the bitter memories. "Your father said, 'What do birthing women think they need a doctor for? He's too busy for your kind.'"

Looking down at his weathered hands, Jesse remembered the boy's hands that had fought to save his mother's life.

Jesse felt the soothing heat of Sarah's hand on his and wished she could warm the last remaining cold spot in his heart. "After she and the baby died," he said, "I dreamed about how someday I'd get revenge on your father, make him suffer like she had to."

"Maybe he's already suffered more than you know."

"It doesn't look like he's hurting to me," Jesse scoffed.

"Maybe not, but you are, and not everyone could recognize that, either."

He nodded, remembering how defenseless he'd felt against Morgan's men. He'd been determined never to allow himself to be so vulnerable again.

Then Sarah had come back into his life, bringing up the same helpless feelings in him—first, when he'd thought she was dying and again when he saw her leaving Simon's room. He'd been afraid he was going to lose her, too, despite his best efforts.

"There are no guarantees," she said as if reading his mind. "But by blaming yourself and holding a grudge against John Morgan, you're only hurting yourself."

"Maybe." He wished he could forgive and forget, but if he let down his guard, what would stop Morgan and others like him from taking advantage again?

"You'll think about it, at least?" she asked.

"We'll see."

"That's all I ask. Now I have something I need to tell you. The day you left me, I went to Simon Brolyn's room to get Sarah's diary. He'd stolen it from me and I didn't think he'd willingly give it back. The reason I was so anxious to get the diary was I thought it held the secret to my leaving Prairie Bend."

She could see the restraint in every taut muscle in Jesse's body. The silence underscored the tension coiled in his hands, the one clutching the curry comb and the one fisted at his side.

"I saw you coming out of Simon Brolyn's room," he said. "You looked like you'd just been in a windstorm. Or made love to him."

"I'd just fought Brolyn for the diary. I was foolish to go to his room alone." She didn't know how

much she should tell him. If she told him everything and Jesse sought revenge, he could get hurt
and it would be her fault.

"The truth, Sarah," Jesse said. "The whole
truth."

"Simon attacked me. Before I could stop him,
he kissed me. I wished it had never happened, but
it did. I should have told you, but I was afraid of
what you'd do."

"Did he force you . . . further?" Jesse asked, his
voice going hoarse.

"No. I was able to stop him. I know how bad this
must sound—"

Jesse cut in. "The appointment your father had
at the bank was with Simon. They were laughing
and shaking hands. While I waited, not knowing
if I'd get the loan or not, I watched your father give
Brolyn a large amount of money. Then when I saw
you leaving Simon's room, it all seemed to make
sense. I thought Simon and your father had
cooked up a way to drive me off my land so Simon
could have you. Before my father died, I promised
him two things. One was that I wouldn't let his
dream for his farmland die with him."

No wonder Jesse had bristled so when she sug-
gested he give up farming. "You said there were
two things."

Jesse spoke in a hoarse voice. "I promised him
I would take good care of my mother. Since I
broke that promise early on, I vowed I would do
everything in my power to keep farming the land.
When you tried to talk me into going into ranch-

ing, I didn't know how I could trust you anymore. You've changed so much from the girl I once knew."

"How did you know where to find me?" Dierdre asked quietly.

"Becky sent a note to the hotel. The clerk gave it to me on my way back from the bank. The note said that even before the wedding, you'd been plotting to get into Simon's room."

"Just to get the diary. Becky knew that." Dierdre bit her lip. "I should have confided in you." She sagged against the stall fence.

"Why was the diary so important to you?" Jesse asked.

She pulled the journal out of her pocket. "I thought it was my link with Sarah. That if I got it back, I could somehow use it to return to the baby I'd struggled so hard to conceive."

"So what you're saying is—even after you married me and made love to me—you were still trying to find a way to leave?"

She nodded miserably. "You'd been so good to me and it wasn't right to lead you on. By the time I realized it was Sarah you had always cared for and wanted, not me, it was too late."

Dierdre took a shaky soul-searching breath and let it out. "The truth is . . . as impossible as all this is to believe, I've fallen in love with you." She collapsed on a hay bail.

Jesse turned back to his horse and began brushing her again. He was silent for a long time. "That's it?" he said.

Dierdre hadn't known what she'd hoped would happen, but after realizing that she loved Jesse, waiting for his reaction was horrible. "Well, not exactly. If all else fails, I still want those riding lessons." She tried to smile, waiting for her fate.

"I don't know," he said finally. "I couldn't trust my Lucy to just anyone."

Dierdre sat up straighter on the hay bale. "I wouldn't expect you to."

"Of course," he said thoughtfully. "I couldn't let just any horse carry my wife, either."

Wife. On his lips, that single word sounded as sweet and warm as a caress. "I know you must think I'm a little crazy, but I have to know. Was it me you wanted that day by the creek or the Sarah you once knew?"

"Since you seem to have all the answers, why don't you tell me?"

She could only think of one way to know for sure. She stood up and opened the gate to the stall. "Is this fresh straw?" she asked, closing the gate behind her.

"Yep. Does it matter?"

Dierdre inhaled the heady mixture of leather and hay and male. "Not really."

She walked up behind him and put her arms around his chest so that her fingers met in the middle. The feel of his body against hers was magic.

"What are you doing?" Jesse asked, his heart beating hard enough that she could surely feel it through his shirt.

Sarah—or whoever she was—didn't answer.

Her fingers started working on the buttons of his shirt. Then she slipped it off his shoulders, and moved her hands down his front until they were . . . damn, she knew how to get his attention.

The forwardness of her behavior was so unexpected that he wanted to throw her onto the straw, reassure himself she was really here. But he couldn't let himself be that gullible, could he? To believe that she'd really changed? He turned around, determined to slow things down and give himself a chance to think.

Around Sarah's neck hung his mother's locket. Seeing the necklace he'd held in safekeeping a dozen years now hanging from his wife's lovely neck, Jesse felt a catch in his throat. The pendant had been his mother's prize possession, symbolizing all that she and his father had meant to each other. Neither hardships nor disasters had been able to diminish their love for each other.

He fingered the heart pendant, feeling Sarah's warmth in the metal. Its surface had been recently buffed to a high shine, though he didn't know if that was by design or if Sarah had constantly carried it in her pocket. Was it too much to hope that she'd worn it for the same reason he'd given it?

He watched in amazement as she lifted the heart locket to her lips and kissed it, then let it fall between her breasts again. The curry comb dropped onto the straw-strewn stall unnoticed.

Sarah unfastened the top button on his jeans, the sure movements of her hands intensely sensual. She moved down to the next button, her fingers brushing his thigh as she loosened the constraints of his pants. She slipped her hand beneath the denim encasing him and nearly brought him to his knees. In his wildest dreams, he'd imagined taking her in the barn, the kitchen, and just about everywhere he could think of; but he'd never thought it would really happen.

Hands shaking with each frenzied beat of his heart, he unfastened the first few buttons of her dress, accidentally tore one off and stopped. He was acting like an impatient schoolboy. He was usually so in control of his feelings, he wasn't sure who he really was anymore. He hadn't known her either, and every time he thought he did, she surprised him—just like now.

Catching a ribbon of her chemise between his fingers, he tugged, inch by inch revealing her firm, ripe breasts until he could see the valley between them and the dark edge of her nipple.

With Sarah's hands tracing the sensitive patch of skin just below his waistband, he released the cotton ribbons one by one, until her breasts lay exposed in the golden sunlight filtering through the eaves. His breath quickened.

"What I'm doing should be quite clear." Dierdre closed her hand around his hardness, and saw him shudder in ecstasy. His unabashed reaction to her touch spurred her on. She stroked his velvety skin the length of his shaft, evoking an unguarded groan from him.

As he began to move against her hand, he

Victoria Bruce

smoothed a thumb over previously unexplored areas of her breasts. Exquisite sensations darted through her as unfamiliar to her as the body in which she now lived. And yet, making love to him here in the most rustic of surroundings seemed the most natural thing in the world.

She felt safe here, and since she knew how harsh living in this land could be, it must be Jesse making her feel that way. Now if she only knew that she was the one he really wanted—not Sarah. She released him long enough so he could peel his jeans down over his flat stomach, and off. A dusting of reddish brown hair extended up his long, lean legs, growing denser between his thighs.

His obvious anticipation, coupled with the loss of his usual self-control, proved a potent stimulant. She increased the pressure of her grasp until Jesse fanned out a horse blanket upon the straw and drew her down onto the ground with him, his masterful arms caressing her into submission.

He sought out her most sensitive areas. The hands that so determinedly worked the land pleasured her with equal fervor. Here, in the barn, among the relatively primitive tools of his trade, she felt his masculinity at its strongest. Unwilling to restrain her desire any longer, she opened to him, arching up to meet him as he entered her.

Their union felt as if her other half had finally melded with her, completing her. Body tingling, she could almost believe that Jesse's hunger was for her only. His hips rocked in perfect time with hers, coaxing, driving, pumping. He read her

324

every nuance as if she were an open book.

"You want to know if I love you," he asked, gently tugging on her earlobe with his teeth. The sensuous combination of his hot breath and the movements of his lips raised her temperature higher, until she nodded, admitting it was true.

"I do . . . love you," he said simply, peppering her neck with warm, wet kisses that escalated her ragged breathing.

His expression one of sheer bliss, Jesse climbed, taking her with him, closer to the point of no return. She wavered on the brink of ecstasy, but something held her back.

She'd thought such a declaration of love all she'd ever need from Jesse, but doubt still gripped her. Was Sarah the one meant to hear those words? Or did he really mean them for her?

Without missing a stroke, he slipped an arm under her, and raised her up until she was looking directly into his clear blue eyes. She wrapped her legs around his back and clung to him, grinding her sweaty body against his.

"It was you, darling," he ground out through a deep moan. "It was always you."

The last of her fears obliterated, an explosion rocked through her with the intensity of a thousand suns. Her moans joined his in a strain as wild and feral as the coyotes that ranged on her land. Floating out of control, she felt him pulsing into her, filling her with liquid heat. She might have traveled here by mistake, but no one could tell her that she didn't belong in Jesse's arms.

*   *   *

In the afterglow of their lovemaking, Jesse watched dust motes dancing in the light shaft all the way from the hay loft to the barn floor. He'd never before tarried in the barn without thinking of how much work he had left to do. Yet lazing here with Sarah, he couldn't think of even one chore that needed to be done.

Sarah turned in his arms. "When you left me at the hotel, I thought I would die."

The simple confession struck him deeply. It didn't really matter who she thought she was. She'd captured his heart. "It took everything I had to leave you," he said. "I couldn't do it again."

A scratching noise outside of the barn diverted his attention. He raised up on an elbow. "Did you hear something?"

"Nothing but the sound of your voice," she said dreamily. "And my stomach. I believe I've worked up quite an appetite."

He listened for a moment, but all he heard was Lucy stamping at a fly. "Must have been my imagination," he said.

He'd been imagining a lot lately. And usually much more than noises. While he'd been making love to Sarah, he'd even wondered if he could have planted a baby. He'd never understood how Kitty and Ben Dickens managed to find time for each of their brood, but suddenly the thought of raising a little Sarah or Jesse didn't seem so frightening.

Maybe he'd talk to her about that tonight. Make

sure it was what she wanted, too. Then, if it was . . .

Well, supper could wait.

Jesse helped Sarah find her clothes and led her back to the house. The radiant glow on her face lit up his kitchen—usually a lonely place where he ate alone—making him want to lose himself in her arms once more. "I can live on love if you can," he said, drawing her to him.

"Oh, darn," she said. "And just when I'd finally grown accustomed to your cooking."

"I'd be glad to give you lessons." Drawing her close, he took a deep, satisfying breath, savoring the smell of lavender mixed with the familiar scent of hay and . . . something else he couldn't make out. He inhaled again.

"Something's burning," he cried, jumping back.

He ran to the window, taking in the horror at a glance. Smoke rolled out of the open door of the hay loft. "The barn's on fire. Lucy's in there. I've got to get her out."

Chapter Thirty-three

Jesse darted out the door to the horse trough. He didn't bother with the bucket hanging from the pump handle. Instead, he dove into the water, came out dripping wet and ran toward the barn.

"Jesse," Dierdre cried, but he'd already rushed into the burning building. She scooped up a bucketful of water from the trough and rushed with it to the barn, spilling precious drops as she ran. Smoke clouded her vision. Embers rained down around her from the blazing hay in the loft. She could feel the heat roaring inside.

With a loud creak, a portion of the loft burned through and fell, narrowly missing her, dropping fire onto a stack of dry hay. She threw the pail of water onto the burning straw and ran back to the pump for more.

As she reached the barn the second time, the heat forced her back. Smoke surrounded her like a thick gray mantle. Heart in her throat, she watched the barn door, wondering if the happiness for which she'd searched so long would be over, almost as soon as it had begun.

Inside, after releasing his other horse, Jesse made his way through the dense smoke to Lucy. "Easy, girl," he said as he felt for the peg that held her halter. He couldn't see to the end of his arm. He'd have to be careful or he could lose his bearings as the fiery fog thickened. He found the halter and slipped it in place.

When he tried to lead Lucy out of her stall, the mare reared back, jerking the reins through his sweaty hands. "Come on, Lucy. You've got to help me," he said, using precious breath to try to soothe the frightened horse. "I'm not leaving without you."

At the sound of his voice, the mare settled enough so Jesse could lead her from the stall where so recently he'd made love to his wife. The heat of burning wood and hay seared his lungs. He hurried to escape the inferno, arm over his nose, lungs screaming for fresh air. He tried not to breathe too deeply, but the smoke crept into his eyes and nose, drawing deep, ragged coughs from his throat. The coughing dragged more poisoned air into his lungs. Rafters crashing down all around, he plunged on into the gray fog, in a weak moment wondering whether he would ever see his wife again.

That devastating thought drove him toward the barn door and daylight. His first realization that safety was within his reach came in the way of a heavenly vision. He saw his wife anxiously waiting for him outside. Cloaked in a haze of smoke, she looked purely angelic as obvious relief transformed her worried features.

As he gasped for fresh air, a new wave of spasms wracked him. Dierdre took Lucy's reins from Jesse and led him and the horse away from the hellish blaze. When his coughing subsided, Dierdre threw her arms around his neck and smothered him in kisses, holding him so tightly the coughing started all over again.

Bent over, hands on his knees, he struggled to catch his breath, while she petted Lucy and gave the horse a hug. "Aren't you going to kiss her, too?" he asked when he could finally straighten up enough to talk.

"I just might," she said, rewarding him with a smile that made him feel like a hero.

A loud crash behind them sobered their celebration. Clinging to Jesse, Dierdre turned around, feeling his helplessness as he watched his barn go up like so much paper.

"I'm sorry, Jesse," she said simply. What else was there to say? He was alive—which was all that mattered to her—but everything he'd worked for seemed to be falling down around him.

During the barn's death throes, she kept vigil with him. As the last skeletal supports finally collapsed, a wagon pulled up. A large woman crawled out, followed by a tumble of children. "You boys stay out of the way and do whatever Jesse tells you to do."

"They're my friends. Kitty and Ben Dickens," Jesse told Dierdre, before leaving her side.

"We could see the flames all the way from our place," Ben said. He shook Jesse's hand, then quickly moved to the horse tank, instructing two children to take turns pumping while the others threw buckets of water on the smoldering embers. The oldest put Lucy and Jesse's other horse in a corral, safely away from the barn.

"Sarah Colburn." The woman put an arm around her. "Are you all right, honey?"

Sarah Colburn. It felt odd being called by Sarah's married name. And yet, especially after her reconciliation with Jesse, it was as comforting and cozy as a warm winter coat. "I'm fine. Old blind Lucy was in the barn. Jesse risked his life to get her out." Dierdre blinked back tears that might have been the result of the debris in the air.

Kitty looked at her as if she wasn't fooled. "Jesse's a good man. My youngest is almost old enough to learn to ride and he won't let anyone else but Jesse teach him. Benny would have been heartbroken if anything happened to old Lucy. For that matter, so would Jesse. That horse belonged to his mother, you know. She saved it after its former owner beat it blind."

"I didn't know," Dierdre said. Learning the significance of Jesse's confronting Simon, she felt her love for Jesse grow. There were a great many

331

things she still had to learn about her husband.

"We've been friends with Jesse—and his mama—a long time." Kitty looked her up and down. "I can't say I'm not surprised to see you here. When I heard it was Jesse you finally married, I didn't figure you'd stick it out. I'm glad you did."

Dierdre smiled, feeling as if she'd just been welcomed into one big, happy family. "I feel as if you're someone I'm going to enjoy knowing very much," Dierdre said.

Kitty nodded, hanging on to her with caring arms as sturdy as an oak. "Fire's almost out. Nothing left to burn. The ashes will smolder for days. We'll stay and help make sure it doesn't spark up again."

"That's very kind of you," Dierdre said.

Ben and Jesse abandoned the rubble that used to be the barn, a half-dozen children trailing behind. "The fire was set," Ben said. "Whoever did it left tracks you could follow in the dark."

"You going after them?" Kitty asked Ben.

"I'm going," Jesse answered. "It's my fight, not yours."

"What do you mean, your fight?" Dierdre asked.

Jesse exchanged a knowing look with Ben before glancing back at her. "The tracks lead straight to the Morgan Ranch."

Chapter Thirty-four

"You don't have to go," Sarah cried, grabbing him by the arm. "You could get hurt."

He was losing valuable time. If Morgan had thought to burn him out, this time he'd find he couldn't hide behind a bunch of hired cowhands. "This doesn't concern you. This is between me and him."

Sarah stood in his way, arms crossed, looking more stubborn than he'd ever seen her. "Maybe it started out just between you and him, but I'm involved now. If you're determined to meet John Morgan before you've had a chance to cool off, I'm going with you."

"I want you to stay here with Ben and Kitty where you'll be safe," Jesse insisted.

"If there's a risk, I'm willing to take it. But what

I'm not willing to do is let you go off half-cocked and get yourself shot."

He wanted to confront Morgan, not stand here arguing with his wife. "If I listened to you, I'd give John Morgan the benefit of the doubt and let him drive me off my land."

"If Morgan's responsible for the fire, he should pay for it."

"But he won't, unless I do something to stop him. Who else is going to stand up to him?"

"I will."

"You're a woman. Your place is . . ."

Her eyes flashed. "Don't say it. Don't even think it. I'm your wife and that means we're in this together. If you're not willing to play as a team, tell me right now."

He was astounded, although pleased. She was talking as if this was her fight as much as his. He glanced at Ben. His friend started to say something until Kitty jabbed him in ribs. When Ben shrugged, Jesse realized he'd have no help from that quarter.

"I still can't allow you to go," Jesse said, setting her aside. "Ben, can I use your wagon?"

"You bet. We'll be here when you get back."

Sarah reached the wagon and climbed up into it before Jesse could stop her. He shook his head. "You can't go. Remember what I just said?"

Smiling, she looked down at him, the heart locket shining through the gloomy haze. "You said you loved me and that you'd never leave me again."

He opened his mouth to argue. Then just like poor Ben, he closed it again. She was right. Together, he and Sarah made a good team. Against her, he didn't have a prayer.

John Morgan leaned back between the ample arms of his leather chair, watching the burning embers in the fireplace. Strange, how cold his bones got in the late afternoon. There'd been a time when he could ride the length and breadth of his ranch, sleeping on the open range without thought of comfort. Those days had long since passed.

Like every payday, he'd given the hands their money and they'd fled to town to spend their fortunes, scattering like rats leaving a sinking ship. Even with the continuous lowing of cattle, he felt acutely alone.

He'd thought this venture into farming might spark the fire that used to burn within him, but he'd begun to doubt that anything could rekindle his ambition to amass power and possessions. With Mason getting on in years, John had no one he could trust to oversee an expanded operation. And with his daughter determined to go her own way, he had no one to leave his fortune to anyway.

A wagon rode up the path, probably just one of the men returning early, bringing back supplies from town. Still, he found himself thankful for the distraction from his melancholia.

*   *   *

Jesse bounded up the steps and threw open the door to Morgan's house. He'd followed the tracks from his farm to the turn-off for the Morgan Ranch where he'd lost them among dozens of other hoofprints.

"Morgan," he bellowed.

John Morgan appeared in the hall, his usually florid face going white as a sheet when he saw him. "Where's my daughter?"

"She's safe, no thanks to you."

Sarah stepped through the door and a margin of color returned to the old man's face. "Jesse's barn burned. It's a total loss," she said.

"Why bother me?" Morgan asked, turning cold. "I told you not to expect my help."

"But you also promised you wouldn't stand in our way," Sarah said evenly.

"I'll handle this," Jesse said firmly. "The fire was deliberately set. The culprit's tracks lead to your doorstep. What do you know about it?"

"I know nothing," Morgan boomed.

"What about your men? Where are they? If the barn had gone up minutes earlier, Sarah could have been caught in the blaze."

"You're supposed to be taking care of her." John cast a worried look at Sarah, as if to reassure himself that she was all right. "Except for Mason, my men are in town. But they'd never do anything to hurt my own flesh and blood. They just follow orders."

"Like the hands that worked me over the day my mother died?"

"I didn't know anything about that," Morgan sputtered.

"But you did nothing to stop it, either. Just like you did nothing to stop my mother's death."

"I didn't know how sick she was."

Jesse clenched his fists, only the most extreme control keeping him from closing his hands around Morgan's throat. It was a good thing Becky had taken his gun as collateral because he'd be tempted to use it.

"I never wanted anything to happen to your mother," Morgan said.

"That's an excuse—and too little, too late. If you had really cared for her, you would have let me take the doctor to her."

Morgan's proud broad shoulders bowed as if burdened by the weight of Jesse's accusation. "I thought if I ignored you and your mother, somehow you'd go away. I did everything but run you off your land, but you just kept sticking. You're the dad-blamedest stubborn boy I ever laid eyes on."

Suddenly, he straightened. "But I didn't order anyone to start a fire. And, whether you believe me or not, I never meant for Annie and the baby to die."

Jesse let Morgan's words sink in. They were probably as close to an apology as he'd get. "Who set the fire then?"

Before Morgan could respond, a new voice spoke. "More importantly, who killed Becky Simmons?"

Everyone turned. Simon Brolyn stood in the doorway.

Dierdre gasped. The shock of seeing the man who'd nearly raped her was as horrible as hearing of Becky's death.

Simon strode in, and stopped a little too close to Jesse. "Seems the storekeeper who found Becky's body in the back of the General Store overheard you threatening her. She'd been beat up pretty bad. Lindsey Seymour says you have a nasty violent streak. He saw you attack me unprovoked."

"And if I see you beating another lame horse, I'll bust you in the mouth again."

So Simon was the man Jesse had brawled with. Dierdre had been satisfied enough with the way she'd held Simon off at gunpoint, but knowing that Jesse had brought him to heel just raised her estimation of her husband higher.

Simon's eyes narrowed. "It's that kind of talk that's got you in a whole lot of hot water. I'd be more careful what you say if you're still here when the posse arrives. You might find yourself strung up from the nearest tree."

"That's enough," Dierdre said. "Jesse didn't have anything to do with Becky's death. He was with me."

"Last night, too?" Simon asked.

No, she'd slept alone at the hotel, and like everyone else in town, Simon probably knew it.

When she didn't answer, Simon smiled evilly. "I'm sorry to hear that," he said.

"If Jesse's a suspect, then why hasn't the posse

shown up?" Maybe Simon was just bluffing.

"I told them he rode south. Seeing how you and I were once betrothed, the least I could do was give your new husband a head start. In spite of your rejection, I still hold you in the highest esteem."

"No, you don't," Dierdre said, remembering her coarse treatment at his hands, and the horrific thing he had done to Sarah. "You just need my father's money to pay off your gambling debts."

Simon's expression went cold. Playing a hunch, Dierdre went on. "You gambled away the money he advanced you for farm equipment. What are you going to do when it never arrives?"

"Is that true?" Morgan bellowed. When he stepped forward, Simon pulled a gun.

"It's Jesse Colburn who's the criminal here." Simon turned the gun on Jesse.

"No," Dierdre cried. She'd already come too close to losing Jesse once today. "Don't do this."

The words died in her throat. She felt a sudden fluttering of the eyelids. The symptom was reminiscent of other episodes long ago, other lost memories, always accompanied by a blurring of the edges of reality. She'd spent three long, lonely days trying to trigger a seizure, but now that she realized she loved Jesse, she couldn't leave him. Feeling herself losing consciousness, she unwillingly slid to the floor.

Simon laughed. "Just like a woman to faint under pressure."

"That's my gun, Brolyn," she heard Jesse say in the distance. She fought to stay alert.

"Is that a fact? Then when the posse finds you and Morgan dead, they'll think it righteous justice for you both. I'll generously offer to marry the widow and take over the Morgan Ranch."

"How'd you get my gun?" Jesse asked. "Becky had it last, kept it as security."

"Well, it didn't do her much good, now did it? Or you either for that matter." Simon aimed the pistol at Jesse's chest. Dierdre heard the click as he pulled back the hammer.

With a roar, Morgan charged Simon for the gun, bravely shielding her and Jesse with his body. As her energy ebbed, Dierdre found herself thinking that John Morgan couldn't die trying to save her—it was his own daughter he should be standing up for, something he had never done when Sarah had been here.

Through the thickening fog, she saw Jesse push Morgan out of harm's way. Fiercely he struggled to wrest the weapon from Simon's grasp. His fingers closed over Simon's and the two men spun around in a bizarre dance of death.

The gun went off with a deafening crack and the stench of gunpowder filled the room. A red stain slowly spread over Simon's groin area. He looked down in amazement at the enlarging pattern of blood before tumbling heavily to the floor. Left with the gun, Jesse shoved it into his waistband and rushed to Dierdre's side.

Kneeling beside her, he scooped her into his arms and held her against his chest. She tried to fight off the seizure but, even in his arms, the darkness stealthily moved in on her. The sensation of his warm breath on her cheek and the feel of his callused hand on hers grew faint. The wrenching away from Jesse felt unbearably painful, worse than anything she could imagine.

Over his shoulder, she saw Simon move. With all her remaining strength, she cried out a warning as he pulled a pistol from an ankle holster and began shooting.

Still trying to shield her, Jesse stiffened, and she sensed rather than felt the impact as a bullet entered his body. And then she was floating in a dark tunnel. Alone.

Chapter Thirty-five

Dierdre shaded her eyes against the bright light next to her bed. The clock radio was blaring, its digital readout flashing off and on in jarring neon red. Feeling strangely mesmerized, she watched the flickering lights, wondering why she felt so disoriented.

Finding her glasses on the nightstand, she automatically put them on and glanced around the cavernous bedroom. The expensive tapestries, the heavy scarlet draperies, Sebastian purring on the bed at her feet. She had to be in Sam's Long Island mansion. But what had happened to Jesse?

The sound of shots echoed in her ears, and the heartbreaking memory of being wrenched away from Jesse slammed into her like a punch in the stomach. She clutched her hands over her protruding belly, even knowledge of the baby she'd created unable to soften the onslaught of emotional anguish flooding through her.

Sarah must have experienced a seizure, Dierdre decided. *Petite mal*, the little death. The pain of separation from Jesse felt more devastatingly permanent than death.

The massive oak door creaked open, and a woman wearing a white uniform carried a breakfast tray in from the hall. Dierdre waved her away and the maid quickly retreated, leaving her to her inconsolable suffering.

She never wanted to get out of bed again. Given the size of her girth, she doubted she could have moved even if she'd had the will.

The growing pressure in her bladder proved her wrong. Answering its urgent call, she sat up and ambled to the bathroom adjoining her suite. Funny thing about time, she thought, clumsily lowering herself onto the commode. She'd apparently switched places with Sarah in her eighth or ninth month, but according to the time she'd spent in the past, she hadn't been gone nearly that long. How much time had passed since she'd left Jesse? she wondered. Was he even alive?

Unfamiliar with the changes in her pregnant body, she struggled to her feet on the third try, and washed her face and hands with an individually wrapped lavender soap. She closed her eyes and thoughtfully raised the miniature soap to her nose, recognizing Sarah's signature scent from the past. The fragrance reminded her of her waltz with Jesse—and later when they'd made love.

Sighing, Dierdre returned to the bedroom, and collapsed onto a velvet stool. Feeling the sting of unshed tears, she blinked furiously, but a tear splashed off her cheek and onto the antique dressing table. Drying the spot with her nightgown sleeve, she noticed her lotions and creams that lined the mirror, along with her collection of porcelain powder jars and a dozen of her antique perfume bottles.

Sam must have brought them here to make Sarah more comfortable, she realized. Reflected in the glass, among the knickknacks that had once meant so much to her, lay an old journal, its cover aged by at least a hundred years from when she'd last seen it.

Heart pounding, Dierdre picked it up, unsure what she would find within its yellowed pages. She skimmed through Sarah's entries—up through the day of her miscarriage. Turning the page, she was startled to discover her own soulful pages, written after Jesse had left her at the hotel.

She hadn't consciously been trying to communicate with Sarah, but Sarah had obviously found the diary. She'd most assuredly read how Dierdre felt her only hope for a baby of her own was to return to the future. Three days later, everything had changed. Sarah couldn't have known that, though. Not unless Dierdre had written about it.

Could Sarah's belief that Dierdre wanted to leave the past have anything to do with their switching places again? Dierdre wondered. Had she been the cause of her own misery?

Dierdre shook her head, the weight of her carelessness adding to her burdened heart. She wished she at least knew whether Jesse had survived the shooting. It wouldn't heal her wounds, but it might help her go on for the baby's sake.

Perhaps Sarah had tried to correspond with her from the past, Dierdre reasoned. Fearing what unwelcome news she might find within those fragile pages, she leafed to the following entry and found a letter in Sarah's fanciful script dated 1887. Heart beating an uneven tattoo, she began to read.

My Dear Dierdre,

I am carrying Jesse's and your baby. I am eating well, avoiding skipping meals and adhering to a strict no-alcohol diet, as instructed by the doctors at the clinic on Long Island. I continue to practice my breathing exercises, although I don't allow anyone to hear me for fear they will think me insane. I hope you will agree that I am doing a capable job.

Since medicine has no knowledge of ultrasound or amniocentesis yet, I have no accurate way of predicting the gender of the child. If I were to guess, I would say that it is a girl. She, or he as the case may be, remains quite active, stubbornly so, despite my appeals for respite. This is probably not surprising given the robust nature of her father and, from all accounts, the independent streak of her mother.

I rent a small house in town so I can be near

my father, who is confined at the doctor's quarters. He is very ill and may lose his leg. Jesse is also being held there until he dies or is well enough to leave. Simon Brolyn lived for several days after being shot, and upon his deathbed, finally confessed to killing Becky Simmons. I understand from Jesse that she was not such a good friend to me.

I wish I had better news, but I hope the prospect of your forthcoming child will sustain your spirits. I don't know how this might be, given my melancholy over the separation from my child in the future. I hope you won't think me presumptuous, but I had grown very close to the babe and had come to think of him as my own. Not an hour passes that I don't think of him. I considered him a gift to replace the child I lost in the past.

While in your time, I had secret aspirations of marrying Sam Vanderbrief. Initially, his stiff mannerisms and impressive moustache reminded me of the tutors my father brought from the East Coast to teach me literature and Latin.

Beneath his austere exterior, however, resides the most sensitive man I've ever known. He treated me with respect and so much caring, all my doubts about whether I could trust a man again were put to rest.

If I ever get a chance to return to the future, I will never leave. For that is where I feel I truly belong. I will remain on the medication, should

*that be the key, and not chance any more chil-
dren. My son will be all I need.*

*As I pen these words, I am holding my china
doll from childhood. Should staying here be my
destiny, I will someday present her to your
daughter—just as I was told my mother pre-
sented her to me.*

Dierdre reread the last sentence of the diary, remembering a doll with its hair painted to match
her own brown curls, its flawless porcelain face
something she could never aspire to. The woman
who gave her the doll had brown hair too, but instead of the same delicate pink coloring of the
doll's cheeks, her skin had been sickly and pale.

A twinge shot through Dierdre's swollen belly
and she took a deep breath, vainly trying to relax,
her mind racing. The lady's name was Elizabeth.
She wasn't sure how she knew, but she could see
her lying in bed, unable to get up. Though the day
had been warm and sticky, she'd been covered
with a quilt. Its bright pink and white swatches
couldn't even enliven her wan coloring.

The design seemed so familiar, Dierdre thought,
touching her throbbing temple. She'd once lain in
the dark, pulling the same comforter up over her
head to shut out the bad memories.

Confusion intensified the pounding in her head
as forgotten memories swirled out of the shadows.
Struck by the memory of where she'd seen that
quilt, she allowed the fragile journal to slip out of

her usually careful hands. *She'd seen that same quilt on Sarah's bed.*

Clutching her stomach, she rocked to and fro, recalling a scene from the past as if it were yesterday. Near death, Elizabeth had handed the beautiful Victorian doll to her and told her that someday she'd pass it on to her own daughter. Then she'd closed her eyes and . . .

Tears sprang unbidden to Dierdre's eyes.

Elizabeth Morgan had been *her* mother! *She* was Sarah!

The unleashed memories came rushing back. She realized that she wasn't the one who'd had seizures. During those times of neurological short-circuiting, she'd found a way to escape the pain of her mother's death and her father's inattention by switching lives with a girl in the future—a girl named Dierdre.

She'd experienced the beauty and danger of the Sand Hills as a child, and her memories had led her back there again, to Jesse. As a child, he'd given *her* the robin egg. She could remember telling him that blue had been her favorite color because it reminded her of her mother's eyes.

Dierdre's chin quivered. By Jesse's own admission, he'd cared about her from the first time he'd seen her. He'd watched over her through the first grade, then unknowingly waited for her until she returned. Tears spilling onto her cheeks, she realized where she truly belonged.

She belonged in the past. With Jesse.

Suddenly, she felt a jab in her stomach, followed

by a painful tightening down lower. Please don't let it be labor pains, she thought, struggling in vain to gain control of her breathing. It was too soon. She wanted Jesse's baby. She had to find a way back to him.

As she tried to fight the pains, the room spun around her, and the contraction went on and on.

Chapter Thirty-six

Puff, puff, whew! Dierdre blew out a cleansing breath as the nurses rushed her gurney into the delivery room. She screamed out.

"Are you in pain?" Sam asked, the picture of concern.

"Yes. You're breaking my hand. Don't squeeze so hard."

"Sorry," he mumbled, lightening his touch. "I've really been getting into this coaching stuff."

Dierdre tried to smile, but her forced gaiety was cut off by a wrenching that tightened her back muscles until they felt taut as a bow. This should be the happiest event of her life, but sadly her heart wasn't with this child. Her heart was in the past with Jesse and their baby.

"Your mother just called," Sam said. "She'll be here within the half hour."

Dierdre tightly shut her eyes. In bits and pieces, she was remembering more details of the Victorian doll and the woman who'd given it to her. Her *real* mother.

While her mother lay dying, Dierdre had grieved at her bedside, not understanding what was happening. She'd depended on her mother for everything. Elizabeth Morgan had stood in the gap, breaching the chasm between her and her father, a man with an unbending will who could make her feel small with just a look of displeasure.

When her mother died, she'd known she'd never survive unless she escaped, too. She'd dreamed of a place where she would never again grow so dependent on the strength and love of another person. In the future, she'd thought she'd found that place.

"Your mother said on the phone for me not to worry," Sam continued, "that from the time you were seven years old, whenever she tried to help you dress, or fix your hair, you'd always say 'I do it myself.' She told me you were so strong you never really needed anyone else."

Dierdre grimaced and shook her head. She'd thought being strong meant not needing anyone else. Now she realized that she'd merely taken the easy way out. By never allowing anyone in, she'd avoided the pain of heartbreak—and all but ruined her chance for true love.

"I'm afraid we're going to have to give you something for the pain," a nurse said.

Dierdre did laugh then. Her heart was finally breaking, and the only drug that could heal it was the life and love she could have had with Jesse and the child they'd created in the past.

"My, aren't we being brave," the nurse said, administering the injection. Sam kept a comforting grip on her hand.

"Hardly," Dierdre murmured.

"Let's prep you for delivery," the nurse said.

The drug was taking effect. Dierdre couldn't feel her legs, and she couldn't see what the nurse was doing to her. The lights overhead were too bright. She wanted to close her eyes, but one of the light bulbs seemed to twinkle with a life all its own. As she watched, she felt mesmerized by the flickering light. Consciously, she knew it was just a bulb burning out, but when she tried to pull her gaze away, her eyelids began to flutter.

"Nurse!" Sam cried, sounding so different from his usually restrained self. "She's having a seizure. Get a doctor. Now!"

The pain was gone. Her back muscles were finally relaxed. "I love you," she murmured, saying a special goodbye to the baby, her first. Then the glow filling her vision faded, replaced by total darkness.

Chapter Thirty-seven

Jesse propped himself further up against the pillows and looked at his irascible roommate. "I should have let that no-good sawbones cut your blasted leg off. You wouldn't have known a thing . . . until you woke up a leg short."

"I can't believe you let him treat me at all." Morgan seemed to shudder at the thought. "Doc Mabe hasn't had a steady hand for nearly a decade."

"No one else would have anything to do with you," Jesse retorted. Actually, there hadn't been time to get anyone else. Jesse had been shot twice in the back, and Morgan had gone into shock after losing a lot of blood. Although the bullets had missed Jesse's spine, if Sarah hadn't gotten him and her father in the wagon, they'd likely both be dead.

"You can believe I never spoke to my elders that way," Morgan grunted.

Jesse realized that underneath his bluster, John Morgan had suffered nearly as much as he himself had for his stubborn pride. Despite his foolish actions, the blowhard *had* actually cared for Annie. Knowing that somehow seemed to help.

The door opened and Sarah walked in, carrying a tray. She had explained what had happened, but also that she had changed places and times again with Dierdre—the woman with whom he'd fallen in love. She shyly smiled at him and set the tray on the stand between the beds. He smiled back, wishing like hell that she could make him feel the way Dierdre had.

She bent down and gave him a kiss. Shocked, he pulled back. When she had first switched back, there had been no affection between him and Sarah.

"Lawsey," Morgan roared. "Can't you keep your hands off one another until I recuperate? It's enough to give a man a permanent setback."

"Admit it, you old reprobate, you're too ornery to die," Sarah said.

Wondering whatever had possessed her, Jesse raised an eyebrow, but Sarah merely smiled and sat down on the edge of his bed.

"You gonna let her talk to me that way?" Morgan complained from across the room.

Before Jesse could respond, Sarah raised a spoon to his lips and told him to open his mouth. When he jerked back to see what she was feeding him, he felt her place her hand high up on his thigh for balance. When he gasped, she shoved the spoon in his mouth.

"Straight sorghum," he sputtered, swallowing the bittersweet syrup. "What's gotten into you? Have pity on a sick man. It's bad enough I'm holed up like a wounded animal with your father . . ."

She leaned close again and pressed a scorching kiss to his lips, making him forget the stinging pain in his back. He stared into her chestnut brown eyes. She did look especially radiant this morning.

"Dierdre?" he asked. "Is that you?"

"No," she said, feeding him a slice of cornmeal mush. "It's Sarah."

The slab of fried mush was burned black, but he could taste the liberal use of sorghum, just like he'd made it for Dierdre. "My God," Jesse said fiercely, pulling his wife into his arms. "It *is* you. Are you here to stay?" He didn't know what he'd do if she left him again.

"I'm staying. This is where I belong. Besides, I couldn't let our child be born without me." She laughed and placed a hand on her gently rounded stomach.

"There you go again, acting like two fools . . ." Morgan hollered. "Wait. Did you say child?"

Jesse's composure dissolved. "Are you . . . ?"

Sarah smiled at him. "Sometime next summer, there's going to be a little Jesse. Or Jessica."

"Whoever heard of a name like Jessica for a baby?" Morgan demanded.

"I like it," Jesse said proudly. Forgetting his wounds, he rolled over, pulling his wife onto the bed with him.

"Are you sure you should be overexerting like this?" she asked mischievously.

"Don't worry about me," he said. "I'm making up for lost time."

As he covered her warm, lush lips with his mouth, he finally felt all the darkness inside disappear, chased away by the blinding light of her love. All the time he'd thought he was nursing her back to health, her love had been healing the pain of his own past, leaving the rich promise of the future.

A future he fully intended to spend loving Sarah.

Epilogue

Sarah looked up from her stitches and smiled as Jessica toddled toward her grandfather. With blue eyes and a strong jaw, Jessica was the spitting image of her father. With Becky gone, the town seemed to have forgotten the rumors she'd spread about Sarah.

"Where in blazes have you been?" Morgan asked Jesse from where he was sitting with Mason Diggs. The younger man had just ridden up on Sage.

"Out checking fences," Jesse said. "I wanted to make sure the latest shipment of Herefords was taken care of."

From the porch of her new frame house, Sarah watched Jesse dismount and lead his horse to the water trough for a drink. Overhead, the windmill whirled in the stiff breeze, its shiny blades reflecting the brilliant rays of the sun.

"And that took you so long?" Morgan demanded to know.

"I stopped to dig up a soap weed." He glanced at Sarah and winked.

"You did what? You've got the responsibility of the entire Morgan Ranch and all you can think of doing is digging up a weed?"

"Didn't want a calf too young to know any better poking one of its eyes out."

"Who cares about a calf? You're going to give me heartburn, boy." Morgan rubbed his leg.

Mason chuckled under his breath and finished the wooden pony he was whittling for Jessica by carving his initials in the saddle blanket.

Jesse tousled his daughter's hair. "Gotta protect the children," he said, smiling at Sarah over Jessica's head.

"Up, Grandpa." The child lifted her hands toward the old man.

A rusty smile broke out in every crease of his ruddy face. "Oh, well, of course you do." He grunted and raised her onto his lap. "Keep up the good work.

"That reminds me," Morgan said. "When are you going to get to work on another grandchild for me?"

"Soon," Jesse said, admiring the gently expanding waistline of his wife.

Her cheeks flushed, just like they had the day he'd married her. "Very soon."

Pregnant with her second child, she smiled up at Jesse, thinking how happy he looked since he'd invested his money in ranching and was finally doing the kind of work he loved; his ghosts from the past were laid to rest. She'd still never mucked out a stall, but thanks to Jesse's patient lessons, she'd learned to ride horses far less tame than Lucy.

She had no doubt that he loved her as deeply as she loved him. And for miles around, not one blade of thistly soap weed could be found.

Journal of Dierdre Vanderbrief

This evening, before a roaring fire in the library, I looked on as my husband read a fairy tale to our son. Healthy in every way, Samuel Vanderbrief III, named for his father and grandfather before him, pretended to listen intently while he surreptitiously fished a nut from the candy bowl. Then, just as his father reached the part where they all "live happily ever after," Sam reached up and flipped the page of the valuable first edition with his sticky hand, leaving a greasy fingerprint.

Surrounded by his collection of rare books and first editions, my husband glanced up at his father's forbidding glare, looking down from the portrait over the mantelpiece. His gaze then drifted to me. He shrugged and turned the page of the priceless book, a resigned smile on his face.

And I returned to writing in my journal, thinking how in time, things always seem to work out for the best.

Lady of the Night

Cordia Byers

Manacled to a stone wall is not the way Katharina Fergersen planned to spend her vacation. But a wrong turn in the right place and the haunted English castle she is touring is suddenly full of life—and so is the man who is bathing before her. As the frosty winter days melt into hot passionate nights, she realizes that there is more to Kane than just a well-filled pair of breeches. Katharina is determined not to let this man who has touched her soul escape her, even if it means giving up all to remain Sedgewick's lady of the night.

___4404-8 $5.99 US/$6.99 CAN

Dorchester Publishing Co., Inc.
P.O. Box 6640
Wayne, PA 19087-8640

Please add $1.75 for shipping and handling for the first book and $.50 for each book thereafter. NY, NYC, and PA residents, please add appropriate sales tax. No cash, stamps, or C.O.D.s. All orders shipped within 6 weeks via postal service book rate. Canadian orders require $2.00 extra postage and must be paid in U.S. dollars through a U.S. banking facility.

Name_____

Address_____

City_____State_____Zip_____

I have enclosed $_____ in payment for the checked book(s).
Payment <u>must</u> accompany all orders. ☐ Please send a free catalog.
    CHECK OUT OUR WEBSITE! www.dorchesterpub.com

TIMESWEPT

Victoria Chancellor

Across the Rainbow. When, at the behest of his six-year-old daughter, seasoned pilot David Terrell flies into a rainbow to wish for a wife, he emerges in 1886 Wyoming, the world of the beautiful Analisa. But their lives can never be fulfilled until she realizes that David's love will take her to a place where dreams really do come true.

___52236-5 $5.50 US/$6.50 CAN

Miracle of Love. When Erina O'Shea's son is born too early, there is little the doctors can do in 1896 Texas. But then Erina's desperate prayers are answered when she finds herself and Colin hurtled into the future, into a world of medical wonders—and into the strong arms of Grant Kirby.

___52144-X $5.50 US/$6.50 CAN

ELIZABETH CRANE

Time Remembered. Fed up with the boring wimps she dates, Jody Farnell puts all her energy into restoring a decaying antebellum mansion. And among the ruins of Whitefriars, the young architect discovers the diary of a man from another century who fascinates her like no other and a voodoo doll that whisks her back one hundred years to his time.

___52223-3 $5.50 US/$6.50 CAN

Reflections in Time. When practical-minded Renata O'Neal submits to hypnosis to cure her insomnia, she never expects to wake up in 1880s Louisiana—or fall in love with fiery Nathan Blue. But vicious secrets and Victorian sensibilities threaten to keep Renata and Nathan apart...until Renata vows that nothing will separate her from the most deliciously alluring man of any century.

___52089-3 $4.99 US/$6.99 CAN

YESTERDAY'S GOLD BOBBY HUTCHINSON

BESTSELLING AUTHOR OF

A DISTANT ECHO

With her wedding to Mr. Right only two weeks away, Hannah Gilmore has more on her mind than traveling to a ghost town. Yet here she is, driving her widowed mother, an incontinent poodle, and a bossy nurse through a torrential downpour. Then she turns onto a road that leads her back to the days of Canada's gold rush—and into the heated embrace of Mr. Wrong.

Logan McGraw has every fault that Hannah hates in a man. But after one scorching kiss, Hannah swears that nothing will stop her from sharing with Logan a passion that is far more precious than yesterday's gold.

___4311-4 $5.50 US/$6.50 CAN

Desperado's Gold
Linda Jones

Jilted at the altar and stranded in the Arizona desert by a blown gasket in her Mustang convertible, Catalina Lane hopes only for a tow truck and a lift to the nearest gas station. She certainly doesn't expect a real live desperado. But suddenly, catapulted back in time to the days of the Old West, Catalina is transported into a world of blazing six-guns and ladies of the evening.

When Jackson Cady, the infamous gunslinger known as "Kid Creede," returns to Baxter, it's to kill a man and earn a reward, not to use his gold to rescue a naive librarian from the clutches of a greedy madam. He never would have dreamed that the beauty who babbled so incoherently about the twentieth century would have such an impact on him. But the longer he spends time with her, the more he finds himself captivated by her tender touch and luscious body—and when he looks deep into her amber eyes, he knows that the passion that smolders between them is a treasure more precious than any desperado's gold.

_52140-7 $5.50 US/$6.50 CAN

THE OUTLAW HEART

VIVIAN KNIGHT-JENKINS

Bestselling Author Of *Love's Timeless Dance*

A professional stuntwoman, Caycee Hammond is used to working in a world of illusions. Pistol blanks firing around her and fake bottles breaking over her head are tricks of the trade. But she cannot believe her eyes when a routine stunt sends her back to an honest-to-goodness Old West bank robbery. And bandit Zackary Butler is far too handsome to be anything but a dream. Before Caycee knows it, she is dodging real bullets, outrunning the law, saving Zackary's life, and longing to share the desperado's bedroll. Torn between her need to return home and her desire for Zackary, Caycee has to choose between a loveless future and the outlaw heart.

_52009-5 $4.99 US/$5.99 CAN

Janeen O'Kerry
QUEEN of The SUN

Riding along the Irish countryside, Teresa MacEgan is swept into a magical Midsummer's Eve that lands her in ancient Eire. There the dark-haired beauty encounters the quietly seductive King Conaire of Dun Cath. Tall and regal, he kindles a fiery need within her, and she longs to yield to his request to become his queen but can relinquish her independence to no one. But when an enemy endangers Dun Cath's survival, Terri finds herself facing a fearsome choice: desert the only man she'd ever loved, or join her king of the moon and become the queen of the sun.

___52269-1 $4.99 US/$5.99 CAN

Dorchester Publishing Co., Inc.
P.O. Box 6640
Wayne, PA 19087-8640

Please add $1.75 for shipping and handling for the first book and $.50 for each book thereafter. NY, NYC, and PA residents, please add appropriate sales tax. No cash, stamps, or C.O.D.s. All orders shipped within 6 weeks via postal service book rate. Canadian orders require $2.00 extra postage and must be paid in U.S. dollars through a U.S. banking facility.

Name_____
Address_____
City_____State_____Zip_____
I have enclosed $_____ in payment for the checked book(s).
Payment <u>must</u> accompany all orders. ❑ Please send a free catalog.
    CHECK OUT OUR WEBSITE! www.dorchesterpub.com

Don't miss these passionate time-travel romances, in which modern-day heroines fulfill their hearts' desires with men from different eras.

Traveler by Elaine Fox. A late-night stroll through a Civil War battlefield park leads Shelby Manning to a most intriguing stranger. Bloody, confused, and dressed in Union blue, Carter Lindsey insists he has just come from the Battle of Fredericksburg—more than one hundred years in the past. Before she knows it, Shelby finds herself swept into a passion like none she's ever known and willing to defy time itself to keep Carter at her side.

__52074-5 $4.99 US/$6.99 CAN

Passion's Timeless Hour by Vivian Knight-Jenkins. Propelled by a freak accident from the killing fields of Vietnam to a Civil War battlefield, army nurse Rebecca Ann Warren discovers long-buried desires in the arms of Confederate leader Alexander Ransom. But when Alex begins to suspect she may be a Yankee spy, Rebecca must convince him of the impossible to prove her innocence…that she is from another time, another place.

__52079-6 $4.99 US/$6.99 CAN